FAUXFRIENDS

FROM BESTSELLING AUTHOR
A.J. McCARTHY

Black Rose Writing | Texas

ISBN: 978-1-68433-725-5
PUBLISHED BY BLACK ROSE WRITING
www.blackrosewriting.com

Printed in the United States of America
Suggested Retail Price (SRP) $19.95

Faux Friends is printed in Book Antiqua

*As a planet-friendly publisher, Black Rose Writing does its best to eliminate
unnecessary waste to reduce paper usage and energy costs, while never
compromising the reading experience. As a result, the final word count vs. page count
may not meet common expectations.

To my mother-in-law, Pauline Bigaouette McCarthy.
Because of her loving nature, generous spirit, and ability to make
people smile, she is our greatest treasure and inspiration.

FAUXFRIENDS

Prologue

She saw the light. It wasn't at the end of a tunnel, and it didn't resemble a train.

It was more of a blinding flash. Flying car parts, a deafening blast, and various types of debris accompanied it. She had a limited view of the explosion. She lay facedown, grass filling her mouth, with a large male body on top of her. The aforementioned body took the brunt of the force, and she feared he was dead or injured.

He rolled to the side, and they exchanged a few shouted words. She flicked a glance over him to see if he lacked body parts. Satisfied his injuries were not life-threatening, she took in her surroundings. Black smoke billowed and flames spewed from the vehicle. An acrid stench clawed at her nostrils. Screams and shouts erupted from every direction.

Fate had stood on the sidelines and saved her life. She could have been closer to the vehicle. Worse, she could have been in it. The sequence of events leading up to that moment put her at a distance to survive unharmed.

One matter was certain. Things had changed. She hadn't signed up for this. They had billed this as an easy, safe job, as far from danger as possible.

This moment marked the turning point. The job was officially dangerous and life-threatening.

At last, things were looking up.

Chapter 1

Nine days earlier

Chantal Pouliot took a slow sip of coffee from her thermal mug and flipped through the pages of the file. As usual, everything was in order. No important forms had disappeared, and signatures were in the proper place. She tossed the folder onto the 'To Scan' pile as her gaze strayed toward the window. A good time for a run, she thought. The air was cool, and the midday sun hadn't yet heated the paved track.

With a sigh, she shifted her attention to her beat-up fake-wood desk. As a high-energy person, restraining that energy proved difficult, but Chantal harnessed it when necessary.

The police department had gone paperless. The new requirement was to scan and store documents in digital form on the encrypted network server. They would toss out old-fashioned filing cabinets and make room for more beat-up desks or meeting rooms. The department would save trees and brag of environmental awareness.

It was a noble cause, but at this moment, Chantal considered the sacrifice of a few trees a fair exchange for an interesting case. Poring over ancient file folders made her want to pull out her hair.

Chantal's mind wandered to an idyllic scene in a restaurant with real linen tablecloths and servers in tuxedos, an expensive bottle of red breathing on the table. A handsome, unknown man sat across from her.

Jolted out of her reverie by a familiar voice, she straightened and pretended interest in a file.

"Chantal, mon bureau, s'il te plaît."

An invitation to her supervisor's office wasn't unusual. He reveled in doling out boring jobs, but she couldn't imagine how it could get any worse. The end of her six-month ordeal was on the horizon.

Chantal hurried to follow him, praying he would take her out of purgatory a few weeks early.

The door slid shut behind her as she settled into an uncomfortable plastic chair. Henri Godet was tall and thin to the point of being cadaverous. He leaned forward and folded long arms on the desk, a comb-over threatening to topple over his forehead.

"I have good news for you," he said to her in French. "I have a case."

Chantal smiled. This was excellent. She could get out of the office and on the streets; with any luck, working with Jeff. But she wouldn't complain if they assigned her to someone else for the time being. Anything would be better than this.

"Great. What is it? When do I start?" She inched closer to the edge of the chair, her back straight.

Godet chuckled. "I knew you'd be happy. You'll like this one. It's a fraud case. You'll work with… what's wrong?"

Chantal had known Henri long enough she didn't have to conceal her true feelings. "White-collar?"

Her boss settled his palms flat on the desk. His expression held sympathy. "Yes. For now. You need more time."

"I don't. I'm ready." Her eyes pleaded with him.

"Captain Bouchard and the psychologist don't agree."

"You do. You know I am."

"It doesn't matter what I think. It's their decision." Normally affable, Godet's voice took on a hard edge. Chantal got the message. He had his orders, whether or not he agreed with them. His expression softened. "Besides, you'll enjoy it. You'll work with the RCMP. They have an email fraud task force, and they'd like to incorporate one of ours into a smaller team they've put together."

Chantal had been an officer with the Quebec City branch of the Sûreté du Québec police force for almost ten years. She knew of cases where the Royal Canadian Mounted Police, the national policing body, joined forces with provincial or local law enforcement, yet such a case had never involved her.

Chantal dragged a deep breath into her lungs. She reminded herself a white-collar case was an improvement over her present duties. If she proved herself with this one, she could return to her old job as a homicide detective.

"Okay. Fill me in."

Relief swept over her supervisor's face. He had expected a bigger confrontation.

Perhaps they were right, she mused. She might need more time before she returned to her old self.

• • •

When Chantal entered the conference room, stacks of files welcomed her, and her shoulders slumped. Here we go again, she thought. It would be more of the same, except in a different room. *Why did people think she enjoyed pushing papers?*

Chantal pasted a brave smile on her face when Henri lifted his head and spotted her. "Ah, there you are. Everything's ready for you. You'll have time to look over things before your new partners arrive."

"Mm." Chantal imagined the hours of boring reading. Henri had given her an overview of the case. It was white-collar through and through, classic email fraud that diverted funds from a Canadian company meant for a supplier in Hong Kong.

A common crime in the cyberworld, but the fact it affected three companies in the same city within a month made it noteworthy.

Thus, the invitation issued to the provincial police from the RCMP cyber-crime task force. With digital technology and the intelligence of the criminals behind it, the common link could be hard to find, but combining efforts might provide an advantage.

With an inward groan, she crossed to the table. Chantal would spend most of her time here, her rear-end almost permanently attached to a chair. It was a huge shift from six months earlier when she had worked undercover, dealing with violent crime.

Of course, her previous work was the reason she spent most of her time these days behind a desk, but it didn't mean she couldn't miss the excitement. It was what she had trained to do.

"Chantal? Did you hear me?"

She blinked twice and focused on her boss. "Sorry. This fascinated me," she said, straight-faced, gesturing toward the mounds of paperwork.

Godet's eyes narrowed as he studied her. "I'm glad you're enthusiastic. You'll get through it faster. Your colleagues will arrive after lunch. We expect you to work well with these people." A stern tone accompanied his last sentence.

"I will." Chantal resisted the urge to make a face at his back as he left the room.

Chantal learned her RCMP partners were from a Toronto branch, and the job might involve travel, which could make it interesting. She might see the inside of someone else's conference room, she thought wryly.

Chantal realized a reason they chose her for this assignment was because of her relative fluency in English. Mastering the second language had become easier in the past several months with the help of her new best friend.

Tori, an import from Florida and newly married to Chantal's ex-partner, Jeff, was involved in a previous case in Quebec City. Although a traumatic episode for Tori, she found love and made her home in a city she now appreciated.

Chantal and Tori had withstood a rocky relationship during the case but came out on the far side as fast friends. Now, they spent a lot of time together as Tori tried to learn French, while Chantal worked the kinks out of her English.

Chantal's lips curved as she pictured the computer geeks making their way to SQ headquarters. She imagined they spent their time with their noses stuck in dusty filing cabinets or pressed to computer screens in an enormous downtown Toronto office building. Quebec City would be a welcome experience for them.

It was a beautiful, historic city and a popular tourist destination. Founded in 1608, it was one of the oldest cities in North America and the only one on the continent with fortress walls surrounding the historic core. The stone buildings and narrow streets of the Old City held a European flavor. With a population of five hundred thousand, it was small compared to Toronto, but Chantal suspected it would be an interesting diversion for the visitors.

At noon, Chantal hurried out of the building, looking forward to fresh air, a change of scenery, and a chickpea salad at a nearby bistro. Judging by the line-up at the door, she wasn't the only person to crave health food.

Forty-five minutes later, her stomach replete but her anxiety level high, Chantal jogged back to the office. Her heels, although low, were not intended for running, and several times she risked falling on her face. Inside the building, she ran up the stairs two at a time, not bothering with the elevator, her skirt hiked halfway up her thighs.

Chantal stopped outside the conference room, aware she was fifteen minutes late and a little disheveled. Maybe more than a little. A strand of blond hair fell across her cheek, escaping the bun she had pinned with precision that morning. She felt telltale patches of wet under her arms and knew her face was likely flushed from heat and exertion.

Chantal tugged on the hem of the skirt that had traveled up her left leg. She tucked in her off-white blouse on the right-hand side. Someone could get the impression she rushed from a meeting with a lover, perhaps in a broom closet, she thought.

Chantal yanked open the door.

Two men had their backs to her. They turned as she clattered over the threshold. Chantal questioned whether she was in the right room. Had they changed the venue while she was at lunch?

She heard the low rumble of suppressed laughter, but she wasn't able to figure out which cop she amused.

One was a couple of inches taller than the other. Dressed in dark suits, both were handsome, with dark hair and eyes. Any similarity between them ended there. The shorter of the two, in his late twenties, had short, cropped hair, eyeglasses, and an appealing smile.

The taller man sported a shaggier look, his hair lying over his collar in the back. His smile was impossible to assess; it was nonexistent. He didn't scowl, but no expression graced his face as his gaze swept over her.

Having been through worse, Chantal straightened her spine and stepped forward. She didn't extend her hand. Instead, she held both hands by her side, an unspoken signal handshaking was no longer usual for her. Since the coronavirus pandemic first rocked the world two years earlier, fewer people shook hands. French Canadians were habitual huggers and cheek-kissers. Many threw the practice to the wayside, perhaps for several years.

She addressed the friendly one first, hoping to boost her confidence level.

"Hello. I'm Chantal. It seems we'll work together."

The man's smile grew even more disarming. "Mark Pratt. It's a pleasure to meet you." He respected her wishes not to shake hands, but she was certain she missed out on an enthusiastic grip.

Buoyed by his reception, Chantal turned to the taller man, offering him the same grin. His smile remained missing-in-action. "Owen Lockwood," he said with a slight bow of his head.

"Sorry for being late. I was tied up at lunch." Chantal gave her skirt another little tug south.

Mark seemed to stifle a laugh before he spoke. "No worries. We arrived a few minutes ago."

Owen's right eyebrow made a sharp move northward. He either didn't accept her apology or he didn't tolerate tardiness, Chantal mused.

Feeling uncomfortable under Owen's disapproving scrutiny, Chantal tucked in her hair with her right hand as she waved her left toward the files covering the conference table. "Why don't we look at these?"

"Why don't you fill us in on what you have so far?" Owen countered.

Chantal circled to the opposite side of the table and took a seat, feeling more at ease with a large object between them. "Don't we have the same information?"

"Probably. But I'd like your take on it."

Chantal glanced at Pratt to gauge his reaction to his arrogant partner. An expectant smile brightened his face.

Although tempted to let Lockwood understand she was his equal and not his subordinate, she remembered Godet's warning to play nice with her new friends. Chantal cleared her throat, feeling like a teacher called upon her to do a class presentation on her first day of school.

"We have three cases of fraud so far, all similar," she said. "The suspect hacked into an email conversation between a Hong Kong supplier of electronic parts and a Quebec purchaser. In each case, the supplier and purchaser have a relationship and, because of the time zone difference, communicate by email. He intercepted their conversations and asked for a change in the bank account. To another bank in the same city. From there, the money disappears."

"A typical BEC case," Mark said.

"BEC?" Chantal's brows furrowed.

"Business Email Compromise, a type of social engineering. It's considered the most low-tech and easiest form of cyber-crime. People can buy a domain name, or spoof one. Often, they hire money mules to bounce the funds from one country to another until it ends up in a place that's hard for anyone to access. Have you found a link between the cases?" Mark asked.

"Not yet. I took my first look at the documents this morning. The only common factor I can see is location: Quebec and Hong Kong."

Owen lowered himself into a chair beside Mark. "There has to be a link between them," he said. "It's too much of a fluke."

"I agree." Chantal glanced at each man. "Any ideas?"

Mark spoke up. "It must be a person, or a group, that has physical access to the Canadian company."

"Have we checked employee lists? Common suppliers?" Owen asked.

"Not yet," Chantal said.

"That's our starting point."

• • •

The man sat alone in the gloomy room with the drapes drawn. Three computer screens provided the only light. He moved from site to site, his fingers dancing across the keyboard. Images flashed and flitted on the monitors.

His environment was basic. A bed and other essential furniture for comfort and immediate needs. His time here was limited and meant to serve a purpose. He focused his attention on his mission. Nothing would distract him from it.

He squinted as a box popped up in the top right-hand corner of his middle screen. He leaned back in his chair and cracked his knuckles, one by one, as his thoughts raced.

Who was this? Had someone stepped into his snare?

A rush of adrenaline coursed through his veins.

His fingers moved faster. He closed websites, while others popped open at his request. Apps only known by the most nefarious of individuals appeared on his screens. He peered through virtual doors and digital windows.

Leaning back, he stretched out his legs, but his gaze never left his screens. It seemed his meticulous plan had worked. A smile spread across his face. Victory was within his grasp.

CHAPTER 2

They split the work between them, going through payroll reports and client and supplier lists ad nauseam.

Chantal learned Mark was a tech wizard, sent to Quebec because of his talents. He spent much of his day accessing various systems, transferring information to spreadsheets, and sorting data.

"Isn't this great? This is one of the best cases I've worked on."

Chantal looked up from her file and stared at the beaming young RCMP officer. She didn't know him well enough to gauge if he joked or not. Her gaze shifted to Owen. He leveled a skeptical stare at Mark, as if he was an exotic creature in a museum exhibit. It seemed she wasn't the only one who found it hard to believe someone enjoyed this type of assignment.

The squeak of the door distracted Chantal from her study of the tech nerd.

"Still hard at work?" Captain Bouchard said. "It's almost six o'clock. You must be tired and hungry."

The stout, balding captain was her supervisor's boss, but in Chantal's previous life as a detective she had worked directly under him, and they still enjoyed a close relationship. He had popped into the investigation room earlier in the day to introduce himself and ensure the team had everything they needed. Since the case involved a federal contingent, he was the supervising officer in charge.

Chantal glanced at her watch in surprise. She hadn't realized how much time they had spent in the stuffy room. The afternoon went better than she had anticipated. Mark did his magic on his laptop while keeping up a lively conversation. His warm smile and upbeat chatter reminded her of her younger brother, bouncing from one subject to the next, happy to be around people.

In comparison, Owen barely opened his mouth all afternoon. His expression remained noncommittal throughout, as he concentrated on the documents before him. If he said anything, it was related to the case.

"Where did you make reservations for dinner, Chantal?" Captain Bouchard asked. "I hope you're going to show our visitors around the city."

Chantal's stomach plummeted. She hadn't planned on playing tour guide tonight, but her boss left her with little choice in the matter. "I didn't reserve anywhere yet. I didn't ask where they'd like to go."

"No need to bother about us. We can take care of ourselves," Mark said, attempting to let Chantal off the hook. A stab of guilt pierced her. He was such a nice guy, and she knew her reaction gave her away.

"Not at all. I'm looking forward to it." She forced a smile onto her face.

"You should take them somewhere on Grande Allée. There's lots of action there with the *Festival d'Été*."

Chantal tried to catch Captain Bouchard's eye. She didn't need more suggestions from him.

"That sounds like fun," Owen said.

Chantal sent him a curious look. He didn't seem like someone who liked to have fun. Was he making a joke at her expense?

She returned her attention to Bouchard. "Would you like to join us?" Chantal asked her boss with a raised brow.

"Unfortunately, I'm not available tonight." His response was a bit too fast. Chantal suspected he had expected her invitation and had contrived to avoid it. "But Chantal will entertain you." He added this for the benefit of the men, missing Chantal's slight grimace.

"What did he mean?" Mark asked as Bouchard left the room. "A festival?"

"*Le Festival d'Été*," she said. "It's a summer music festival in Quebec." She frowned. "It'll be difficult to find a place to eat on Grande Allée. It's in the center of the action. But I'll try something."

Chantal crossed the room to place a call. A few minutes later, she returned with a satisfied smile. "We're in luck. I have a friend who owns a restaurant. He'll hold a table for us. But we have to be there by seven thirty."

"Where are you staying?" she asked the Torontonians as they prepared to leave. Owen walked a few steps to pick up his briefcase, and Chantal noticed he moved with a pronounced limp. She thought she had detected something earlier. She made a mental note to find out what had happened to his leg.

"At the Hilton, uptown," Mark said.

"Great, you're close to the restaurant. We'll meet there."

Chantal's apartment was located one street over from Cartier Avenue, a trendy artery lined with shops, markets, restaurants, and bars. Its unique streetlights looked like giant circular lampshades, hanging over the street, each of them painted with different vibrant patterns.

Chantal sprinted up the steps to the outer door of the quadplex building and up another interior flight of stairs to her apartment door. She stripped off her clothes, jumped into the shower to freshen up, and changed into something a little less office and a bit more evening.

The skirt was black, tighter and shorter than the one she wore to work. She paired it with a sheer black sleeveless top and wore a black camisole underneath. Slipping her feet into a pair of high-heeled pumps and running a brush through her hair, she checked her lipstick and grabbed her purse.

Fortunately, she lived within walking distance of the restaurant.

Within minutes, Chantal didn't feel so fortunate and cursed her vanity. She rarely wore heels, and though the restaurant wasn't far, she still had a few blocks to go. She concentrated on the sights and sounds to draw her mind away from the pain. Some streets, including Grande Allée, were closed to vehicles and crowded with tourists and locals of all ages, shapes, and sizes.

Street artists performed for spare change, while others were part of the festival offerings. A band tuned instruments for their upcoming performance, and she knew they would have plenty of music to entertain them.

Chantal hoped to arrive first, but again, luck wasn't with her. However, when she spotted the two men sitting at a coveted table on the outside terrace, her delight overshadowed her discontent.

Owen seemed more mellow and affable than witnessed to date, although he lagged behind Mark by a considerable margin. Relaxing with a glass of wine in her hand, Chantal set aside her misgivings about the man and vowed to enjoy the evening.

After the server took their orders, she focused her attention on Mark.

"Tell me about yourself? Were you born and raised in Toronto?"

"I'm from Nova Scotia. I was a military brat."

"Did you ever live in Valcartier?" Chantal referred to the Canadian Forces Base, north of Quebec City.

"Sure did. We were posted there for four years." Mark's smile held a trace of wistfulness. "We loved it here."

"So, you're familiar with the area. Did you pick up French?"

Mark frowned. "Not much. I was ten when we arrived, and my parents registered me in the English school on the base. I wish I had put more effort into it."

Chantal glanced at Owen. He listened to the exchange with a lack of expression. "And you? Have you ever been here before?"

"No, but it's everything I expected."

His cryptic remark intrigued her, but she suspected now was not the time or place to dig further.

"How long have you worked together?" Chantal moved her gaze between the men.

"Never," Mark said with a smile. "We met this morning."

"But you're both from Toronto, aren't you?"

"Toronto's a big place," Owen said. "We're not from the same detachment."

He spoke as if Chantal should have been aware of these details. She mentally kicked herself. He was right; she should have known. She also suspected he had more time to prepare for this case, while her boss had dumped it in her lap yesterday.

Their meals arrived and eased the moment of awkwardness.

Excellent food and smooth, free-flowing wine helped. The warm night air, combined with the milling groups of people and the festive atmosphere of Grande Allée, gave the evening a magical quality.

As the night progressed, Mark and Chantal's level of giddiness increased in proportion to the amount of wine they consumed. He insisted she teach him a few lines of French, with which he practiced on the servers and other patrons. The results were hilarious, at least from Chantal's point of view. She clinked glasses with people at neighboring tables and shouted words of encouragement at the street performers.

Owen didn't join in the merriment, although Chantal thought she detected a glint of suppressed laughter in his eye.

When Mark waved his arm to order another round of drinks, Chantal raised her hand in protest. She had reached her limit of alcohol consumption. One more drink and she wouldn't make it to work the next day.

She stood, unsteady on her feet, and knew she had made the right decision.

"I'll be on my way. I'll see you two tomorrow."

Mark stood. "Are you okay to make it home? Do you need me to walk with you?"

Chantal smiled at his earnest expression. "I'm fine. Thanks."

She flung her bag over her shoulder and shoved her way through the crowd. She made it six feet when a hand snuck around her waist and a beer-laden voice made a lewd suggestion in her ear.

Chantal aimed her narrowed gaze at the drunken smile that advanced closer.

"Remove your hand and move away," she told the man in French.

He either didn't hear her or he didn't care. He laughed and hauled her closer.

"If you don't remove your hand, it'll soon have a handcuff on it."

His eyes sparkled. "I like your style, *ma belle*."

"You won't if the other handcuff is on a guy named Jean-Guy who's covered in tattoos and wants to share a bunk with you."

Chantal withdrew her badge from her purse and held it inches from his nose. The man squinted and peered at it. Seconds later, he held both hands in the air and an embarrassed grin lit his face.

"Excuse me, officer. I was just being friendly." He took two steps back.

Chantal glanced over her shoulder to see an alarmed Mark and a composed Owen watching the incident. She waved and left the bar. Another night on the town.

• • •

The pain increased with each step. Chantal considered removing her shoes and walking barefoot the final block before her apartment building. But when she weighed the chances of stepping on a piece of broken glass against having blisters, she chose the blisters.

However, as soon as she unlocked the outer door of the building, she slipped out of her shoes and dashed up the stairs to her apartment. Chantal tossed the offensive shoes by the door, wondering if she should put them in the garbage bin, and hung her purse on a coat rack.

She massaged the back of her neck as she went to the kitchen to fill a glass with ice water. She needed to hydrate after drinking so much wine, she thought. Chantal returned to the living area and lowered herself into an armchair, crossing her tortured feet on a matching ottoman.

She laid her head back and smiled. The evening hadn't been as bad as expected. Mark had entertained her, and she had witnessed a tiny softening of Owen's nature. Chantal considered that an achievement worth celebrating.

Her brows lowered in a perplexed frown when she focused on the sofa across from her. Chantal unfolded herself from her comfortable spot and crossed to the offending piece of furniture. As she bent to move it back into position, she drew herself up and lifted her gaze to the wall. Chantal reached for her cell phone.

CHAPTER 3

Chantal stood to the side, her arms crossed, as she kept her eye on technicians who brushed doorknobs, tables, and other surfaces with fingerprint powder. She knew she faced a long night as she cleaned up the mess.

Despite her desire to change into comfortable clothing, Chantal had disturbed nothing in the apartment. She cursed herself for sitting in the armchair, but if she hadn't, she would never have noticed the sofa being out of place.

Now, a cop swept the rooms with a detector, finding a tiny camera installed in a painting above the sofa and two microphones, one in a plant and the other on the back of her night table in the bedroom.

Chantal had little doubt this invasion of privacy was related to the case, but the rapidity of the offence and the knowledge of the intruder shocked her. She got the assignment two days earlier. *How did someone gain that information so fast? What did they hope to overhear in her apartment?*

Two things were certain. She wouldn't sleep tonight, and there would be a full sweep of the offices at SQ headquarters first thing in the morning.

● ● ●

"Why didn't you call us?"

For the first time in their brief association, Chantal witnessed something other than good cheer in Mark's expression.

"Why would I? What could you have done?"

Chantal had filled in Captain Bouchard and her RCMP associates about the events of the previous night at her apartment, and she faced a grim line-up of cops. Mark had spoken up first.

Bouchard took advantage of the pause to insert his opinion. "Given you support, advice, protection, to name a few."

Chantal clenched her teeth as she considered her response. She reminded herself to accept their words for what they were; expressions of concern and not doubts of her abilities.

"Thank you," she said with a sigh. "I appreciate that, but I was fine. It wasn't an act of violence. Someone invaded my privacy. And I'm sure it involves this case."

"We've only been working on it for a day."

Owen mirrored Chantal's thoughts from the night before.

"You're right," she said. "Someone already knows who's on it and is trying to get ahead of us."

"We knew we were dealing with a cyber expert," Bouchard said. "We have to work harder and faster to gain the upper hand." His gaze swept over the trio. It was his signal to get back to work.

• • •

By late morning, Chantal was on the brink of losing her mind. They had spent the rest of the morning hours buried in paperwork. The legal documents, bank statements, and written statements morphed into an incomprehensible blur of words and numbers. She glanced at her partners. As suspected, Mark loved sifting through data the way dogs loved to find themselves inside meat lockers. Chantal couldn't understand it, but she was relieved at least one of them enjoyed it.

Owen, as was his way, was harder to read. If he thrived on it, or if it bore him to death, his outward demeanor revealed nothing. Stoic was too soft a word for him. Several times, he shot her a look when she paced the room, incapable of sitting any longer. It was neither disapproving nor sympathetic, but it was almost enough to make her sit down. Emphasis on 'almost.'

As the hours crawled by, her restlessness grew. The agenda didn't include action, but at least a good rousing discussion was in order. Yet, whenever she suggested discussing theories, Owen shut her down.

"It's too early for that. We need to find a connection."

A surge of irritation drove Chantal to pivot toward him. "Excuse me, I didn't get the memo that put you in charge of what we do or don't do."

Owen gave a small shrug. "Someone has to do it. Otherwise, we'd get nowhere."

"I have an equal say. We all do."

"Fine. When it's time, I'll listen, but there's no point tossing out theories with nothing to back them up."

"I'm finishing the second company now," Mark said as he tapped on his keyboard, his fingers a blur of motion. The tremor in his voice betrayed his reaction to their heated conversation. "You can check for matches soon, while I get the third one set up."

Chantal rolled her eyes. Another round of tedium.

"I have to talk to Captain Bouchard," she said. "I won't be back until after lunch. You'll be all right to take care of yourselves?"

Mark waved her off with an uneasy smile.

Chantal found her boss in his office, and he didn't seem surprised to see her. He removed his glasses and sighed. "What can I do for you?"

"This will take forever. Can't we get a team together to help us go through these documents? The phone book is more exciting."

"Police work involves more than car chases and gunfire. You've served long enough to realize that."

Chantal frowned. She wanted to argue, but Bouchard was her boss, and she would take the hit without flinching. "I think we could move this along faster. Get some results, you know."

"I don't have the personnel to put on this. You guys are it, and it will take as long as it takes."

"Because there's no risk to human life, there's no rush."

Bouchard considered her observation for a moment. "That would be it, yes."

Chantal stood. "I'm not babysitting them at lunchtime. I have something to do."

He glared at her over his glasses. "There's no need to 'babysit', but I want to see a team player."

"I will be, don't worry."

Checking her watch, she saw it was noon. Chantal bypassed the conference room and went to her locker. Five minutes later, she wore her running outfit, had completed her stretches, and headed out the door. She hit the running track behind the building, joining a handful of officers and other staff, despite the heat and humidity common to Quebec this time of year. Running the circuit several times would eliminate her agitation and put her in a better mood for the afternoon.

A quick shower, a sandwich eaten on the run, and Chantal was only five minutes late to resume their 'oh-so-scintillating' work.

The run helped. Her focus returned, and though Chantal rarely sat during the afternoon, she read documents as she paced, stopping at intervals to scribble notes on a pad.

"I think that's enough for today." Owen stood and stretched, shaking out his right leg. Chantal had noticed the habit during the day. She assumed, whatever the injury or affliction, it caused his muscles to stiffen if he sat for a long period. "We'll pick up tomorrow where we left off," he said.

Chantal bristled, wondering who had given him permission to determine their work schedule. "You guys go ahead. I'll continue for a while."

The two men stared at her. Mark's eyes widened as Owen's brows lowered. Chantal knew she came across as being restless and eager to leave the dreary room. But Owen's imperial decisions made her balk.

"Suit yourself." Owen shrugged and turned to Mark. "You feel like stopping somewhere for a drink?"

"Sure." Mark's voice sounded doubtful as he cast a last glance at Chantal. "See you tomorrow."

Chantal sent him a half-hearted wave as she lowered herself into a chair and watched them leave. After her stupid declaration of independence, Chantal needed to make a dent in the stack of files before she left for home.

Out of sheer stubbornness, Chantal attacked the papers, determined to dig herself out of the hole into which she had cast herself.

"What are you doing here?"

Captain Bouchard stood in the doorway wearing a stunned expression.

"I wanted to get on with this." Her tone sounded as lame as her words.

"It's seven o'clock. Go home."

"I didn't realize it was so late." She lied. She had checked her watch every five minutes for the last hour, but the pile didn't appear low enough to justify leaving.

Shaking her head, she grabbed her purse and left the rest for the next day.

• • •

The bar was busy for a Tuesday night. Owen and Mark looked out of place, dressed in dark suits. Their ties were in their pockets, and they had loosened the top buttons of their shirts. It helped, but their style of clothing and rigid posture made them stand out.

The bar was named *'Le Bureau de Poste'*, which translated to 'The Post Office.' It was housed in what used to be an actual Post Office. It served the usual pub fare and drinks at a reasonable cost, and it drew a young and rowdy crowd. Thus, the strangeness of two English-speaking uptight-looking RCMP officers.

"I guess things would be different if Chantal was here." Owen's gaze circled the room, taking in the crowd as he took a long sip of his beer.

Mark emitted a burst of laughter. "That's an understatement. She'd probably know everyone in here."

The hostess showed them to a table, and they placed their orders. The food arrived in short order, and they devoured it.

"I didn't realize how hungry I was," Owen said, as he sat back in his chair with a sigh. He sent a questioning look across the table. "How about we make it an early night?"

"I agree," Mark said, his smile sheepish. "I was a little fuzzy today. It wouldn't have hurt to cut back on the wine last night."

"I'll go to the washroom and then we'll grab a cab." Owen stood and pulled on his suit jacket.

"We'll meet outside." Mark made his way through the crowd that had grown denser as the evening wore on. Outside, he filled his lungs with fresh air and welcomed the sense of space that was lacking inside the bar. He pulled his phone from his pocket and scrolled through his apps to see if he had new messages.

A large body careened into Mark from the side and hurled him to the hard asphalt. It followed him to the ground and lay on top of him, a dead weight.

"What the…" Mark was in an awkward position on his side, with his right arm pinned beneath him. The man was unmoving, unconscious. At least, Mark hoped he was unconscious, and not dead.

High-pitched, agitated voices surrounded him, but he didn't understand a word. When the weight left him, he flipped onto his back and got a glimpse of the guy who had crashed into him.

He was young and shorter than Mark, but heavyset. He wore jeans and a t-shirt, and he had sandy-brown, longish hair. His hair was all that Mark saw of his features as his head flopped atop his shoulders.

Two young women shouted at Mark in rapid-fire French, their eyes animated and their arms flailing in every direction.

"Is he okay?" Concern replaced Mark's aggravation as he struggled to his feet and brushed dirt off his pants. His right shoulder ached, but he had no injuries. At his words, the women stopped and shared a wide-eyed stare, before one of them spoke in halting English.

"I saw… a man… hit." With this, she made a chopping motion with her hand. "And push!" Again, she simulated a harsh shove. Mark got the picture.

"Where is he? What does he look like?"

The woman lifted her shoulders and held her hands out, palm up. "I didn't see good." She held a hand high above her head. "Tall. I only see back."

"What's going on?" Owen appeared behind Mark's left shoulder.

"Somebody clocked that guy and shoved him into me. Knocked me to the ground."

Owen looked him over. "You okay?"

"A lot better than him." He gestured toward the still-unconscious man. Someone had placed a rolled-up jacket underneath his head. The sound of sirens reached them, growing steadily louder.

"Let's go before we have to answer questions from the locals," Owen said.

"But shouldn't we stay for that reason?"

"Not if we're trying to keep a low profile on this case. Quebec is a small city. Word could get around. Come on." He tugged on Mark's sleeve.

Mark patted the pockets of his jacket. "Wait. I don't have my phone. It was in my hand when I got knocked over."

They searched the area for the cell phone, knowing it was unlikely to survive the fall and the moving feet during the excitement of the attack.

A young man approached Mark with an outstretched hand. He held a cell phone in his palm. *"C'est à vous, Monsieur?"*

"Yes… I mean, *oui. Merci.*" The Good Samaritan returned Mark's smile before heading into the bar. The RCMP tech took time to check the device before returning it to the safety of his pocket. "That was pure luck."

"Okay, let's go," Owen said. A police car had arrived at the scene with an ambulance following behind. No one seemed to notice them slipping through the crowd to cross the street and climb into a taxicab.

CHAPTER 4

"I have an idea."

Two heads lifted and pivoted in Chantal's direction.

"We made no headway with employees. We've looked at common suppliers, but what if it was someone working for a cleaning service?"

"We included service companies. They don't have any in common," Owen said. He returned his gaze to his computer.

"We haven't looked at the employees of those service companies. What if someone worked for all three? Or gave up a job with one to work with the other?"

After a moment of silence, Owen spoke. "Mark, find us the names of their cleaning services. Chantal, we'll need you to set up meetings for us. We have to examine their payroll records."

Chantal set up a meeting for that afternoon, with two others the next day. By the end of the following afternoon, they got lucky.

A young man, Luc Beaudet, appeared on the payroll of the three cleaning service companies. The first breached company had employed Beaudet as a service technician before they fired him for unprofessional behavior.

A month after his dismissal, he started a job as a night shift employee for the cleaning company, guaranteeing that his former daytime colleagues would not see him. During that period, someone hacked the company emails. Beaudet quit his job and turned up a couple of weeks later with another company. The cycle repeated.

"He probably used a keylogger."

Chantal shot Mark a questioning look.

"It's a plugin that's inserted into the keyboard port between the CPU box and the keyboard cable. It intercepts all the signals as the person types. He'd get the passwords, logins, everything he needed to take over emails."

"As a janitor, he'd have easy access to anyone's computer," Chantal said.

Owen turned to Mark. "Would it still be there?"

"We can check, but it's not likely. He probably removed it and used it for the next victim."

"We'll bring him in." Owen's expression was grim.

Chantal interceded. "I understand this guy is technical. Installing keyloggers is a piece of cake for him. Downloading passwords and accesses would be easy, but he's young. He's twenty-four years old. He worked in the service department. What would he know about wiring funds through Hong Kong to offshore banks?"

"He had an accomplice," Owen stated. "That's obvious. We'll find out who it is."

With little effort, they picked up the suspect at his apartment and brought him in for questioning. Owen and Chantal would interrogate Beaudet, while Mark would watch the live video feed in an adjoining room.

Luc Beaudet was thin and wiry, of medium height, with a mop of brown hair that was longer in the front and flopped in front of his eyes. Every thirty seconds, his hand shoved his hair off his face while his right leg jittered. He chewed on his lower lip as his eyes shifted from one police officer to the other. Chantal sat across from him and was certain his heart pounded in his chest.

They informed him of his rights. When asked if he wanted a lawyer present, he hesitated, weighing the advantages and disadvantages, but decided against it. Chantal wrote off his reasoning as youth and inexperience. She was quite happy not to deal with a lawyer.

Beaudet was bilingual, eliminating the need to translate for Owen and Mark. Captain Bouchard handed the reins of the interrogation to Owen, leaving a disappointed Chantal to represent the SQ.

"Mr. Beaudet, do you understand why you're here?"

"No." His leg jiggled faster, and his eyes skittered between the cops and the tabletop.

"You worked for Macrem, didn't you?" Owen clasped his hands behind his back as he stood over the young man. It forced Beaudet to look up at the cop.

"Yeah. So?"

"From what I hear, it didn't go well. They fired you, didn't they?"

"It didn't matter. I didn't want to work there, anyway."

"Why was that?"

"They don't pay well." He moved his gaze from Owen and fixed it on the table.

"After you left Macrem, you worked for an office cleaning company as a janitor. You were better paid there?"

He shrugged a shoulder without lifting his head.

"Answer him." Beaudet flinched at the sharpness of Chantal's voice.

"It was temporary, and I like working nights."

"You moved from one janitor job to another," Owen said. "If you wanted a different job, why didn't you return to customer service or try something else?"

Beaudet straightened in his chair, his expression annoyed. "I have trouble staying in one place. I get bored. Since when is that against the law? What's this about, anyway?"

Owen leaned forward and placed his palms on the table. "What it's about is fraud, email fraud, hundreds of thousands of dollars' worth."

"I don't have that kind of money." His eyes flashed with triumph. "You can check my bank account. Go ahead."

"That'll happen in good time," Owen said, erasing the gleam from the young man's expression. "Can you explain why trouble followed you from one company to the next? When you worked as a janitor at…let me see…." Owen opened the file. "NetJet Services, they sent you to clean the offices of Macrem, the employer that fired you and soon after became a victim of fraud. Then you moved onto other companies, and by some bizarre twist of fate, they were also victims of fraud and lost a ton of money." He met Beaudet's anxious gaze.

The young man swallowed. "I had nothing to do with it. You can't prove it."

"You had help." Owen ignored his plea of innocence.

"I did nothing wrong." He turned a panicked gaze to Chantal, as if she could protect him from the stern cop.

"We're not after you." Owen softened his tone. "We want the people behind it and would appreciate any help you could give us."

"I did nothing," Beaudet repeated, but doubt and misery rang in his voice.

"So, if you didn't do anything, you wouldn't object to us looking at your computer files." Owen slid into the seat beside Chantal and leaned his elbows on the table.

The young man's brows lowered. "That's personal. You're not allowed to do that."

"With your permission, we can."

"You're not getting permission from me." He crossed his arms over his chest and thrust his chin out, but his gaze ricocheted around the room.

A long silence stretched between them until Owen spoke.

"I guess we're finished here, but if more money disappears, we'll knock at your door."

"I can go?" Beaudet shifted his gaze to Chantal, seeking confirmation. She remained expressionless. She had her own questions to ask.

Owen raised his hands, palms upward. "We have no proof, do we?"

The man smiled and stood, his chair almost toppling over in his haste. Owen and Chantal did the same, at a slower pace. They called a uniformed officer to escort Beaudet from the building. Before the taxi arrived to pick him up, another officer was in an unmarked car, prepared to follow him.

"We could've tried for a warrant to search his place," Chantal said.

"Based on what? His job as a janitor? Perhaps things are different here, but in Toronto we'd need more to go on."

Chantal tightened her lips. He had a point, but her gut told her Beaudet was connected to the crime and letting him walk away felt wrong.

"Do you really think he'll lead us to his accomplice?" Chantal stood facing Owen, hands on hips, challenging him. Mark came from the adjacent room to join them.

The taller man shrugged. "It's worth a try. He's young and scared. He'll want to talk to someone. Who better than the guy who got him into this mess? We'll watch him for a while. In the meantime, we'll look at those files again."

Chantal opened her mouth to protest, unsure if she could handle another session of dredging through paperwork. But she didn't have any better suggestions to offer. She crossed her eyes at Owen's departing back and caught the grin Mark sent her way.

CHAPTER 5

"Can we find his contact through his IP address?" Owen faced Mark. They had returned to the investigation room.

"It's possible. It'll depend what kind of protection he put in place. He may not be as smart as he thought he was. But, if he used a bulletproof server, we could be in trouble. I'm good, but I'm not that good."

"A bulletproof server?" Chantal asked. "What's that?"

"It's a VPN or Virtual Private Network. If the server's in North America, we'll be in luck, but if it's in a country like Russia or North Korea, it'll take forever to get access to it, if at all."

"Mark, you work on that while Chantal and I check out the banks."

Chantal's smile disappeared, and she shot Owen an irritated glare. His bossiness knew no bounds.

Mark appeared sympathetic as she walked past him. Chantal glimpsed his wallpaper on his computer screen and did a double take.

"Is that you?" She leaned over Mark's shoulder to get a better look.

A lush paradise of turquoise waters, white sand, and palm trees covered the screen. Mark stood in the foreground of craggy rocks and tropical growth, dressed in a casual t-shirt and shorts and wearing an enormous grin. He held a small container filled with indistinguishable items.

"Yeah, that's me, in Fiji." A proud smile lit his face.

"Fiji? It's beautiful. That's a nice trip."

"It was. I was geocaching."

"Geo what?" Chantal asked.

Mark's comment caught Owen's attention, his head turning in their direction.

"Geocaching. It's a hobby of mine," Mark said.

"I've never heard of it."

"I have," Owen said. "Doesn't it involve traipsing around the world looking for treasure?"

"Treasure?" Intrigued, Chantal pulled up a chair and focused on Mark. "Tell me about this."

Mark laughed. "I don't traipse all over the world, although I've had nice trips. But you can do geocaching anywhere, even here in Quebec City." He pulled out his cell phone. "I have an app on my phone. I can hunt for the cache, near or far, wherever I want. When I find it, I log it in. If I take a souvenir from the cache, I leave something behind to replace it."

"That's amazing." Chantal had a tough time imagining this young man as a world traveler hunting hidden treasures.

Mark shrugged self-consciously. "It's a hobby. I like it. Globally, millions of people do it."

Chantal blinked in disbelief. "That's fascinating."

Owen stood and hovered behind her right shoulder. "Almost as fascinating as our next task. Let's go, Chantal."

• • •

With privacy laws and bureaucratic red tape, getting information from a Canadian bank was a challenge. But working with a bank in Asia was just short of impossible. Simply dealing with the difference in time zones gave Chantal heartburn.

As the door shut behind them, Owen pulled his cell phone out of his pocket. Chantal ignored him. She settled into a chair and logged into the computer, pulling up her files to find the name and contact number of the bank. Her concentration broke when she overheard Owen's side of the phone conversation.

"Li Jun, it's Owen. How are you and your family?... Yes, fine... Listen, I need a favor."

Owen had captured Chantal's full attention. Her gaze drilled into him, but he refused to glance in her direction.

"I need a trace on a transaction through the Hong Kong Commercial Bank. All I have is a date, an amount, and what company it originated from. Can you help me?... Great, I owe you one—again."

His smile and his chuckle appeared genuine, much to Chantal's astonishment.

She shook her head. An inside contact would make her life easier, but it baffled her that this man could pull strings with such ease. Chantal listened to him rhyme off the banking information to his source and realized she would have to compliment him on his impressive skills.

"Nice," she said, after he disconnected the call. She had pried the simple word from her throat like a bird dragging an unwilling worm from a hole.

Owen's brows lifted. "Something wrong?"

"Of course not. You just saved me a lot of time. It's great. Who is this guy?"

"Li Jun Cheng. He works for one of the big banks in Hong Kong, and he's got connections. I should have the info within half an hour."

As predicted, Owen's cell phone chirped twenty minutes later, and he jotted down the information. He stared at the notes for a few moments after setting his cell phone on the desk.

"It seems the funds were briefly in an account with the Hong Kong Commercial Bank before being transferred to an account in the Cayman Islands." He lifted his gaze to Chantal's.

"Was he able to give you the name on the account?"

"WS Corporation."

Chantal grimaced. "That sounds like a generic name someone would give a shell company."

"We'll check it out. There may be something there."

"Do you have any connections in the Cayman bank system? You could save us time."

"Do I detect sarcasm?"

"Not at all. Your initiative is impressive." Chantal stood and stretched. "I appreciate anything that can move this case faster. I hate wading through paperwork."

"For the next step, we'll need clearance. That's the only way the banks will cough up information." Owen hit speed-dial on his phone, and within seconds, he instructed someone to prepare the papers requesting the warrant. He ended the call and turned to her. "I hope Mark made some progress on his end."

As if he had conjured him, Mark Pratt appeared in the doorway. "I spoke to my guys. They'll gain access to the victim's network and try to trace the IP address. We won't have any news until tomorrow at the earliest."

"Same here," Owen said.

Chantal's phone jangled on the table beside her. She answered and spoke in French. Her brow furrowed, snagging the interest of the RCMP officers. She disconnected with a sigh. "That was from the officer tailing Beaudet. Our friend went home and stayed there."

"Yeah. That was a long shot." Owen's frown matched Chantal's. "He could've called or texted his partner, or he could've done nothing. Maybe he's more afraid of his co-conspirator than he is of the police. In which case, we've got a dangerous person to find."

They pondered the thought for a long moment before Owen looked at his watch. "It's six o'clock. I suggest we knock off for the night. Do you want to join us for dinner?"

Chantal appreciated the invitation, but she needed to defuse some energy. Sitting around a restaurant all evening wouldn't do it. She politely declined, offered restaurant suggestions, and left.

Chapter 6

Gunfire echoed off concrete walls. A wide stance braced Chantal against the recoil of her handgun as bullets pounded into her target without mercy. Lips set in a harsh line, she fired her weapon until a telltale click signaled the end of her ammunition.

Chantal lowered the gun and shook out her shoulders as her eyes narrowed on the shape that advanced toward her.

"Not bad," she mumbled, examining the cluster of bullet holes in the black cardboard silhouette.

Glancing over her shoulder, Chantal noted all firing lanes were occupied, and three cops waited their turn. She removed the earmuffs and protective eyewear and returned them to the range supervisor on her way to the locker room.

As Chantal retrieved her bag and shut the orange metal door of the locker, a familiar voice spoke from behind her.

"Good shots. It's obvious you've been practicing."

She turned and encountered the man's gaze. His face, with its dark scruff of beard and sharp blue eyes, was as familiar to her as his voice.

"Paul."

"You seem surprised to see me here."

"I thought you had someone waiting for you at home."

His mouth curved in a grimace. "Not anymore. Does that make you happy?"

"Why do you think I'd care?"

His leering grin displayed white teeth and reminded Chantal of why she avoided him. "We both know you miss me."

Chantal shook her head and brushed past him. "I miss you like I miss food poisoning."

"Do you want to grab a drink?" He fell into step beside her.

"No. I got things to do." Chantal wished her car wasn't at the other end of the parking lot. She knew he would follow her all the way.

"Still scanning papers?" The derision in his voice reverberated loud and clear.

"No. Transferred to white-collar." Ironically, it thrilled Chantal to announce her change of position.

"Oh, you've moved to the big time." A chuckle accompanied his words. "I bet you'll think twice before walking into a trap next time, won't you?"

Rage swelled in her chest, but Chantal wouldn't give him the satisfaction of witnessing it. Her training as an undercover cop kicked in, and she graced him with a serene smile. "There won't be a next time."

Chantal settled into her car and left Paul Morrisette to stare after her.

• • •

The man didn't notice the stifling humidity. His baggy beige shorts and pale blue t-shirt kept him cool. Black sneakers encased his feet. He dressed like men in this neighborhood. The store's awning shaded him from the sun as he drank from a Coke can dripping with condensation.

People swept past without taking notice of him. The man didn't care about them either. He focused his gaze on the quadplex across the street. Through the window on the top right side of the building, he spotted movement. Someone carried on with their day, expecting it to end like any other. There was no sign of people in the other apartments.

The man tossed the empty can in the garbage receptacle beside the door. He slung his backpack over his shoulder and crossed the street, circling behind the building. The back alley was quiet. A quick glance assured him no one paid any attention.

With soundless shoes, he climbed the stairs to the back door. The thumping music emanating from the speakers inside the apartment more than drowned out any sound he made. It also reassured him the other occupants weren't home. If they were, they had hearing problems or were long-suffering.

The man smiled. How easy this was, he thought. The target had prepared everything, with no need to deaden or mask noise. A problem solved.

His smile widened as he peered in the window and didn't see anyone in the kitchen. He pulled latex gloves from his pocket and slipped them on.

It took mere seconds to circumvent the lock on the flimsy door. He slid over the threshold and crossed unseen to the living area at the front of the apartment. Turning his back to the window, he removed the gun from the pocket of his shorts. With his senses on full alert, he waited for the occupant to enter the room.

His reward appeared in a matter of minutes. The man didn't waste time with greetings or explanations. He raised his gun as his victim passed six feet in front of him, and he pulled the trigger. It was a clean shot to the temple. The body hit the floor with a thump.

The man stood over his victim for several minutes and admired his handiwork. Moving to the hallway, he found the deceased's office. He deposited the laptop and all storage devices in his backpack.

"Time to go." He scanned the room.

In the kitchen, he stepped over the body, exited through the back, and trod down the stairs.

Chapter 7

Judging by the redness in his eyes and the slowness of his movements, Chantal assumed Mark had overindulged the previous evening. She glanced at Owen, but he didn't seem to suffer the same fate.

"Did you guys go somewhere last night?"

"Yeah, to a pub on Rue St-Jean," Mark said from his position by the coffee machine as he stirred sugar into the murky brew.

Chantal didn't know whether to be amused or concerned about Mark's nightly excesses.

"Let's get to it. Mark, any news from your team?" Owen's orders put an end to Chantal's musings.

"They're working on it," Mark answered. "They hope to contact me later today."

Chantal nodded. She admitted this was one advantage of working with the RCMP. A request for IT help at the Sûreté would increase the backlog and create a frustrating delay. The federal body possessed more resources and better connections.

"And you?" Chantal said to Owen. "Any news of the warrants?"

"They're being signed as we speak. That's the simple part. The hard part is badgering the bank to give us priority."

"Now, what do we do?" Mark said.

"We find Beaudet's accomplice. It's someone who has knowledge of money laundering."

"OC?" Chantal asked. Organized crime's involvement had already occurred to her.

Owen shrugged. "Maybe. Maybe not. It could be an independent operation with two or three people hoping to make a fast buck. It's not that complex to dream up a hacking scheme. And it's not that difficult to hide or launder the money, especially in the Caymans."

"We'll check the airlines to see if Beaudet had travel plans to soak up the sun," Chantal said. She tapped out an email as she spoke.

"Have them search for a traveling companion too," Owen added. "We're already checking family, friends, and acquaintances. We'll add co-workers to the list, both current and past."

Two hours later, Chantal leaned back and drove her fingers through her hair. "Beaudet didn't show up in any airline register," she said, staring at her email inbox.

"He took care of the hands-on stuff and left someone else in charge of everything else. I'm not surprised." Owen's fingers drummed on the tabletop, his expression pensive.

"Who?"

"We'll know soon," Mark said. "I just got word from the techies. They'll send me a list of his social media contacts."

Chantal smiled. This assignment might progress faster than expected, and she would impress Bouchard so much he'd put her back on active duty.

Beaudet had an impressive list of contacts, and they divided the names between them for further scrutiny.

Hours later, they whittled it down to one person.

"Nelson Griggs, the lawyer, hangs out with some unsavory types," Owen said.

"Oh?" He had piqued Chantal's interest. "Like who?"

"Like construction bosses rumored to be on the take. Like city officials known for the same. He may be Mafia-connected. It deserves a closer look. I'll call him." Owen cast a meaningful glance in Chantal's direction. "Our next step is to find out who heads the company that received the bank transfers."

She grimaced. Her talents weren't in financial forensics. Someone else would better handle the tracing of the company or individual that received the cash. Mark was busy with other things. If Owen made the executive decision she needed to track shell companies, she would handle it her own way.

• • •

"Hey, long time no see. This is a pleasant surprise." The brunette set aside her magazine and rose from her deck chair to give Chantal a hug. "Did you take the day off too?"

"No, I'm still on the clock. I called Jeff. He said he was running errands, and he'd be here soon. I didn't think you'd mind if I dropped by. How're you feeling?"

Tori laid a gentle hand on the tiny bump in her stomach. "Apart from being tired, I feel great."

Jeff's wife was in her fourth month of pregnancy and suffered traditional ailments, ranging from morning sickness to fatigue. But the couple's joy over the upcoming birth outweighed any minor inconveniences.

"Jeff went to pick up some paint for the nursery. Pink, of course."

Chantal laughed. "I've never seen him so happy. He wanted a girl, didn't he? He's going to be the most protective dad."

"Poor kid. She won't have a moment's peace." An indulgent smile lit Tori's face. Pregnancy suited the woman. She was small-framed, of medium height, trim and supple, with a healthy, fresh-faced appeal. It had only improved since her pregnancy began.

Chantal envied Tori's happiness. She hoped to have a family but didn't think it was in the cards. She was ecstatic for Jeff and Tori. Their road to bliss had been rough, and they deserved their new reality.

Chantal had known the woman for seven months, since a previous case involving the three of them. It had been harrowing, and it was the assignment that landed Chantal on the desk duty she itched to leave behind. But the friendship she gained from it helped to balance the difficulties that followed.

The crunch of gravel in the driveway alerted them to an arrival, and shortly after, Jeff's tall frame strolled into the backyard, a large German Shepherd following on his heels. Jeff aimed his smile at both women, but his first stop was to give his wife a kiss before he greeted Chantal.

"You checking up on me?" A wink accompanied his teasing tone.

"Someone has to. I hear you're being lazy today." She scratched the dog behind his ears, and he rewarded her with a big doggy grin. Six-year-old Riley was Jeff's shadow and helped satisfy Chantal's occasional need for animal companionship.

"I guess I am, if you think tackling Tori's honey-do list is lazy." He grinned when the two women laughed at his put-upon expression.

Chantal hadn't noticed the small brown bag in his hand until he presented it to his wife with a gentlemanly bow. Tori's cheeks took on a pretty pink color.

"You're giving away my secrets, kind sir," she said.

"It's either that or it'll get cold. Besides, it's only Chantal. You shouldn't keep secrets from her."

The aroma wafting in her direction satisfied Chantal's curiosity. "Tori, you didn't tell me."

"A lot of women have uncontrollable urges when they're pregnant." She straightened her shoulders.

Chantal laughed. "I'm not pregnant, and I often get uncontrollable urges for poutine. It's nothing to be ashamed of."

"I'm doing my best to limit them." She slid the aluminum container out of the bag and removed the lid to display French fries covered with gravy and heaps of cheese curds, a popular dish that originated in Quebec.

Tori retrieved a plastic fork from the bag and dug in. She swallowed her first mouthful before looking at them with a sheepish expression. "Would anyone else like some? I can share."

Chantal and Jeff laughed and declined her offer.

"What about you?" Jeff said to Chantal as he lowered his frame onto a chair between the two women. "I didn't think you had time for social calls."

"This isn't social." Chantal rolled her eyes. "I'm working on an exciting case. White-collar email fraud."

"Yeah, I can see how that would thrill you." Jeff's grimace matched his wife's. They both knew how much Chantal hated sitting at a desk.

"It's better than what you were doing, scanning files." Tori, ever the optimist, dug deep for a bright side.

"It is, but I work with two RCMP guys."

Jeff's expression turned to one of horror. Tori laughed. "What's wrong with that?"

The cops turned their gazes to the uninitiated civilian.

"They think they're better than us, and they know everything." A pained expression twisted Jeff's face when he turned back to Chantal. "That sucks for you."

Relief coursed through Chantal. It was nice to have someone who felt her pain and commiserated with her. "One of them is okay, Mark Pratt. He's a computer geek, but he's nice and pleasant to talk to."

"You're saying the other one is not so great." Chantal's ex-partner's dark brown eyes held pity.

"Arrogant and bossy."

"Is either of them good-looking?" Tori asked before scooping up another forkful.

Chantal frowned. "What does that have to do with it?"

"Everything. If they're easy to look at, it'll brighten your day."

Jeff's frown matched Chantal's as he looked at his wife with skepticism. "She won't hook up with an RCMP guy."

"Never," Chantal agreed.

Tori waved her fork at them. "I didn't mention hooking up. I asked if they're good-looking." She stared at her friend with raised brows.

Chantal sighed and gave in. "Okay. Sure. They're both handsome, I guess. That's it. Nothing else."

A satisfied smile settled on Tori's lips. Chantal wasn't sure if it was in response to her statement or because of the disappearing contents of the aluminum container.

"On top of that," Chantal said with a frown. "I met up with Paul at the shooting range yesterday."

Jeff's attention jerked toward her. "Paul Morrisette?"

Her husband's tone distracted Tori from her snack. "Who's he?"

"Just a guy I used to date," Chantal said, putting a casual spin on it.

"Oh. How come I've never heard of him?" Tori sent an accusatory look toward Jeff.

"Because it ended a long time ago," Chantal said. "It's been over a year since we were together. What do you say about rivers and bridges?"

"Water under the bridge," Jeff offered, but his frown contradicted his words. "What did he want?"

"He didn't want anything. We chatted." Chantal regretted mentioning her encounter with her ex-boyfriend. And, judging by the curiosity on Tori's face, she was in for an interrogation. "Anyway, I…"

"Wait, who is he? Jeff, how do you know him?"

"He's a cop," Jeff said in answer to Tori's question. "SWAT. He's also an ass."

Chantal laughed. "You're right. He is. And he's in my past with a lot of other things. Let's move on to the real reason I'm here."

Chantal wanted to change the subject. She should never have brought up Paul's name, she thought. Sometimes she wondered if Jeff took their breakup worse than she did. While Chantal's heart suffered a bruising, Jeff's sense of protectiveness raged.

She pitied any boy who showed an interest in the baby girl Tori carried.

Chantal slapped her hands on her knees. She had a job to do. "So, apart from me wanting to get out of the office, Mr. Owen Lockwood assigned me the important task of tracing shell companies. And, as you know, I'm not well-versed in financial maneuvers, so I wanted the name of your contact. Didn't you have a guy that helped you out once?"

"Yeah. He knows his stuff, but he doesn't spend much time on the right side of the law. I'm not sure your RCMP friend will like it."

"He won't even know about it. I plan to take the credit." Chantal grinned.

CHAPTER 8

At headquarters, Chantal found a quiet room in which to make her call. Jeff had given her the number for Daniel Boivin, an expert in shell companies. An ex-lawyer who served a few years for fraud, he worked as a travel agent. This held a certain irony, since the government had revoked his passport and limited his travel plans to destinations within Canada.

Chantal hadn't met the man, but judging from his voice, she imagined he was in his mid to late forties. When she introduced herself as Jeff's ex-partner, she detected the wariness in his tone, which was perhaps understandable, given his history.

"What do you want?" Boivin said.

"Information. I need to know how to trace key people involved in offshore shell companies."

"Why would I tell you that?"

"Because I'm asking nicely, and we're both friends of Jeff."

"I wouldn't say I'm a friend of his."

"He helped you out on a couple of occasions, and you owe him. And since he sent me to you, you now owe me." As the words came out of her mouth, she realized they made little sense. She pressed on. "So, what can you tell me?"

A deep sigh swept through the line. What followed was a concise method for tracking experts in bank fraud.

Chantal disconnected the call, leaned back in her chair, and studied her scribbled notes. She spent a few minutes organizing them before returning to the conference room to join her RCMP partners.

Both men raised their heads when she entered, one grinning and the other scowling.

"Where were you?" Owen said.

"Hello to you too." Chantal graced him with a broad, insincere smile. "I did what you asked me so nicely to do. I looked into shell companies, and I have a strategy." She held up her pad with the newly written notes. "It'll take some computer time."

Owen nodded toward her laptop. "You'd better get at it. I don't plan to spend weeks here."

Chantal wanted to ask him why he was so grumpy, but she bit her tongue. She remembered promising Captain Bouchard she'd play nice.

She threw a speculative glance in Mark's direction. He could do the computer work in a fraction of the time, she thought. He winked and nodded in response as he caught her unspoken request. When Owen stood to take a phone call, Chantal slid the pad across to Mark. He took it with a smile and skimmed over the notes.

"Perfect. I'll get on it," he said in a low voice.

"I owe you one."

"Don't worry about it."

"That was Griggs' secretary."

Owen's voice came from behind Chantal's left shoulder. She swiveled to face him. The lawyer's quick reply surprised her. Was he desperate for business or was someone else pushing him to respond? "And?" she asked.

"We'll meet him the day after tomorrow in Montreal."

Chantal's eyes widened. It left them with little time.

* * * *

Her bag sat at the door, packed with a mixed wardrobe. Chantal needed to portray a savvy businesswoman, but she threw in casual clothes for her off-hours. Her traveling outfit consisted of a pair of haute couture jeans topped with a pale blue Ralph Lauren blazer and a cream-colored blouse.

A loud buzz propelled her to the window. A black Mercedes was parked at the curb. They would travel in style to their destination, a two-and-a-half-hour drive. It wouldn't do to show up in anything other than an expensive vehicle.

Opening the door, she faced an Owen who had also put thought into his clothing. He wore beige chinos, brown leather shoes, and a tailored sports jacket over an open-necked shirt. Casual chic.

"Ready?" A quick appraisal of Chantal's attire accompanied his curt greeting. Whether it earned his approval hung in the air.

Without another word, Chantal grabbed her bag and wheeled it out the door. Owen took it from her with a trace of a smile curving his lips.

"We have to practice keeping up appearances, don't we?"

Chantal wondered how far he expected her to go to keep up appearances. The bare minimum would be a challenge for her. Pretending to be in love with Owen would be like climbing a ten-foot brick wall covered in grease.

Settled in the luxury car, her manicured hand, laden with fake diamond rings, trailed over the soft leather seat as Owen pulled into traffic. "It's obvious the RCMP is footing the bill," she said. "The SQ wouldn't dig this deep into its pockets."

"There's no point in going through it if we don't appear authentic."

Chantal's gaze fell to her Gucci handbag, nestled at her feet. She had stayed up late, studying the profiles created for them by the RCMP. The organization left nothing out.

According to common databases and registers, they were Mr. and Mrs. Danvers, or John and Michelle. They came from well-to-do families. John was the offspring of a moneyed investment advisor from Toronto, and Michelle was the spoiled daughter of a Quebec City real estate tycoon. Raised within their respective family businesses, they had learned the tools of the trade. As a married couple, they wanted to try their hand at making quick money.

The law enforcement officers threw together the strategy in a day and a half. Owen and Chantal would meet Griggs under their new identities. Owen had already set up the appointment using the fake name and a vague reference to a business proposal.

The RCMP whittled out the vagueness and put together a solid proposal. Presuming their suspicions were on target, the lawyer would take the bait and agree to a fraudulent money scheme. If they pinned the email fraud on him, the investigation would end there. If he wasn't the top man in the scheme, the police hoped to move up the chain of command.

The highway between the two cities was not scenic. It involved a lot of flat land, trees, farms, and a scattering of smaller cities and towns. Chantal had driven it many times, and it sparked no interest in her.

If she expected jovial conversation to pass the time, Owen disappointed her. Chantal attempted to banter, but it led nowhere, and she gave up.

In Owen, Chantal increasingly saw a man who studied his surroundings and the people in them before venturing too close. *Was this why he was cut out for white-collar crime? Because of an intensity for details?*

At the Queen Elizabeth Hotel in downtown Montreal, the valet opened the passenger side door with a respectful bow. Chantal slid out of the vehicle and gave him the slightest hint of a smile, leaving Owen to hand him a tip once he ferried them into the vast lobby of the luxury hotel.

Inside their room, Chantal relaxed. She didn't need to play the haughty, pampered, want-to-be businesswoman when they were alone. She could gaze with wide-eyed awe at the opulent 20th story suite of rooms and the magnificent view of the city of Montreal.

"Lifestyles of the rich and famous." Owen spoke from behind her.

"I'd hate to get used to this. It would make my own life appear very boring."

"Rich people have problems, maybe more than regular people."

"I suppose," she said, moving her gaze from the view to encompass the room. "One bedroom. But there's a comfortable-looking couch."

Owen responded with a noncommittal shrug. "We'll deal with it later. We've got a couple of hours before our appointment with Mr. Griggs. I suggest we change, have lunch in the hotel restaurant, and head over."

A tight-fitting black-and-white striped dress with a black bolero jacket replaced the trendy jeans. Black high-heels replaced the patent-leather loafers. Owen donned a dark gray Armani suit.

At Rosélys, the restaurant on the ground floor of the hotel, the hostess escorted them to a private corner booth. Chantal indulged in the most exquisite, expensive Niçoise salad she had ever eaten, while Owen decided on a steak.

They weren't the only well-to-do businesspeople in the restaurant. Individuals of both genders surrounded them, dressed in expensive clothing and jewels. Many carried on cell phone conversations, and no one seemed to mind the rudeness.

Both English and French circulated in equal measure. That was one difference between Montreal and Quebec City, Chantal reflected. A business hub in Canada, the much larger city of Montreal attracted individuals from everywhere, and the English language was more prevalent than in the province's capital city.

An hour and a half later, the cops stood in front of a white brick building with grimy windows in the Notre-Dame-de-Graces borough of the city, not as upscale as the area surrounding the Queen Elizabeth Hotel. The ground floor housed a coffee shop and a small health food store. The two other floors were home to a real estate agent, a yoga studio, and a computer repair shop, along with Nelson Griggs, attorney-at-law.

Despite the dissimilarity of his co-tenants, or perhaps because of it, Mr. Griggs strove for the look of a high-level law firm. Although small, his reception area was well-appointed with comfortable leather chairs, low tables, and plants. A well-dressed brunette with a wide, welcoming smile worked as his receptionist.

The man greeted them from behind an imposing desk free of everything except a laptop computer. A credenza sat to the side, also devoid of paper or photos.

Nelson Griggs circled his desk to meet them, his hand outstretched toward Owen.

"Mr. Danvers. Pleased to meet you. And you must be Mrs. Danvers," he said as he shook Chantal's hand, a wide smile on his face. She mentally registered the need for hand sanitizer after the meeting.

Chantal returned his smile but noted with asperity he had relegated her to 'the missus.' It gave her an important insight into this man's character. In his late forties to early fifties, he wore an expensive dark suit and shoes. His cologne preceded his person, which made Chantal grateful for the light touch Owen used to apply his fragrance.

"How can I help you?" the lawyer said after the usual exchange of pleasantries concerning the weather, the trip from Quebec City, and their impression of their accommodations. Chantal leaned back in her armchair and laced her fingers across her abdomen. Griggs' signal was clear. John Danvers was the man to deal with, and Michelle, the trophy wife, came along for the ride. She didn't intend to let him think otherwise.

The width of the man's smile and his apparent eagerness suggested he had researched the couple's resources and would bill them inflated rates for whatever services they required. The fact he didn't question why they would drive almost three hours to seek a mediocre lawyer when they no doubt had an abundance of high-level ones at their disposal in Quebec City testified to the size of the man's ego.

Owen set out to dispel any curiosity the man may have had. "My wife and I need assistance, and I believe you have the unique experience we're looking for."

If possible, the man's smile widened more. "I certainly hope so. I have a vast amount of knowledge in many areas. It's obvious you're not fooled by the fact I'm not part of a large law firm. I like to rely upon my own skills."

"That's what our research told us," Owen said.

"So, what can I help you with?" The lawyer interlocked his fingers on the desk. He assumed a serious expression designed to instill faith in his prospective clients.

Owen glanced at Chantal, as if seeking encouragement to move forward. "We have plans for some business dealings, and we need someone to help us with the money end of things."

If Nelson Griggs found it strange two people steeped in financial connections needed help to handle money, he gave no sign. He nodded sagely, but Chantal was certain he dreamed of a healthy cut of whatever they offered.

"What type of dealings are we talking about?" he said.

As planned, Owen kept his answer vague. "Business dealings. We'd like to invest the proceeds abroad, perhaps in the Caymans."

"Ah, I see."

It was obvious he understood, but as his gaze shifted between them, Chantal knew he would insist on another meeting while he did a more in-depth investigation of them. *He couldn't risk walking into the hands of the RCMP, could he?*

"Maybe you could fill me in on what transactions you're considering." The man's voice held a note of caution.

"Construction," Owen said with a smile that implied two could play the game. "We own a construction company, and we'd like to expand. The expansion may require some overseas transactions, and we want to make sure they're taken care of in a proper manner."

"Who referred you to me?" Mr. Griggs tilted his head as his gaze bore into Owen's.

This was where they banked on Beaudet having remained silent about the police interrogation, afraid of the consequences a power greater than his might mete out.

"A young man who used to work in the technical service industry. He's a friend of a friend."

Griggs' eyes glimmered with understanding as he nodded. The police also banked on him being too greedy to bother checking with Beaudet as to the veracity of their claim. If he did, they had Mark on standby to intervene.

"How long are you in Montreal?" The lawyer made a show of looking at his Rolex watch. His schedule was tight.

"We'd like to leave by the end of the day tomorrow." They had decided beforehand if Griggs wanted the business, he would accept the pressure of a deadline. Otherwise, Owen would contact his boss to request the budget to pay for another night in Montreal.

"There's another client arriving in a few minutes, but could you drop by tomorrow, say at one-thirty, and we'll discuss the details?"

"Honey?" Owen turned to Chantal.

"One-thirty doesn't suit me. I have another engagement. Two-thirty would be better."

Griggs laid his hands flat on the desk, three large, diamond-studded rings winking in the fluorescent lighting. "Two-thirty it is. I'll make sure my schedule is clear. We can take as much time as we like."

"Excellent." Owen stood and held out a hand to Chantal. She demurely took it and rose from the chair, a satisfied smile curving her lips. "We'll see you tomorrow."

Chapter 9

The sparkling city lights accompanied their evening meal at Portus 360, a high-end restaurant in the heart of Old Montreal. Known for its panoramic views, its menu specialized in Portuguese cuisine.

They couldn't assume Griggs or his associates were not watching them, so they maintained their personas of a wealthy couple enjoying a meal during their brief stay in Montreal. Their initial discussions centered on the meeting with the lawyer and the one to come the next day.

"He definitely comes across as smarmy."

"What? Smarmy? What is that?" Chantal wore a mask of confusion.

"Oily. Creepy. Untrustworthy."

"Ah, smarmy. I'll remember that one. It'll impress my friends. Thanks."

"Glad to help."

Owen's smile transformed his appearance, Chantal thought. He radiated good looks and charm, and she was certain many women in the room regarded her with envy. She dragged her mind back to the case. "Did you hear from Mark?"

"Yeah. There was no contact."

If Griggs had called Beaudet, Mark was prepared to intercept the call. He would divert it to a fake voicemail, lost forever. They hoped the lawyer's greed would prevent him from getting antsy if he called the young man and didn't get a response.

Chantal and Owen expected Griggs to dig into their background, but the RCMP had created foolproof profiles for them. They would pass the lawyer's inspection.

From under her eyelashes, Chantal studied the man seated across from her. The nighttime cityscape behind him highlighted his dark hair and eyes. Her curiosity got the better of her, and she hoped the wine and light conversation put him in a congenial frame of mind.

"Tell me the story of your limp."

Owen's eyes lifted to meet hers. Her boldness could have astonished or angered him. His expression revealed nothing.

"Are we getting into personal questions?"

A tenseness invaded their small space in the expansive restaurant. Chantal prayed the dim lighting hid the redness that crept into her cheeks. She would rather not get into a back-and-forth session of sharing intimate details of their lives, but she maintained eye contact, determined to see where their conversation led.

Owen was the first to give in. He rolled his eyes and sighed. "It happened while working a case."

Chantal couldn't hide her surprise. "Really?"

"I'm a cop. It happens." A casual shrug accompanied his words.

"White-collar rarely results in a lot of injuries, unless you count paper cuts."

A slight smirk appeared on his lips. "I worked drugs and OC before. They transferred me to fraud to give myself time to heal."

It took a second before Chantal realized her mouth had dropped open. She kicked herself for not doing her homework and looking into his background. Assuming he had always worked white-collar was an amateur's mistake.

Owen's smile told her he read her thoughts.

The server arrived with their plates as Chantal was about to ask for specifics. Politeness forced her to wait until the woman left and Owen took his first bite, but her patience only went so far.

"What happened?"

Owen's gaze jumped from his plate to her face. Chantal leaned forward, her food untouched, her utensils clutched in her hands.

"It was a drug bust," he said with another shrug. "It went downhill fast. Shit happened. That's it."

"You're big on detail." Chantal knew he detected her sarcasm and wondered if he intended to drive her insane with curiosity.

"It's not appropriate dinner conversation." His focus returned to his meal.

"I'm a cop. That's regular dinner conversation."

Owen's gaze bore into hers. He set down his utensils and laid his hands on the table. "We were undercover and infiltrated the gang. A raid was in the works. We thought everything was under control. When the deal went down and the cavalry rode in, someone pulled a knife. Another one had a gun. Two of the perps got away, we arrested two others, and I sustained an injury. I don't think you need any more details."

"Who's 'we'?"

"My partner, Eric, and I."

"Was he hurt too?"

"No. For me, it was the wrong place and time."

"Does the RCMP consider that a successful mission? You caught two and lost two?"

"Not really, no. But, like I said, shit happens, and you deal with it."

Chantal dug into her meal and contemplated this new reality that was Owen Lockwood. She needed to reclassify him and picture him as a cop who handled violent crime cases, with a story that resembled hers.

"Do you ever see him?"

"Who?"

"Your partner."

"Eric? Yeah, sometimes. Socially."

Another oxymoron. Owen with a social life. Chantal nodded and resumed her meal.

"You miss your partner?" he asked.

"Yeah, I do. I miss seeing him. I miss working with him every day. I miss the work, period. Paperwork is not my thing."

"I got that."

Chantal glanced at him, looking for a telltale smile, but his expression remained blank. "You? Do you miss working with your pal? Do you miss the action?"

"Of course. It doesn't compare. Eric was the best partner, and he will be again. I'll get over this injury and be back at it."

"You have a physiotherapist?"

"Sure. I run and train as much as possible. It's coming along."

"Good. We'll both be back at our regular jobs soon enough," Chantal said. The conversation satisfied at least part of her curiosity, but the fact he didn't seem interested in her history preoccupied her.

Was it a general lack of interest or had he already investigated her background?

Whatever it was, they had danced close enough to a line she wasn't willing to tiptoe over. Chantal gave up her line of questioning until the meal wound down and they headed back to the hotel.

In the luxury suite, Chantal glanced at Owen as he removed his suit jacket and set it on the back of an armchair. He wore wealth well. It might be temporary and for show, but he slid into the role with ease. Did he come from a monied background? Or was he an excellent actor?

He intrigued her, she admitted, but Chantal sensed he would balk if she continued her inquisition. Baby steps, she thought.

When she noticed his smirk, Chantal blinked and realized he had caught her staring.

"Something bothering you?" he said.

"No, not at all." She swung her gaze to the window and pretended an interest in the magnificent view of the city. "Just thinking about tomorrow."

"While you're thinking about that, I'll have a shower."

Chantal waved her hand in dismissal. "Sure. Go ahead."

With the sound of the shower running in the background, Chantal relaxed. She kicked off her heels and released her hair from its restrictive bun. Despite having wished for a change of scenery, Chantal yearned to be in her apartment. An uneasy feeling snaked through her gut, and she couldn't put her finger on the source. Was it Owen? Why? Was it the case? It was straightforward and a step up from what she had been doing. Why would it bother her?

One thing Chantal had learned in her years of police work was to trust her gut.

Her gaze settled on the couch, and she decided it would be fine for her. As large as it was, Owen would find it difficult to fold his long frame into a comfortable position. With a resigned sigh, she crossed to the bedroom to retrieve bedding and a pillow.

Chantal had problematic timing. Owen stepped from the bathroom as she moved over the threshold. They both came to a dead stop. Owen wore nothing but a towel around his waist and a question on his face. Droplets of water glistened on his chest.

"I..." Chantal said. She looked at the bed, decided that wasn't a good idea, and steered her gaze to the window. For a moment, she forgot why she was there, until a harsh throat-clearing yanked her memory to where it belonged. "I need the bedding."

She swung to the closet and pulled out a sheet and blanket. "Sorry," Chantal said over her shoulder as she left the room. Bent over the couch, tucking in the sheet, a pillow landed in front of her face.

Her wide-eyed gaze turned upward. Owen stood beside her. He wore the hotel-issued bathrobe and an enigmatic smile.

"I thought you might need that. Have a good sleep."

CHAPTER 10

At two-thirty the next afternoon, they once again sat in Griggs' office. Owen had donned a different suit while Chantal wore a classic black pencil skirt, a white blouse with black pinstripes, and heels. The stylish, yet businesslike, outfit gave her confidence, something she needed after a long, restless night on the couch.

Griggs wore an ingratiating smile, enough for them to understand he had done his homework, and what he found satisfied him. He expected to make money from whatever scheme the couple had in mind.

"I have the afternoon set aside. Take as long as you like. Why don't you tell me what I can do for you?" he said. He wore a tailored, navy-blue suit and sparkling diamond cuff links that matched his rings. Chantal didn't remember the last time she had seen cuff links on a man's shirt.

Since, as expected, the chauvinistic lawyer focused his attention on Owen, he took the lead. "As I mentioned yesterday, we're in real estate. To be specific, we're interested in constructing office buildings."

"Yes, you said you have your own construction company."

"We set one up a few weeks ago. We have contacts in the industry that gave us some leads. There are projects in the funnel already. We intend to contract out the work," Owen said. "First, we need to create companies that will bill the sub-contracted services."

"Ah, I see."

The glint in the man's eyes confirmed he understood their explanation. It was a common scheme. They would register various companies in foreign countries and bill services never required and never fulfilled, inflating the cost of the construction and reducing the taxable income of the construction company. Meanwhile, the sub-contractors made a full profit for work they never performed.

"And then," Owen continued. "We want you to deposit the proceeds, or most of it, in overseas accounts. Of course, none of this would concern government authorities."

Jeff's contact had educated Chantal in the intricacies of hiding illicit funds. It involved an elaborate game of hide and seek where they transferred money through banks and countries that were uncooperative in revealing information about their clients. If the authorities navigated the labyrinth, the funds would have vanished and be impossible to trace.

"That won't be a problem, Mr. Danvers. I have extensive experience in this area."

"That's what we counted on."

"I charge a flat fee for creating the companies plus a small percentage of the funds that leave the country."

Owen made a show of negotiating the rate, enhancing the impression that he was a savvy entrepreneur. He frowned when Griggs asked him to pay a retainer on the spot.

"You don't trust me."

"It's standard practice. I have costs to pay upfront, people who'll demand payment. Your retainer will help pay them."

"Just give him a check, honey, and stop arguing with him," Chantal said, shifting in her chair. "I have an appointment for a massage, remember?"

A grudging scowl on his face, Owen handed over the check, and they stood to leave.

"How can I contact you?" the lawyer said, his fingers stroking the check in his hand.

"Your assistant has my number. I'll call you soon to see how things are going." Owen's voice held the right amount of authority to discourage any further questioning. "I hope to see progress by then."

Owen and Chantal held hands on their way to the car. Once inside the vehicle, the tension eased.

"It should go smoothly from now on."

"I still think he's connected," Chantal said. "He doesn't seem big-time enough to pull this off on his own."

"Mafia? Probably. Lower level, certainly. He admitted he's not working alone, and OC would be the most likely scenario. We'll insist on dealing with someone higher in the food chain."

Chantal's pulse kicked up a notch as she considered the fact a Mafia connection was no longer a distant possibility, but a distinct probability. The organization had wheedled its way into many levels of business and government. The prospect of dealing with the tentacles of organized crime sent a frisson of apprehension through her veins.

Using the car's GPS system, Owen maneuvered the vehicle through Montreal traffic and onto the highway that would lead them to Quebec City.

Owen and Chantal had made a deal. When they were outside the metropolitan area and convinced they weren't being followed, they pulled into the parking lot of a coffee shop. After a purchase of a caffeine boost for the road, Chantal slid into the driver's seat. She could pretend to be the submissive wife, but only for a limited period. She itched to drive the luxury car.

From now on, the undercover couple needed to operate under their new identity. If Griggs had the connections they suspected he had, someone would check into their manufactured background. It was also likely someone would monitor their movements to make sure their story held water.

Owen and Chantal would live in an expensive home overlooking the St-Lawrence River in the Quebec City suburb of Sillery. The police force had rented it for ten days and had moved in everything they needed while the couple met with Griggs in Montreal.

Ten days was the time limit federal authorities gave the undercover investigation. If the team discovered nothing substantial, they would move to another plan.

Meanwhile, Mark would split his time between the hotel and police headquarters. They used a secure cell phone for any communication the couple had with him or the team.

"I'll call Griggs in a couple of days," Owen said, drawing Chantal into thoughts of the case. "By then, he should have set up the shell companies, and I'll press him for next steps. We might get names of his contacts."

"With any luck, we can have this wrapped up within a week." Chantal had mixed feelings about her statement. It was gratifying to tie up an operation, but would it mean she'd go back to scanning files until some other white-collar project came along?

"Tell me about your most interesting case," she said as she pulled into the passing lane to overtake a van.

When there was no immediate answer, she glanced at her passenger. He wore a thoughtful expression. She smiled. He wasn't ignoring her, after all.

"Hard to say. Most of them are interesting or have a certain amount of intrigue."

"Which one stands out the most?"

His mouth twisted. "It was my last one, but we discussed it, and I don't feel like getting into it again. How about a funny one?"

"Great." Chantal straightened in her seat and threw him another glance. A smile lit Owen's face, and as usual, the effect it had on his appearance astonished her.

"It was a while ago. I was working robbery. Two masked men broke into a liquor store after hours. The cameras picked them up, and it sent out an alert. It was in a rural area. Not too many roads for them to take to escape. We set up a couple of roadblocks, caught them right away."

Chantal's smile faded. "What was so funny about that?"

"Do you know what gave them away?" He flashed a smile in her direction and caught her head shake. "They had painted their masks on with permanent markers."

The laugh erupted from deep inside her. "Oh, no!"

"You've got to be a special kind of stupid, don't you?" He chuckled.

"I've got a good one. It wasn't mine, but news got around. It was a guy who robbed a banking machine. He wore a mask over his face and had his hat pulled low, but he had his name and birthdate tattooed on his neck." She barely had the words out before she had a fit of giggles. Owen's deep laugh filled the car.

The mood remained light for the balance of the journey until they pulled into the driveway of their stately rented house. It acted as a stark reminder that they were cops from different parts of the country working on a case neither of them really wanted.

CHAPTER 11

A different place; a different attire. He had discarded the casual shorts and t-shirt, along with the sneakers, in a garbage bin over fifty kilometers from the crime scene. The gun, he kept.

Dressed in a dark suit and tie, with black dress shoes, he carried a briefcase in his right hand. A misty rain fell. Not a drenching rain, but it relieved the heat of the day.

Another good sign, he thought, with a slight smile.

Glancing at people on the sidewalks, he realized he could blend in no matter what he wore. In this neighborhood, there was everything from teenage girls in skimpy outfits to business executives in suits.

He paused outside the door and pretended to scroll through his phone. When a woman in yoga pants exited the building, he avoided her gaze and slipped through, touching nothing. He chose the stairs instead of the elevator, only needing to climb one level to reach his destination.

He had chosen the timing of his visit with care. The secretary that manned the desk always left the building at four-thirty, while her boss stayed behind for another hour.

He tugged his sleeve over his hand before using it to pull open the door. The squeak of hinges alerted the person occupying the inner office to his presence.

"Are you back? What did you forget?"

The carpet muffled the man's footsteps as he moved toward the sound of the voice. When he stepped into the office, the person behind the desk looked up in surprise and rose to his feet.

"Wh…"

The bullet struck him between the eyes with precision and interrupted the rest of his question. His body toppled onto the chair, his arms flopping by his sides.

The man put on his gloves before he approached the desk. He slipped the laptop into his bag beside the still-warm gun and searched the office for USB keys and backup drives. He clutched a much heavier briefcase when he descended the stairs and left the building.

• • •

Owen didn't have to reach out to Griggs. Instead, he received a phone call from the lawyer at three o'clock the next day as the group reconvened in the SQ conference room. Owen put the call on speakerphone so Chantal and Mark could hear the conversation.

"I'm leaving for Quebec City in half an hour," Griggs said. It was obvious he was in a car. Traffic noises distorted his voice. "I'd like to take you and your lovely wife to dinner tonight. My treat. I've got a lot to discuss, and I have a private table reserved at Le Continental. I've arranged for a car to pick you up at seven. No need to worry about drinking and driving."

The prospect of having to spend an evening with the lawyer didn't appeal to Chantal, but it was an opportunity to move the case forward. The man's almost jovial manner sparked curiosity in her. Something was up, and she wanted to know what it was. But she had a problem. "We have to call him back and tell him we can't go."

CHAPTER 12

"Why do you think you can tell me what to do? Since when are you my boss?" Chantal stomped down the steps of the house, shouting loud enough to draw the attention of the man who stood beside the open rear door of the black Lincoln. She was loud enough to reach the ears of the nearest neighbors as well. However, the tall stranger in the dark suit remained straight-faced and solemn.

"It was just a suggestion. I wasn't telling you to do anything." Owen also wore a dark suit that contrasted with Chantal's tight red dress. Her black patent-leather heels clicked on the paved driveway as she headed toward the car.

"Just a suggestion? You never make suggestions. They're always orders. I don't have to listen to you. I'm an equal partner here, you know."

"Of course, you are." Owen used a mollifying tone.

Chantal went to lower herself into the car before swinging to face him. "Now you're patronizing me! Treating me like a child!"

"Not at…"

The slamming of the car door reverberated through the early evening air. "I'm not going," Chantal said with her hands on her hips and her chin jutted toward Owen. "You can go by yourself. I've had enough of you." She waved her arms as if flies swarmed around her head and marched toward the house with a contrite Owen following behind. Footsteps pounded behind them and she wondered if the driver intended to convince them to get in the car or if he would give up.

She didn't have time to wonder much longer.

Chantal glared over her shoulder to shout more angry words at her partner as the blinding flash and resonating boom surrounded them. The impact of Owen's body ramming into hers thrust her onto the lawn, and his crushing weight flattened her. She struggled to breathe, fearing for the life of the man who had saved hers.

Seconds passed as Chantal strained to detect a sign of life from the body on top of her.

"Are you okay?" A voice shouted in her ear. It sounded as if he bellowed through a tin can. The blast affected her hearing, but a rush of relief shot through her as Owen shifted his weight to his elbows and gave her room to breathe.

"I'm good. Are you hurt?" Chantal wheezed the words. She flipped over and stared into eyes that were mere inches from hers. She witnessed concern and an indeterminate amount of pain, but as he rolled onto the grass beside her, she was almost certain he suffered no serious injuries.

In the background, the sleek black car was ablaze, the flames shooting high into the sky, the heat intense. Bystanders gathered to take in the sight, many filming the spectacle with their phones. Chantal hoped one of them took the time to call 9-1-1.

Her gaze searched for the driver. The man was closest to the vehicle when it exploded, and he lay unmoving on the stone-paved driveway twenty feet from the burning car. Chantal shoved herself to her feet and spoke to a now-standing Owen. "We have to move him." Owen nodded and ran toward the victim, his limp flagrant. Chantal followed close behind.

She stooped beside the driver and placed her fingers on his neck, detecting a weak pulse. Owen crouched on the opposite side and grasped his arm. The searing heat of the fire was extreme as Chantal averted her face and grabbed the driver's other arm. They pulled him onto the lawn, away from the flames and any further danger.

"We need to call it in."

The words were no sooner out of her mouth when the wail of approaching sirens reached her ears.

With the immediate concerns dealt with, Chantal's gaze scoured their surroundings, looking for another threat. *Was the responsible person watching? Had someone activated the bomb from a few feet away, or had they detonated it elsewhere?*

Questions ran through her mind, with a fast-forward sequence of scenarios and possibilities. She peered over her shoulder to where Owen paced the lawn with his phone pressed to his ear.

His limp prominent and, without a doubt, painful, he seemed impervious to the discomfort. Singed holes in the back of his suit jacket and pants meant burned skin. Chantal needed to convince him to get treatment. He disconnected the call and turned back to her.

"It was an obvious set-up, but your plan saved us, all of us, by the looks of it," Owen said from beside her shoulder. His gaze shifted to the unconscious driver. A team of paramedics surrounded him and prepared the stretcher. "Another few seconds and we'd have been in that car."

They both stared at the burning mass of metal fifty feet away. Within minutes, fire trucks, police vehicles, and an ambulance swarmed the area, which had already drawn a lot of attention from neighbors and passersby. Chantal and Owen stood aside as the police worked on moving the crowds farther away and questioning witnesses. In the meantime, firefighters applied foam to the blaze. The flames reduced to a sizzle.

"There'll be a bunch of questions to answer," Chantal said, her grim gaze riveted on the billowing smoke.

"I called Bouchard. He's alerting everyone this was an undercover police operation. He'll handle it."

Chantal nodded. It wouldn't be the first time their bosses needed to intervene with the authorities when a case veered in the wrong direction.

While the ambulance technicians carted the driver off to the hospital, Chantal fielded questions from police officers. She stuck to their cover story for now, knowing Bouchard would smooth it over when the time came.

When someone suggested they go to the city police headquarters, Owen accepted without hesitation. Chantal placed her hand on his arm. "You should go to the hospital first."

A frown darkened his face. "What for?"

"You're injured. You have burn holes in your clothes."

"I'm fine." He waved his hand.

"What about your leg? Your limp is worse."

"I'm fine." This time, he growled the words between clenched teeth.

The man's stubborn pride aroused a surge of anger in her, but Chantal squelched it. If he preferred to suffer the pain, then so be it. She turned from him and slid into the back seat of the police cruiser.

Once at headquarters, they requested Captain Bouchard's presence, and he arrived a few minutes later, along with Mark Pratt. Two investigators from the city police joined them.

"Start from the beginning," Bouchard said.

Owen gave details of the phone call from Griggs and the planned dinner at a restaurant in Old Quebec. Chantal explained how she couldn't join them for fear of being recognized and destroying their case.

"Clarify, please," Bouchard said.

"I know the owner. Not well, but well enough that he'd recognize me and give away my identity."

The captain frowned and nodded. He waved his hand, telling her to continue.

"We staged an argument," she said. "As we walked to the car, I gave Owen a hard time." Chantal didn't mention how good the talking-down felt. She had released some of her frustrations, while he assumed it was all an act. "The driver stood beside the back door of the car. I slammed it shut and headed to the house. Owen followed. I'm pretty sure I heard the driver moving in our direction."

"I think he followed us, maybe to find out if we still needed him. We put on a good show." Owen's manner was matter-of-fact. "At any rate, it saved his life. Any closer to the car, and he'd be dead."

Yes, Chantal thought, they'd all be dead if it hadn't been for their performance. Judging by her superior's expression, he thought the same thing.

"Anyway," she continued. "The plan was for Owen to go alone to the restaurant. He would've recorded the conversation. It's obvious Griggs never intended to meet us."

"I've sent a car to bring in Beaudet, and we're trying to locate Griggs," Bouchard said. "They're our ties to this, although it reinforces our suspicions of a link to organized crime."

Chantal agreed. Using explosives was a trademark method of killing for the Mafia. Someone didn't want them to stick their noses in the lucrative construction business.

Before she could voice her thoughts, Bouchard's cell phone rang. His expression as he listened to the individual on the other end made her glance at Owen with concern.

Bouchard ended the call and gazed at the group, his eyes bleak. "Beaudet is dead."

No one spoke for several seconds until Chantal regained her senses. "What happened?"

"A gunshot to the head. It's early, but no one seems to have heard or seen anything."

"Damn," Owen hissed. "They're out to eliminate all ties."

Chantal stood and paced the room. "Griggs was in on the set-up. Chances are he never left Montreal."

"We'll know soon enough. They sent cars to his office and home."

When 'soon enough' arrived, they had another shock. Someone had killed Griggs in Montreal. The police found the lawyer dead in his office with a bullet in his head. Preliminary examination determined he died late afternoon, and his receptionist swore he hadn't left the office all day, which meant he never placed the phone call to Owen from a car.

"No wonder his voice sounded distorted. It wasn't him."

Chantal agreed with Owen. "They covered it up with traffic noises," she said.

Bouchard stood, his head bowed. He stared at his phone lying on the table before lifting his gaze to Chantal. "I'd like to speak to you in private, please."

Her brows furrowed into a frown, Chantal followed him to a smaller interview room with white, astringent walls, a table, and two chairs. Neither of them sat.

Bouchard faced her with his fists on his hips. "Everything's changed. This is no longer a white-collar investigation. It's murder and attempted murder. You'll hand it over to homicide. Jeff and his team will take over."

"No," Chantal said, her voice harsh with emotion. "This is my case. I want to keep it."

"It's too soon. You're not…"

"It's not too soon. I'm a week away. What will change?" Her voice trembled with emotion. She couldn't lose this assignment.

"There's still an evaluation to do."

Chantal leaned toward him, laying her palms on the table. "You know I can do this."

"I don't…"

"Yes, you do." Chantal straightened. Her voice took on a pleading tone. "I'm fine. We both know it. I can work with Jeff on this." Her boss lowered his gaze. She held her breath, not daring to speak, yearning for the right response.

Bouchard lifted his head and stared at her. "I'll consider it," he said, his voice low.

"I can do it. I won't push myself."

The older man snorted. "Since when do you not push yourself?"

CHAPTER 13

The tall, dark-haired man locked gazes with Chantal as soon as he entered the room. He looked her over as if to reassure himself she was unharmed. Chantal hoped her smile put him at ease.

He shook hands with Captain Bouchard before introducing himself to the others.

"I'm Jean-François Lafond. You can call me Jeff," he said to Owen as their hands clasped.

Owen's eyes flashed as he recognized the name. "You're on this job?"

"Yes. It's moved to homicide now."

Owen glanced at Chantal. They hadn't discussed the conversation she had with her boss, but his eyes held a question.

"The RCMP will stay involved," Jeff said, reading his mind. "In part, because of the original fraud case, but there's also the likely connection to OC."

Owen's expression didn't change, but Chantal sensed his relief. It left two questions unanswered: would Owen be in charge, and would Chantal remain a part of the mission?

"I saw the initial reports of the crime scenes. It has the characteristics of a professional kill, a single execution-style shot to the head. There's work to do." Jeff's gaze encompassed everyone in the room.

"It was my understanding Quebec City didn't have a large, organized crime element." Owen directed his question to Jeff.

"Not compared to cities like Montreal and Toronto, but sometimes there's spill-over. I can't say I'm surprised. One of the key people involved was a lawyer from Montreal."

"They wiped out our only leads, Beaudet and Griggs," Mark said, despair in his tone.

"True," Owen said, "But we'll have access to their computers."

Captain Bouchard cleared his throat. "They cleaned out Beaudet's office. There's nothing left. No hardware, paperwork, nothing."

Chantal threw herself into her chair and leaned her head back. "Of course."

"We're going to have the same problem with Griggs," Owen said.

"What's next?" Chantal turned to Jeff for direction.

"We'll split up the interviews while we wait for forensics to come in."

"I think Owen and I should stay undercover. We can try to contact someone within the organization."

Chantal watched as Jeff and Bouchard traded glances. A flush of indignation rose within her, knowing what their thoughts were. Jeff's gaze returned to hers. "We'll think about how we move forward with this."

"Besides," Bouchard said. "Your cover's blown. They tried to kill you."

Chantal stood, flattened her palms against the table, and leaned forward. "Not necessarily. We have to dig deeper to eliminate or confirm the OC theory, and we can do that by staying undercover. We'll find Griggs' connection."

"For what it's worth, I think she's right."

Chantal sent a glance Owen's way. It felt strange for him to agree with her, but, she reasoned, he was after the same result as her; to work on an active homicide case.

"I'm willing to consider it, but if I approve, I'll pull you out at the first sign of trouble," Bouchard said, his stern gaze focused on Chantal.

"I don't agree…"

Bouchard's upraised palm stifled Jeff's argument. "We need your support if we want this to work," the captain said. His tone made it clear the support was a requirement not a request.

Jeff held Bouchard's gaze for a long moment before he turned to the others. "Let's work up a new plan."

Chantal heaved an inward sigh as her mind raced with possibilities. She pushed them aside when the Beaudet crime scene photos arrived in Jeff's email inbox, and he pulled them up on the large screen. Everyone sat, except for Chantal; her nervous energy wouldn't allow it. Instead, she stood to the side of the screen, not wanting to miss a detail.

The first photos displayed a brick two-story building in the Vanier district of the city. Curious bystanders pushed the limits of the crime scene tape.

The apartment entrance opened into a small living room furnished with a worn brown corduroy sofa and armchair. A low coffee table and a floor lamp completed the ensemble. The kitchen area had a high counter and bar stools that separated it from the living room.

Blood and human tissue splattered the white laminate cabinets and the door that led to the back stairs.

"That's Beaudet?" Chantal was no stranger to gruesome sights, but the victim didn't resemble the young man she remembered. "How long was he dead?"

Jeff peered at the contents of the email. "Dr. Morin said three to five days."

Bloating and decay distorted Beaudet's body, and she understood why the police officers and crime scene workers wore masks. Chantal was certain they had smeared Vicks under their noses.

"A clean head shot," Jeff said.

Owen nodded. "That confirms what we were told."

The rest of the photos covered the other rooms. Apart from the grotesque body and a bloody footprint near the back door, little showed a violent crime had occurred. Whoever removed the computer and incriminating documents did so without creating a disturbance. There were no overturned tables or dumped filing cabinets.

"He wasn't in a hurry. No worries about someone knocking on the door or calling the police," Owen said.

"The crime scene techs might find out if the killer used a silencer. Walls in those apartments are paper-thin. Someone should have heard something," Chantal said.

Jeff scrolled though the email. "They questioned the neighbors. No one heard or saw anything suspicious."

Owen leaned over and peered at the photos. "The killer was confident. He carried out a cold-blooded murder in an occupied apartment building and walked out with a computer and God knows what else without being noticed. He, or they, murdered two people in two different cities."

"But days apart. Plenty of time for one person to move between sites," Chantal said.

"Tying up loose ends."

Chantal agreed with Owen. Someone decided both Luc Beaudet and Nelson Griggs had reached the end of their useful lives.

•   •   •

The discussion centered on Chantal and Owen staying in their roles as a wealthy couple, looking for help in setting up offshore companies.

There was an even division: Jeff and the captain against Chantal and Owen. Mark stood in neutral territory, a human Switzerland.

Chantal understood her boss and ex-partner had concerns for her well-being. She appreciated the sentiment but, in her opinion, it was unnecessary.

"The way to find out who carried out these attacks is to follow the trail to whoever ordered it, whether it's Mafia or someone else. It will wrap up both the fraud and the murder cases." Chantal stood with her hands on her hips. The position accentuated the smears of grass stains and dirt on her dress.

"It's not the only way. We can investigate without going undercover," Jeff argued.

"The FBI established our identities and backgrounds. We should take advantage of it."

Owen's counterargument held merit, Chantal thought. "We can turn everything to our advantage," she added.

Both Jeff and Bouchard's expressions remained doubtful.

"Give us a week," Chantal said. "If nothing comes out of it, we'll back off."

"A week," Bouchard said. Jeff's brows furrowed at his boss' capitulation. "We'll have someone drive you to the house."

"I'll go to the house, but Owen needs a ride to the hospital. He has burns to take care of." Chantal ignored her new partner's glare as she gathered her bag, bid farewell to the occupants of the room, and headed for the exit.

She had almost reached the door when a firm hand on her arm and a stern voice in her ear forestalled her. "Wait up. I'm coming with you."

"I've got a ride, and you have somewhere else to go," Chantal said to Owen as he fell into step beside her.

"We're going together," he responded, his tone flat. "I'm not leaving you alone."

"What?" She stopped in her tracks, indignant. "Why would you say something like that?"

"I thought, after what happened today, you'd realize someone tried to kill us."

"So? Your solution is to ignore your injuries? You're immune to pain and infection?"

"We need to look out for each other."

"Sending you to the hospital is my way of looking out for you. Besides, I'm an experienced police officer. I can take care of myself." Chantal huffed and walked toward the exit, shaking her head.

"Be reasonable. You can't cut off your nose to spite your face."

Again, Chantal came to a standstill. She reeled around to face him. "What? Cut off my nose?"

"It's an expression," Owen said. "It means you shouldn't hurt yourself or put yourself in danger just to get back at me."

She shrugged her shoulders. Chantal didn't have the time or energy to decipher strange, anglophone expressions. "If you're worried about a bomb in the police vehicle, the only thing we'll achieve is having us killed together."

"I'm more concerned about what could happen at the house."

"They've guarded it since we left. Nobody got in, and I won't let anyone in while you're gone. You don't have to worry about me."

Chantal tried to conceal it from the others, but she needed to decompress after the attempt on her life. She had to let her emotions rage. Being alone would do the trick. Besides, she wasn't an idiot, she thought. She would be armed and ready for any intrusion.

"I repeat," she said as she walked out the door. "I can look out for myself."

It was a punch to her heart when Owen's words followed her. "Yeah, we know how well you can take care of yourself."

● ● ●

The man smiled. Sometimes life took an unexpected turn, and it worked out for the best. Was it possible a higher power had decided it wasn't their time and stepped in to change his plan?

He laughed out loud at the thought. Call it a higher power, fate, or plain luck. He took it as a sign that the game wasn't over. Like hockey, they were in the second of three periods. With any luck, it would play out in overtime.

CHAPTER 14

It was a low blow, and a pang of regret shot through Owen when Chantal looked at him with a mixture of hurt and anger in her eyes. But he knew, at times, you needed a low blow to knock sense into someone's thick skull.

At any rate, he had to muscle his way through this situation. When Owen spotted the flash in her eye, he knew she would come at him with both barrels. He wanted to head her off.

"There's the car," he said, grabbing her by the elbow and tugging her along, thankful the cruiser coincided with his need for a distraction.

Owen opened the door of the car and steered Chantal into the back seat. He climbed in after her and gave the driver the rented house's address.

Chantal leaned forward and said Owen would go to the hospital after he dropped her off. The cop nodded as Chantal folded her arms and stared out the window.

Owen noticed the driver glanced in his rear-view mirror, a tiny smirk on his face. The cop would assume they'd had a lover's spat, Owen thought, which was so far from the truth it was a joke. But, for the sake of peace, he kept his mouth shut.

When they pulled up in front of the white brick house, Chantal thanked the driver and climbed out of the vehicle without a second glance at Owen. He let her think she made a fast escape—for about five seconds—until he exited the car and followed her to the door.

When his footsteps crunched behind her, she spun around to face him.

"*Maudit!* What are you doing here?"

Owen ignored her expletive, which he was certain was a French swear word. He didn't allow it to bother him.

"You can fight me all you want. I'm not leaving you alone."

Chantal's nostrils flared, and her eyes turned cold and flinty. Owen took a perverse pleasure in witnessing the transformation. He supposed he should feel guilty about it, but he couldn't work it up. Her life was at risk. She would get over her mad and be alive to do it.

Owen saw her work herself up to give him a full-scale blast. He unlocked the door and pushed his way through.

"Get out!" Chantal's shout bounced off the chandelier in the high-ceilinged entranceway.

"No can do."

"I hate you." She hissed the words from between her gritted teeth.

"Fine. Hate me as much as you like. It won't change anything."

"*Mon Dieu! Qu'est-ce que j'ai fait pour mériter cela?*" Chantal flapped her arms in frustration. She spun around and marched into the living room with Owen following behind.

Owen settled onto the deep leather couch, grabbing the remote control on his way. She snatched the device from his hand and glared at him.

"What? I didn't understand you." He grabbed the remote from her.

"I said, what did I do to deserve you?"

"Fate or luck, whichever you wish."

A sound that resembled a growl rumbled in her chest.

"Keep out of my sight. I don't want to see you or hear you." She strode toward her bedroom.

Owen would take her advice, he decided.

• • •

Chantal stood in the spacious master bedroom and drew several deep breaths. They did little to calm her. Anger flowed through her veins like lava. Owen's highhandedness pushed her to her limits. The brief, pleasant interlude they shared in the car on their return trip from Montreal was exactly that: brief and long gone.

She didn't appreciate his remark. He had investigated her history. Using it against her made her livid. But she also directed her anger toward herself. He had checked her out, yet she hadn't done the same for him. That was her first mistake in her dealings with Owen Lockwood.

Chantal took another deep breath and flopped into a wingback armchair. Jeff said she was too high strung and needed to focus on relaxing. She tried to take his advice, but eventually jumped from the chair and paced the room to work off her frustration.

Chantal knew herself well enough to realize she had overreacted to Owen's insistence on returning with her. After the explosion, she presented a cool exterior, but it affected her all the same. Fear and stress were the roots of her reaction. She held it in all evening and thought she would implode if she didn't escape the confines of the police station. All she wanted was to be alone and give her emotions free rein. Owen pre-empted that plan, and she reacted to his sabotage.

Chantal threw herself into the chair again, bent over, and placed her head in her hands. A groan escaped her lips. She admitted his intentions were well meant. It didn't excuse his arrogance, but his heart was in the right place.

It had been several months since her work exposed her to brutality of any kind. Chantal thought the healing process was over, but it was obvious she wasn't there yet. She had a long way to go before she could face violence head-on without aftereffects. But she felt ready to start. The adrenaline rush she experienced at the bombing attested to that.

Chantal understood the assignment had taken an about-face. It had changed from a simple, white-collar crime investigation to a dangerous mission. That meant a few things for her. She could work the case in a diminished role, or they could remove her from it. The other alternative would be that she stay involved in the investigation.

The latter choice was the best for her career and the one that gave her the biggest thrill, but the question was if she could handle it. One thing was certain. If she wanted to get through it in one piece, she had to sort through her feelings concerning Owen.

• • •

The next morning dawned bright and awkward. Owen's remark from the previous day hung over their heads like a dark cloud. They hadn't spent enough time as roommates to feel comfortable. The fact they had to share a home, no matter how large, amid a state of tension made it more difficult to handle. Conversation was sparse, barely enough to decide the plan for the day.

Owen winced as he shuffled around the kitchen, making his coffee. His limp was more noticeable than usual, and Chantal felt a twinge of remorse for not helping him with his injuries the night before. Although, she told herself, she had reminded him several times he needed medical attention. As a grown man, he had to take care of his own health.

Chantal needed to shove her negative thoughts aside. She had the chance to test herself, to see if she had recovered and could return to her previous life as a detective.

While Owen showered and changed, Chantal gave herself a mental head shake, tried to concentrate on the case, and think about the threat on their lives.

They were closer to the top than they had thought. And the person at the top wasn't your common white-collar criminal. His collar had blood on it.

CHAPTER 15

"Non."

She paused and ran a frustrated hand through her hair.

"Je ne suis pas d'accord. Je suis capable."

There was another pause as the man on the other end digested Chantal's declaration that she didn't agree with him. Everyone in the room could hear her side of the heated French conversation, but no one understood it.

Chantal accepted the call from her boss for that reason. She had no plan to share his concerns with the team. Owen's comment the previous day had hit hard, and she would not add to her misery by sharing her superior's doubts.

At least she convinced Bouchard she should stay on the case. She didn't want to give it up. It had picked up several degrees of intrigue.

Of course, Chantal had fears. She knew she wouldn't be human if she didn't. But she felt excitement and anticipation, something she had lived without for several long months. The added aggravation of dealing with an arrogant RCMP detective was a necessary evil in the equation.

Chantal pasted on a grin and turned to face her co-workers. Mark sent her a sympathetic smile.

"That seemed like a pleasant conversation." Sarcasm overlaid Owen's tone.

"It was. That's the way we always talk." Chantal concentrated on removing a fleck of lint from her jacket.

"Must be a cultural thing."

"Yes, it is. No need to worry." Chantal crossed the room for a coffee refill. She would do a couple of extra laps on the track to get rid of her caffeine buzz, she promised herself.

"It didn't worry me."

Mark's head bobbed between the two of them like an observer at a tennis match. Chantal assumed the extra layer of animosity between her and Owen was obvious, but she didn't acknowledge it.

"Any news from the tech crew?" she asked Mark.

"Not yet. They're still analyzing the bomb and crime scene."

"We'll be careful how we paint it," Owen said, rubbing the back of his neck. "We can't claim terrorism, or it will set off a wave of panic and political posturing. But we can't declare ourselves the target or it will raise too many questions and blow our cover."

"We'll blame another likely source and say it was bad timing." Chantal took a deep gulp of her coffee.

"Don't you think this already blew your cover? We discussed this last night. Why would they want to kill you if they believed your story?" Mark said.

Owen drummed his fingers on his leg. "They may be aware we're law enforcement. Or they may want to eliminate someone who's nosing in on their territory. Perhaps the plan was for the bomb to explode before we got in the car. They may have wanted to scare us, send us a message. That's what we need to find out."

"There's also the possibility the Mafia isn't involved at all," Chantal said.

"Where does that leave us?" Mark asked.

"We have to take it to the next level. To whoever Griggs worked for, if he wasn't on his own. It'll mean digging around within the Mafia." Owen's gaze fixed on Chantal. It held an 'I dare you.'

The scuffed white walls seemed to close in on Chantal. The over-circulated, artificial air suffocated her. She needed to work off steam or she would say something she'd regret. A change of scenery was in order.

"I'm going for a walk." She snatched up her phone and headed for the door. Someone murmured something behind her, but she ignored it.

Chantal squinted as she stepped outside the main door and cursed herself for not bringing her sunglasses. She didn't intend to return for them.

"Wait up."

She spun on her heel and watched Owen hurry to catch up to her. Chantal sighed. Getting space was too much to hope for.

The sun beat on her head, and she didn't feel like hanging around on the cement walkway. When Owen landed by her side, Chantal resumed her sprint, taking for granted he went the same direction as her, whether or not she wanted him to.

"We have to talk," he said.

Pain throbbed in his voice. She slowed her pace. "Talk. I'm listening."

"Let's stop and have a coffee someplace."

Chantal hadn't planned on another coffee. "It sounds serious."

"It could be."

She cast him a sideways glance. His tone piqued her curiosity. "All right. Let's stop, but I'd rather have something cold than a coffee. I don't like this heat."

It was mid-afternoon, and the shop was quiet. Chantal and Owen took a corner booth, he with his coffee and she with an iced tea.

"Okay, what's this about?" Chantal stared at him over the rim of her glass, the cool liquid doing its magic to refresh her.

"We have to think of the case. We're at a crucial point and can't let anything get in our way. That includes our personal feelings." His gaze met hers full-on, intense and searching.

"Since when do you spend so much time beating around the bush?" Ferreting out hidden messages was not on her agenda for today. There was too much to do.

"Okay." Owen sighed. "I'm not sure you should stay involved in the operation."

Both cups jumped as Chantal's fist slammed on the table. Other patrons sent them curious looks.

"You talked to Captain Bouchard." The words vibrated as they left her lips. She leaned forward, pressing against the edge of the table. "Or was it Jeff? I can't believe this. What the hell… does everyone think I'm *folle*… crazy?"

"I wasn't talking to anyone. And, no, I don't think you're crazy. Things have changed, and you should look at this realistically."

"All I need to look at are our next steps. And I'm not the only one they put on light duty. Maybe you're the one who should step away from the case." The feet of the chair scraped on the ceramic as she stood.

The server sidestepped between two tables when the policewoman swept by. A wave of hot, humid air hit Chantal as she marched through the doorway. She hardly noticed. It felt less stifling than the tension between her and Owen. She hurried toward headquarters. Owen wasn't behind her, but that wasn't the reason for her pace. As usual, she needed to drive away her tension.

If people wanted to undermine her and make her feel inadequate, they succeeded. Doubt tickled the back of her mind, making her question whether she was up for the job. But Chantal was stubborn. Giving in wasn't an option.

The entrance to the imposing building loomed ahead of her. It was too soon; she wasn't over her mad yet. Chantal wasn't aware of Owen's plans, but she wanted to return to the house and manage her emotions from there.

Her anger didn't extend as far as leaving him stranded. She left the car behind for Owen and called a taxi to take her to Sillery.

In the vehicle, she closed her eyes and leaned her head back against the seat. Chantal longed for her apartment and thought of Cartier Street where she was close to her friends and the shops and restaurants where everyone knew her name. And where no one battered or trod upon her confidence.

A sudden flash of anger surged through her. The thugs that had beaten and abused her months ago had taken so much. The physical injuries were temporary, although the memories of them lingered. But they had pummeled her faith in herself, filling her with fear and self-doubt. That was something she could never forgive.

Chantal dragged her attention back to the drive. They passed the stately, old mansions on Grande Allée. On her left were the historic Plains of Abraham, the site of the famous battle between the British and the French in 1759, now a beautiful vista of green space dotted with ancient buildings and battlements.

The taxi pulled into the driveway of the Danvers' pretend home. Despite her despair, Chantal smiled to herself. Few people would yearn to trade a magnificent five-bedroom home in upscale Sillery for a small two-bedroom apartment.

She darted a glance over her shoulder and saw the unmarked police car parked down the street. Chantal was careful not to stare or acknowledge its presence as she climbed the few steps to the door.

Her phone and keys landed with a clatter on the mahogany table in the entranceway. Her purse took up residence on the brown leather tub chair, as she kicked off her shoes.

Chantal released her hair from its clip as she climbed the curving staircase. The shower called to her, and she wouldn't keep it waiting. A ping made her swivel around like Pavlov's dog and head back to her purse to retrieve her phone.

As she walked back up the stairs, she read the text from Mark.

"Don't feel bad. Lots of people would choke after what you went thru."

Chantal stopped mid-stairs and re-read the message. First, she didn't understand what he meant by choking. Another strange expression? And second, does everyone know about her past? Had Owen filled him in on how inept he considered her? Or had it been Jeff? Her temper flared again.

She hit speed-dial on her phone and, seconds later, Jeff's voice carried through the device.

Chantal got right to the point. "Are you gossiping about me?"

"What are you talking about?"

"Have you told Owen and Mark about my past?"

"No. Of course not. Why would I?"

Chantal knew Jeff well enough to believe him. A sigh escaped from deep in her lungs. "I'm sorry. I'm on edge. This case is important to me. But everyone seems to think I can't handle it."

"That's not true. I know you can handle it."

"Then why you are fighting me?"

A long silence followed her question until a sigh reached her ears. "It's still fresh for me."

Chantal swallowed the lump that had formed in her throat at Jeff's words. She reminded herself that she hadn't been the only person affected by the operation last winter.

She cleared her throat. "I don't think the captain feels I'm up for it."

"He does. You know him and his rules. Your waiting period isn't over, and they didn't test you yet. He wants to make sure you meet all the protocols."

Chantal chewed on her lip. "You could be right."

"I'm always right," Jeff said with a chuckle before his tone sobered. "What's important is how you feel about the case."

Chantal and Jeff were always upfront with each other, and she didn't intend for that to change.

"I want to do it. I want my life back, but I'd be lying if I said I'm not nervous or scared. It's more a fear of failure than anything else. Having people wonder if they can count on me or not is killing me. I need them to think of me as a strong part of the team."

"For what it's worth, I count on you. I always will. As for how others think, that's something you'll earn on your own. You can do it."

"Thanks. You're the best."

"I am."

"And you're very modest."

"That too," he said. "I'll see you tomorrow."

Chantal smiled as she disconnected. Her conversation with Jeff had eased her mind and helped put everything into perspective. The spark of anger still flickered. If Jeff was off the hook for gossiping, Owen was on it. She would deal with him later.

Chantal stood under the shower spray and let the scalding water relieve the rest of her tension. She needed to keep the goal in sight if she wanted her career and life back.

She jerked in surprise when she stepped into the bedroom, a towel wrapped around her damp body, and found Owen standing in the room. A renewed flash of irritation seared through her.

"No, I'm not packing my bags, if that's what you hoped to see," Chantal said as she pulled the towel a little tighter.

"You don't know what I hoped to see."

Chapter 16

"I wanted to apologize for my remark yesterday. I didn't get a chance at the coffee shop." Owen held up his hands to ward off any attack Chantal might launch. "I shouldn't have said it. I'm sorry."

Owen's dark suit contrasted with Chantal's off-white casual sweatshirt and blue jeans, although he had removed his jacket, softening the look. She avoided his gaze as she headed to the kitchen and removed a large bottle of water from the fridge. A long sip refreshed her and bolstered her courage.

When she returned to the living room, her stare met his head-on. For once, her expression was as stern and unreadable as his. "You're right; you shouldn't have said it. You don't know me or what I went through. You may think you do, but you're only aware of the basics. I'm certain of that. It's a mistake to judge people when you don't understand."

Owen's eyes reflected his regret. "Touché. And that's one of the few French words in my vocabulary."

"It's a good one. I hope you won't need it often."

"Are you going to keep me hanging on a limb? Is my apology accepted?"

His plea dangled in the air between them.

"What about the rest of it?"

His brows formed a question. "The rest of what?"

The doorbell chose an opportune moment to ring.

"Who's that?" Chantal's heart rate spiked as she realized her gun was in the bedroom.

"It's Mark. He said he'd drop by."

The younger RCMP cop's smiling gaze took in the elegant entranceway as he stepped over the threshold. Chantal saw a nondescript rental car parked in the driveway before the door closed behind him.

The previous day, they towed the burned-out Lincoln to the crime lab for the forensic team's examination. All that remained to indicate a crime had taken place was a scorched area of pavement, the crime scene tape, and a patrol car parked on the street.

"Nice digs."

"Yeah. Not too shabby," Owen said. "Come on in. Would you like something to drink? The bar isn't well stocked, but there's a nice bottle of red if you'd like a glass."

"Sure. Why not?"

Chantal led the way to the sitting area. She retrieved her glass of water and moved to the window. Her restlessness returned, and she yearned to be outside, running in the park, but the darkening sky pointed out the foolishness of the idea.

"Have you thought more about next steps?" Mark asked.

Chantal turned to face the men, swirling the water in her glass. "We're going to look for another contact of Griggs."

"With the added inconvenience of not having a computer to work with," Owen added. They had found no electronic devices at the lawyer's home or office. The killer covered his tracks.

"The Mafia connection is a sound theory." Mark sank into one of the wing-back chairs facing the fireplace. "It'll mean moving up the ladder."

"We will," Owen said. "With care."

Mark's gaze narrowed on the woman who stood by the window. "What do you think, Chantal?"

She drew a deep breath. "I think I want to know why you're talking about me behind my back." Her glance moved from one man to the other. As expected, Owen's expression didn't change, but Mark appeared confused.

"I don't understand," he said. He turned to Owen. "Do you?"

Owen never removed his speculative gaze from Chantal, but he gave a slight shrug in response to Mark's question.

Chantal removed her phone from the rear pocket of her jeans, opened the message, and handed it to Mark. "This text you sent me.

It's obvious you talked to someone. I don't appreciate gossip." She shot an accusatory look at Owen.

"I didn't send this." Mark stared with wide eyes at the screen.

"I don't know anyone else by the name of Mark." Chantal placed her fists on her hips.

Without asking permission, Mark tapped the screen several times before a shocked expression appeared on his face. "It *is* from me," he said in a hushed voice.

"That's what I told you."

His eyes were pleading as he looked at her. "No. You don't understand. I never sent this." Mark yanked his phone out of his pocket, entered his passcode, and handed it to her. "See. No text message to you. Look."

Chantal stared at the phone, bewildered.

Owen unfolded himself from the chair and removed the device from Chantal's limp grasp. He scrolled through it and shook his head. "Nothing." He stared at the other RCMP officer. "How did they do it?"

"You think someone hacked into his phone to send me a text?" Chantal's voice rose higher with each word.

"That'd be the only explanation, don't you think?" Owen said. He raised a questioning brow toward Mark.

"It is." His low voice reflected his chagrin and confusion.

"Wouldn't they access it by Bluetooth?" Owen asked.

"Yes, but I have data encryption. It's protected. I don't understand how they did it, but I'll find out." Mark looked as if someone had insulted his mother. "We're dealing with a highly efficient technophile."

"Or group of technophiles," Owen said.

"Wait. The bar." Mark looked at Owen, his eyes bright. "Remember when someone pushed that guy into me? I lost my phone. About ten minutes later, I got it back. It was a set-up." He jumped to his feet and paced the floor. "They must have planted something in my phone."

"But why would they send a text to Chantal? They're showing their hand. They have to realize it's going to work against them." Owen said, his tone as perplexed as Mark's.

"Maybe because they don't care anymore; they've gotten everything they want. Or they're teasing us." Chantal lowered herself onto the sofa, a dazed look on her face. "And it's someone who knows about my past."

• • •

Chantal was up early and pulling on her sneakers when her cell phone jangled. She recognized Jeff's number on the screen. As Owen appeared beside her, she hit a button and put the call on speakerphone.

"We got the results from the bomb," Jeff said. "It's the same type as the one that killed Tommy Endrizzi six months ago in Montreal."

Chantal recalled the event. Endrizzi had been a kingpin in the Laval chapter of the Mafia. And, as many kingpins discovered, living the life meant taking the risks that came with it. His assassination had rattled the underground network and spurred the violence to escalate between the rival gangs in the area.

"That brings us a step closer." Chantal's gaze narrowed. She flicked a glance at Owen.

"We made one other step," Jeff said. "With Griggs, the killer missed something in his clean-up. There was an after-hours phone message recorded on the receptionist's console. It was brief, but it was from Donovan Boyle from two days ago."

"What did he say?" Chantal couldn't contain her excitement. Boyle was a higher-up in Montreal's Irish Mafia.

"They needed to meet, and he expected a call back."

"It's possible Griggs arranged the meet, and they killed him as a result," Owen said.

"Right. But Boyle also mentioned a name, Martin Dion. He said he'd talked to him, and they had things to discuss."

"Do you know who Dion is?" The name was unfamiliar to Chantal.

"Not yet," Jeff said. "But I'll find out."

"We'll wait to hear from you." She disconnected the call and faced Owen. "That's good news. We'll have a contact soon." She bent to grab another sneaker.

"Where are you going?"

"For a run." Chantal held her arms to her sides to display her jogging clothes. She thought it was self-evident.

"Not by yourself."

"Why not?"

Chantal had fought the urge to work out since the previous evening, at the time of Mark's revelation about the hacked cell phone. They kept the device active in case there were more texts that could lead them somewhere. In the meantime, Mark would get a new phone for regular use.

For Chantal, sleep had been evasive.

"You're asking me why not?" Owen's brows lifted. "Because someone almost killed us a couple of days ago."

"We won't start this again, will we? I'm going to jog around the park in broad daylight. People do it all the time. I'm a trained police officer."

"I know that, but you're on a case."

"So. What does that have to do with it? We're not working right now. I'm sure I can take half an hour to go for a run."

"I'll go with you." He turned and headed to his room.

"No." Chantal said to his parting back. One of the primary purposes of running, apart from the obvious one of getting exercise, was to clear her head. She couldn't do that if Owen ran beside her. He was a reminder of why she needed to run. "I don't need you to come with me."

He either didn't hear her objection or ignored it. A few minutes later, he appeared, dressed in sweatpants and a t-shirt. "Let me grab my sneakers, and I'll be ready."

"There's no need. I'm not a child, and I'm not afraid. Besides, what about your leg?"

"I can still run."

"I don't want to be responsible for you hurting yourself." She tested a fresh approach.

"I'm responsible for myself, and I'm not worried. I run all the time." His tone suggested he wasn't changing course.

"I've never seen you run." She didn't mention the trouble he had to walk since the bombing.

"I do. It's part of my therapy." He finished lacing his sneakers and straightened to face her.

"Why are you doing this?" She flapped her arms by her side.

"My reasons should be obvious. I don't have to explain them."

Chantal wanted to scream with irritation, but she gritted her teeth and led the way outside.

The fresh, early morning air greeted them, but the hazy sunshine promised another hot and humid day.

Chantal hit the trail at a strong pace and didn't turn to see if Owen followed. His negative thoughts could keep him company. Besides, running at his own pace was better for him, she reasoned.

A few seconds later, heavy footsteps beat the path behind her. A quick glance over her shoulder found Owen to her left. He stared straight ahead and kept pace with ease, his limp barely evident. Chantal swung her gaze forward and stayed determined to ignore him. She popped her ear buds into place, adjusted the volume of the music on her phone, and drowned out the sound of his footsteps. She didn't normally listen to music while running, wanting to be aware of what happened around her, but this was an exception.

Half an hour later, Chantal slowed, preparing for her cool-down, and glanced over her shoulder again, certain she would be alone. She wasn't. Owen was close behind, his face shiny with sweat. The tightness around his eyes and the pinching of his lips were evidence of his pain. As he slowed his pace to match hers, Chantal's gaze dropped to his leg. He was all but dragging it. Chantal stopped and faced him.

"Are you okay?" she said, wiping errant strands of hair from her face.

"Am I okay? Do you really care?" Owen's eyes flashed. He leaned over with his hands on his thighs, his breathing labored.

"Well… you should've stopped if it hurt," she stammered.

"Yeah, right. Let's get back." He straightened and wheeled around to head toward the house.

Chantal didn't dare speak, aware of his fury. They crossed the street in silence.

Owen stalked to his bedroom while Chantal headed to the shower. When she emerged, he was in the kitchen pouring a glass of water, his hair damp from his own shower.

"You told me you ran all the time," Chantal commented.

He turned to face her. "I do, as part of my physiotherapy, but I don't run marathons."

"It was hardly a marathon, only half an hour."

"With a bad leg, that's a marathon."

"Look, I'm sorry. But you could've stopped."

Owen placed his empty glass in the dishwasher and grumbled something unintelligible. Chantal wanted to ask him to repeat it, but he limped past her and settled on the couch, lifting his leg onto a footstool. He pulled his computer onto his lap.

His attitude reeked of scorn, and Chantal acknowledged she deserved it. If they reversed roles, she would be the same, but all he had to do was speak up, she thought. She wasn't a monster; she would understand.

But then again, Chantal also understood pride. She had more than her fair share of it and didn't blame Owen for his stubbornness.

If she was honest, it was refreshing to see something other than his forever-prevalent stoicism. At least he possessed normal human emotions, something she had only seen once before, when they had shared some laughs between Montreal and Quebec.

She seemed to trigger negative emotions in her partner. This was foreign to Chantal. She enjoyed a reputation for being an energetic, positive player. Clashes with her colleagues were rare.

Where did the tension between her and Owen come from? Was it SQ versus RCMP? Or was there something beneath the surface that provoked her, something her intuition tried to get across to her?

CHAPTER 17

Chantal wriggled into her dark blue dress and adjusted the neckline to gain a smidgeon of modesty. It rankled that she was only useful as eye candy on the arm of her all-knowing husband. She tamped down her resentment with the reminder she was working undercover once again instead of scanning documents in a sterile office. Chantal held hope that, after this case, things would change.

First, she had to get through this one.

Again, Chantal and Owen had journeyed to the Queen Elizabeth Hotel in Montreal and arrived before noon. Jeff had done his homework. The new contact was another lawyer. He wasn't on the radar of the authorities, but he was a valid candidate for a mob connection.

Martin Dion had never been convicted or investigated for a crime, but it didn't mean he never committed one. It was fortuitous that his name slipped out of the mouth of Donovan Boyle.

Owen contacted him and explained that his lawyer had passed away, and he and his wife needed financial advice. The man seemed to understand Owen's meaning and suggested they meet at a restaurant in Montreal at three o'clock that afternoon to discuss the business deal.

"I'll get in touch with you at two-thirty to tell you where we'll meet," the man said during the call.

Owen agreed to his terms.

"He's cautious, I'll give him that." Owen leaned back in the floral-patterned armchair as Chantal helped herself to a glass of water. "Much more so than Griggs was. He's not giving us time to set up surveillance."

"It'll be somewhere within a half hour drive, that's for sure. I hope we can trace the call."

Owen grimaced. "It'll be brief. I'm certain of that."

He was right. At two-thirty, an unknown number popped up on Owen's cell phone, and a voice rattled off an address.

The meeting place was more down to earth than restaurants the 'Danvers' usually frequented. It was an Irish pub in Downtown Montreal by the name of Butlers. Charlie, the owner and bartender, was a petite brunette and greeted them with a welcoming smile. She seemed like the type to know her customers by name, but she showed no sign of recognizing Dion.

The man sat across from them. A dark mahogany tabletop, polished to a shine, separated the couple from him. Dion was of average height and, although not obese, a paunch strained against the bright gold buckle of his belt. His dark hair, slicked back from his forehead, revealed a receding hairline.

It crossed Chantal's mind that his appearance fit the stereotype of a Mafia member. His voice, however, carried a hint of a French accent instead of the traditional Italian.

"What can I do for you people?"

His stare was dark and intense and held no glimmer of a smile. She glanced at her partner and witnessed the same hard, unsmiling stare directed toward Dion.

"We were working on a business deal with the help of our lawyer, but he met with an unfortunate accident, and we need someone else to take over," Owen said. "Since the services we need are of a financial nature, we thought you might help."

"What are these services?" the man said. His expression didn't reveal any knowledge of Griggs or his 'unfortunate accident.'

Owen rolled out the same story he gave Griggs and asked Dion if he thought he could assist them. The man nodded as he considered the proposition, giving nothing away.

"I've got some people to consult, but I think I have the network available to help. Tell me where to find you, and I'll drop by with an answer."

"Here's my business card," Owen said, handing him one of the fake cards the RCMP had prepared for them. "Contact me at that number." The man's eyebrows lifted to their highest point. Disbursing orders was customary for him, not receiving them.

"I also expect an answer within two days," Owen continued. "Otherwise, I'll go somewhere else."

"I don't think…"

Owen took Chantal by the elbow and tugged her from the booth. "Well, I do think, Mr. Dion. I don't like being jerked around. Losing Griggs delayed this venture longer than acceptable. It's time to get moving. If you can't help us, there are other people willing to earn a commission on what I'm offering."

Dion stood and held his hands out by his sides. "Hang on. Don't go off half-cocked. I didn't say I wouldn't work with you. I have to find the right person."

"Then I suggest you find him as soon as possible."

The couple marched out of the establishment, leaving a stunned Dion standing beside the booth.

"I didn't realize you'd take that direction," Chantal said, almost as astonished as Dion. "You're not afraid of bringing the fury of the Mafia raining down on top of us?"

"The guys at the top respect strength in their dealings. They won't do business with wimps. It may be part of the reason Beaudet and Griggs are dead. If we want to get in with these guys, we have to show them we're worthy."

Chantal agreed, but not without hesitation.

"We'll give him two days. If we don't hear anything, we'll get back to him. But I'm almost certain we'll have an answer before then," Owen said.

A shiver ran down Chantal's spine, a mixture of excitement and fear. She needed both emotions to work a case, along with a healthy dose of caution.

• • •

The monotone female voice repeated the phrase 'Turn left up ahead' until Chantal wanted to yell in frustration.

"She should understand we had no choice. There's construction everywhere." Chantal waved her arm like a tour guide presenting artifacts in a museum.

91

"It's okay. We'll…"

The shrill ring of Owen's phone overrode the mechanical inflection of the GPS system and replaced it with Mark's smooth, stable tone.

"Any luck on the trace?" Owen asked.

"Yes, and no. We pinpointed the phone, but it came from someone at a service station in Pointe-Fortune," Mark said.

"Where's that?" Owen shot a questioning glance in Chantal's direction.

"It's west of the city, on the way to Ottawa, at least an hour from Butler's pub," she said.

"I'm not surprised." Owen's mouth slanted into a frown. They had hoped to zero in on Dion's headquarters. "Keep us up-to-date if anything else comes in."

"What are you guys going to do?" The techie cop sounded wistful, like a kid left out of a ball game.

"Nothing until he gets back to us."

Owen punched a button on the steering wheel to disconnect the call. They had also taken precautions and scrambled their cell phone signals.

Chantal's thoughts turned inward as she let Owen deal with the GPS woman and the irritating late afternoon traffic in Montreal. The serene elegance of the hotel was a welcome reprieve when they arrived.

"Shall we order in?" Owen asked as he removed his jacket and tie.

"I suppose." The thought appealed to her. She didn't feel like dressing fancy and pretending to be rich, no matter how much fun it was. Chantal admitted to herself that the almost combative meeting today had shaken her. Her job chained her to a desk too much these days, she reasoned. "What kind of food do people in our position order?"

"I presume whatever we like."

Relieved to discard the heels and the form-fitting dress, Chantal changed into sweatpants and a T-shirt before they met with Captain Bouchard, Jeff, and Mark via an online video platform. The medium became commonplace during the pandemic and was part of the new normal.

The camera in the conference room in Quebec City picked up the image of her colleagues converged around the table and sent it to Owen's laptop. Their expressions reflected their eagerness to hear the account of the meeting with Dion.

"How'd it go?" Jeff leaned forward and rested his elbows on the table.

Chantal shot a glance at Owen before she spoke. "It didn't last long. Owen made it clear he called the shots, and he insisted Dion get back to him within two days."

Bouchard's brows lowered. "It sounds like you had an aggressive conversation."

"I got my message across." Owen's tone was matter-of-fact.

"Dion's interested," Chantal said, hoping to smooth things over. "There's no doubt about it. It threw him off, but I think he'll pull through for us."

Mark sent a nervous look at the men sitting on either side of him. Matching frowns darkened their faces.

Bouchard's throat-clearing broke the uncomfortable silence. "It's not my business how the RCMP handle their dealings with criminal elements, but I'd rather you do it without dragging one of my officers into a dangerous position."

Chantal wanted to object and remind her boss Owen hadn't dragged her into anything. She may not have expected his approach, but she was a full partner in the operation and took responsibility for herself.

"Chantal and I work together," Owen said, his tone even and reasonable. "And I think you know her well enough to agree she'd tell me if she didn't go along with anything."

Neither the captain nor Jeff contradicted his statement, but only Mark wore an unsuspecting smile when they ended the video call.

Owen poured himself a glass of wine from a bottle room service had delivered. He sent Chantal a questioning look, holding the glass up.

She accepted his offer with a nod. "Do you really think they're watching us?" Chantal didn't need to explain who 'they' were.

"Maybe, maybe not. We can't take chances. You and I both know how careful they are. They check out everyone before they do business with them."

"They must wonder why, with all our money and connections, we came to them." It wasn't the first time Chantal mused over this thought aloud.

"They're greedy. They won't pass up this chance."

"And then, they'll make sure we're tied to them forever, victims of blackmail and extortion."

"That's their specialty." He raised his glass in a toast.

Owen's phone rang as they finished the last bites of delivery sushi. He threw Chantal a glance before he pressed the record button on his phone and answered the call.

Chantal admitted Owen possessed a talent for what he did. He was smooth and calm and gave every impression of being an experienced business owner, used to getting what he wanted. When the call ended, he didn't speak. He hit the replay button.

"Hello."

"Mr. Danvers?"

"Yes."

"This is Dion. I spoke to my business partners. They aren't available for a meeting. We'll do it by conference call."

"I insist we meet face-to-face." Owen's tone didn't allow wiggle room. "We're talking about a significant amount of money. I won't hand over my business to just anyone."

"My partners are very busy."

Chantal detected a vibration of anger in the man's voice.

"So am I, Mr. Dion. If this deal means so little, I'll take my business elsewhere."

"That won't be necessary. Give me time. I'll get back to you." A click signaled the conclusion of the conversation.

It was obvious the Mafia lawyer wasn't happy. Owen pushed him to the limits of his patience. Perhaps his partners were non-existent. Without a doubt, he itched to teach Owen a lesson.

"We'll wait until tomorrow. Then I'll call him back, keep up the pressure."

"He's angry and dangerous." Chantal knew she stated the obvious.

"He's also a low man on the totem pole, or at least a middleman. He's expected to deliver business to the top, not eliminate it."

Chantal agreed, but her mind jumped ahead, picturing different scenarios that might appear. A bomb had almost eliminated them. A gun had taken care of Griggs and Beaudet.

"We've got a strong team backing us up." Owen, once again, seemed to read her thoughts.

"I know." Jeff's face appeared in her mind. Her 'big brother' would wait on the sidelines, looking out for her, and ensuring everyone was on their toes.

Chantal glanced at her watch. It was only nine fifteen in the evening. She had finished her glass of wine. She didn't want another, and an unusual wave of fatigue washed over her. Not feeling up to an awkward conversation with Owen to pass the time, she opted for bed.

When she shared her intentions with Owen, the corners of his mouth lifted. "You don't seem like the type to run off to bed at nine o'clock."

"It's nine fifteen, I'm not running, and I love spending the evening in bed with a book."

Owen shot her a skeptical look.

Chantal prepared for bed, wondering what she would read. She had forgotten to bring a book with her.

• • •

A proud smile turned his lips upward. Everything had fallen into place without a hitch. People were available and prepared for the next step.

He was like a basketball coach, he thought with a deep chuckle. Strategizing, setting up the plays, choosing the best players at the right times. He planned to make it to the championships, but he'd be the only one on the podium to claim the prize. He may use a team, but he wasn't a team player.

No, there could only be one winner here.

CHAPTER 18

There was no need for Owen to reach out to Dion. An email appeared in Owen's fake inbox telling them to meet their prospective business partners at a restaurant, Chez Leoni, the following afternoon.

Owen handed his phone to Chantal for her to read the missive.

"Do you think it's a set-up?" She lifted her gaze from the phone to meet his.

"Could be. Anything's possible. We need to see it through."

Chantal stared at the cityscape through the floor to ceiling windows, weighing the pros and cons of accepting the invitation. She agreed they needed to move forward, but with caution. Their attempt to infiltrate a crime syndicate with technology and unscrupulous people on their side could backfire on them.

The couple dressed in upscale casual attire, assumed their personas, and left the hotel. Owen claimed the keys to the Mercedes from the valet.

On Ste-Catherine Street, they remained conspicuous while window shopping, until Owen glanced at his watch and mumbled a few words to Chantal. They would make it to their one o'clock meeting with minutes to spare.

As they drove along Peel Street, a car pulled out of a parking spot in front of an imposing building in the financial district. The exchange was smooth and convenient, but Chantal knew the cop in the sleek black car had watched for them in his side mirror.

"The perks," Owen said with a smile. Parking in downtown Montreal was often a challenge, and they didn't want to waste time driving in circles, looking for an empty spot.

The strength and warmth of Owen's hand surrounded Chantal's as they strolled toward the office building that housed investment advisors, insurance companies, and financial managers. Within it, the SQ had borrowed an unused office to hold a clandestine meeting with the two undercover cops.

A Montreal contingent of the police force greeted them. A computer screen projected the serious faces of Captain Bouchard and Jeff via an audiovisual link.

Chantal flashed them a warm smile, her spirits lifting at the sight of their familiar faces. She hadn't realized how much she needed the grounding they gave her until she laid eyes upon them.

"We're going to get you set up for tomorrow," Bouchard said. "They'll search for listening devices."

An SQ tech expert stepped forward. He held a small box in his hand. "Chantal, you can carry this in your purse. Bring a pad with you and pretend you want to take notes." He removed a pen from the box and clicked the top of the device. "This turns it on. Be sure the logo faces the subject. It'll record both audio and visual. On your way in and out, turn it off. Scanners won't detect it."

"There'll be a team surrounding the building," Jeff said. "We'll listen to everything. Any sign of trouble, get out of there."

A shiver of nerves crawled over Chantal. The final instructions, the electronic gadgets, and the stern expression on Jeff's face reminded her she was back in the game. It was where she wanted to be, but she struggled to ignore her anxieties.

Within half an hour, they were in the car, heading to the Queen Elizabeth. Chantal paid little attention to the traffic or road construction; her thoughts turned inward.

"How about the hotel restaurant tonight?"

Chantal shook herself out of her introspection. "What? Oh, sure, that'll be fine."

Her mind circled around the case and the upcoming meeting, and she was thankful for Owen's habitual less-than-chatty demeanor. If he noticed the difference in her behavior, he had the sense to keep his comments to himself.

• • •

Chantal suffered through a restless night, troubled by dreams of being captured and beaten. She woke in the morning confused and disturbed. It took her several minutes to differentiate between what was real and what was part of a dream.

Tightening the tie of her dressing gown, she headed to the living area of the suite, her feet bare and her hair pulled back in a loose ponytail. Owen sat on the bar stool at the counter, browsing through the news on his tablet, and sipping coffee from a large mug. Chantal forced a bland expression onto her face and slipped a pod into the coffeemaker.

"Sleep well?"

Was it an innocent question, or was he aware her dreams had disturbed her? Was he clairvoyant? Sometimes, she thought he was.

"Never better," she said.

"Good. We have a big day ahead of us."

As if she needed reminding, she thought.

Chantal took her coffee to the bedroom while she showered and dressed. She checked her reflection in the mirror. The navy lightweight pantsuit was the right mixture of business and businessman's wife, depending on the level of chauvinism with which she had to deal. At the very least, it lifted her confidence.

She did her hair and makeup as fast as possible, wanting to give Owen plenty of time in the bathroom to get ready.

While he was in the shower, Chantal packed her bag. They would return to Quebec City after this meeting. There was no need to spend more of the government's money in Montreal.

Chantal paced the floor as she waited for Owen. When he emerged from the bedroom, he had his suit jacket over his arm and his necktie in his hand.

"We should go," she said, surprised by his lack of urgency.

"There's lots of time."

"We need to check out."

Owen glanced at his watch. "Yep. We still have half an hour. After lunch, we'll head to the meeting."

"We need to be there by two-thirty."

"No worries."

"I thought we'd go over the scenario."

"We went over it twice last night. That should be enough. Why are you so nervous?"

"I'm not. I like to prepare."

If Chantal was honest with Owen, she would admit to her uneasiness. It had been six months since she had worked a case, and it hadn't gone well. Fears of blowing the operation assailed her. But one thing was certain, she would never confess her nervousness to her partner.

For the third time, she opened her purse and checked the contents to ensure she had everything with her. Turning, Chantal watched Owen make himself another cup of coffee. Was she imagining he took more time than usual to do it? When he caught her eye and sent her a sly smile, she realized he set out to irritate her.

Chantal contemplated making herself a second cup of coffee to spite Owen, but more coffee would add to her jitteriness.

The chirping of Owen's cell phone saved her from an overdose of caffeine. The smug smile on his face disappeared, and he was all business. Mark's voice reverberated through the phone. He was with the electronics team who would monitor their meeting with Dion's friends, and all systems were ready.

"Time to go," Owen said as he disconnected the call. He grabbed his coat and knotted his tie on the way to the door. Chantal threw the strap of her purse over her shoulder and hurried to catch up to him, dragging her wheeled bag behind her.

They found a bistro with an available table on the patio where they ordered a light lunch. When Chantal glanced at her watch for the third time, Owen leaned forward to catch her attention.

"We're ten minutes away. Would you like a glass of wine?"

Chantal held up her hands. "No. No alcohol. I'm fine. I'm just concerned because they haven't delivered our food yet."

As she finished speaking, the server appeared with a smile, a sandwich for Owen, and a salad for Chantal.

They arrived at their destination several minutes ahead of time.

Chantal straightened her jacket as she strolled toward Owen. A fond smile lit his face as he waited for her. As usual, the smile transformed him so much that it threw Chantal for a loop. She wondered if he was aware of the power of that grin as they slipped into their roles of husband and wife, knowing cameras and microphones might record their every move and word. Chantal slipped her arm into the crook of Owen's elbow.

The restaurant where they agreed to meet their supposed partners touted itself as Italian but served a varied menu. However, it wasn't the food that interested them today; it was the private room where they could talk over coffee and biscotti.

A red-vested server escorted Owen and Chantal upstairs and down a narrow hallway. He motioned them over a threshold and shut the door behind them. Two broad-shouldered men in dark suits stepped forward, their faces expressionless. One of them held a scanning wand. Chantal put a distressed hand to her chest and appeared confused. Owen squeezed her shoulder as if to reassure her.

"I'm sorry," a man said as he stepped forward. In his mid-thirties, he was short and stocky, but his well-tailored, dark suit fit him well. His smile revealed good dental work. "I'm Steven Walsh. This is routine. We have to take precautions. I'm sure you understand."

"You don't trust us?" Chantal said, her tone showing how affronted she felt by the intrusion.

"It's all right, Michelle. It's painless, and we have nothing to hide." Owen held his arms to the side as the thug checked him for wires. Chantal wore an insulted expression as she did the same. One man took her purse by its strap and removed it from her shoulder. He opened it and allowed the other man to pass the wand inside before handing it back to her.

Chantal snatched it from his meaty hand and lifted her nose in the air, brushing past him to follow Owen as he crossed the room.

Walsh waited beside a table with another man of the same age range. He was taller and thinner, with a darker complexion, and also well-dressed. They both oozed the same practiced, used-car salesmen smiles.

Something struck Chantal as odd. She had expected older individuals, experienced in the game of fraud. More Scarface and less Cadillac Man.

"Please, sit," said Walsh. "This is my partner, Ed Trenton."

Trenton smiled and nodded as he poured coffee from a thermal carafe and set cups on the table in front of each of them. Chantal removed her notepad and pen from her bag and placed them beside her coffee cup, clicking the end of the pen.

"Where's Dion?" Owen said as his narrow-eyed gaze moved between the two men.

Walsh smiled. "He didn't feel the need for his presence. We can take it from here. I'm a lawyer, and Ed is an expert in financing. We're available to answer your questions."

Chantal glanced at Owen, wondering if he felt the same strange vibe she did, but his expression revealed nothing. She expected the men to be nervous, worried about the exposure of their scam. Instead, they seemed relaxed and confident—too much so.

"Did Dion bring you up to speed on what we need?" Owen took a slow sip of his coffee.

"Not in detail. All he said was you required our particular expertise."

Owen emitted a dramatic sigh and exchanged an exasperated look with his make-believe wife. "We need help to set up foreign shell companies. They'll bill sub-contracting work to a construction company that we own, and the proceeds will go offshore. Without a trace, of course."

"Of course," Walsh said with another ingratiating smile. "There won't be any problem. We have special skills and can get it done as soon as possible."

Owen's brows lifted. "It's obvious there'll be a fee for these services."

Walsh's plastic smile broadened at Owen's prompt. He motioned with his hand toward his partner, who had remained silent up to this point. "Ed handles that end of things."

The other man straightened in his seat like a child called upon by a teacher to answer a tough question. "It'll cost ten thousand per company plus ten percent of all invoicing," Trenton said.

"Those are nice round figures." A stern look graced Owen's face.

"We like to keep things round," Walsh said with a chuckle. Trenton joined in with a hearty laugh that seemed inappropriate to the comment.

"I prefer things less round. I suggest eight thousand and seven percent." Owen bared his teeth in a forced sneer.

Walsh and Trenton's smiles vanished. They hadn't seemed to expect a challenge. Walsh's mouth clamped shut and his lips thinned. His gaze shifted to his companion, who gave an almost imperceptible nod.

"We might work that out. We'll discuss it and get back to you," Walsh said.

"Good." Owen pushed back his chair and stood. Chantal retrieved her untouched notepad and pen and returned them to her bag.

"Wait. We need to work out the details." Without the smile, uncertainty transformed Steven Walsh's face.

"As do we," Owen said. His cryptic statement didn't seem to comfort the two men, who exchanged concerned glances. Walsh wrung his hands.

Chantal aimed a bright smile at them before following Owen out the door. Neither of the detectives spoke until seated inside the car.

"Strange, wasn't it?" Chantal said.

"Very. That's why I cut it short. We weren't getting anywhere with those two. They staged it."

"I guess we should've expected that," Chantal said.

"The recording is probably a waste of time, but it could lead us to the source."

Chantal spread her fingers over her purse, unconsciously protecting the pen which had filmed the encounter with the two men, perhaps actors hired to fill a role. She didn't like to think they had wasted their time. The case needed to move forward, not stagnate.

"If we can identify them, we can apply pressure to discover who pays them," Owen said.

"Mark can work his magic." Chantal hoped she sounded more optimistic than she felt.

The looming return trip to Quebec City would be interminable, Chantal thought. She had felt confined the last few days, unable to work off her restless energy. She took a stab at casual conversation with Owen.

"Is your family in Toronto?" Everyone enjoyed talking about their family and home life, she reasoned.

"No."

Chantal stared at him, waiting for elaboration. With none forthcoming, she said, "Do you have any family? Anyone close? Brothers? Sisters?"

"No one close. You?"

Chantal's mouth dropped open. He was a master stonewaller, a foreign trait for Chantal. Her eyes narrowed. She wouldn't give up, she thought.

"I'm from Gaspé. My parents still live there, and so does my sister. I have a brother who works out west as a PI."

"Gaspé? Where's that?" He checked his side mirror as he merged onto Autoroute 20. They would have highway driving for the next two hours.

"About seven hours northeast of Quebec, on the Gaspé Peninsula. You should visit if you have the chance. It's a beautiful drive."

"I'll keep it in mind."

Chantal peered at his expression. Was he being sarcastic?

"Do you travel a lot?" She came at him from a different direction.

"Not much."

Chantal rolled her eyes and gave up. She removed her phone from her purse and scrolled through social media sites to pass the time. Her head flooded with memories of the hours she had passed with Jeff when they did mind-numbing surveillance. They discussed everything and anything, never holding back.

In contrast, Owen was like a closed book. When you opened it, you discovered invisible ink covered the pages.

• • •

They kept up the pretense and returned to the rented house. Owen checked his phone messages as they climbed the front steps with the ornate handrail and the huge hydrangea bushes on each side.

"It's all clear. No one came by while we were gone."

During their absence, the authorities had maintained a patrol officer on the street to make sure no one tampered with the home or installed electronic devices during their absence.

Chantal squelched a sigh as she slipped off her shoes in the entranceway. As she carried her bag upstairs, she wondered if the house felt more like home to her or if what she felt was relief from the tense silence in the car. She believed the latter.

Chantal longed to run, but Owen would insist on going with her, and they would repeat what happened a few days earlier. She didn't feel up to it. A soak in a hot bath might do the trick.

"Should we order in?"

Chantal blinked. She had forgotten they hadn't eaten dinner. They should have stopped somewhere, but neither of them had brought up the subject.

"Pizza?" A questioning shrug accompanied her suggestion.

"Why not? It's fast and easy."

Yes, she could handle fast and easy tonight. Tomorrow, they needed to turn their attention back to the case.

CHAPTER 19

"I got an email from Eric. We're going to videoconference with another officer downtown. Something about an operation he's involved in. I'll be back in an hour or so. Lock the doors and don't leave."

Chantal glanced up at Owen from her chair at the kitchen table. He stood in the doorway, his hands in his pockets.

The website displayed before her absorbed her attention, to where his high-handed manner and most of what he said passed unnoticed.

"Yeah, no problem." She mumbled the words, and her focus returned to the laptop as the front door closed behind Owen.

Ten minutes later, Chantal stood and stretched. She glanced toward the window and noticed the clouds had given way to bright sunshine. It was only mid-morning, but she needed to work out some kinks. It would be the perfect opportunity to get out without Owen. She appreciated him wanting to keep her company, but it was painful for him and guilt-inducing for her.

Within minutes, dressed in her jogging clothes, she sprinted the short distance to the picturesque Parc du Bois-du-Coulonge with its trails that wound through gardens and green space.

Chantal was in her element. The pull of her muscles eased the tension in her body. The heat hadn't descended in full force yet, and she inhaled the still-fresh air.

Since it was a weekday, a smattering of people took advantage of the trails. Chantal passed others, but few passed her. The heavy tread of sneakers behind her signaled a well-trained jogger coming up on her rear. She moved to the right to allow the runner to pass, but the person adjusted to her pace and remained five or six strides behind.

Chantal's gaze darted around her. Surrounded by dense trees, she needed to find an exit point leading to an open area populated with people. She was alone, unarmed, amongst trees, and her evil-detecting antennae were on full alert.

She turned her head to glance at her fellow jogger and realized the distance between them had shortened. He was nothing but a blur as his arms reached forward, and he dived toward her. A body outweighing hers by more than double pummeled into her side as they crashed through the brush beside the trail.

Chantal slid her hands underneath her chest to push herself up, but one assailant became two. Someone yanked her arms behind her back. Another pressed a rag with a chemical stench over her nose. She slipped away.

•   •   •

Another smell engulfed her as she regained consciousness; a musty, damp basement smell. A thin mattress was all that separated her from a hard, cement floor. The dim glow from an exposed bulb hanging from the ceiling threw the corners of the room into shadow.

Her chest tight and her pulse racing, Chantal's gaze bounced around her. The room was bare of everything except the mattress. A window set high on the wall had bars on the inside. She glanced toward the door, but the chances of it being unlocked were slim to none.

Chantal was free of restraints and, although she was sure she sported bruises and tender muscles, she suffered no injuries. That knowledge didn't ease her mind. In fact, her anxiety showed no signs of letting up. A full-scale panic attack headed her way, and she needed to pull herself back from the edge or more misery would rain down upon her.

Giving up the present, her mind threw her back to six months earlier, when criminals had abducted and held her prisoner in another cold, damp basement. That one had been in Trois-Rivières, a town between Quebec City and Montreal.

It involved the case that gave Jeff his wife and Chantal her best friend, but it was also the one that came close to breaking her. Captured by a drug lord and his minions, they had locked her away, beaten her senseless, and bartered her for another victim—Tori. The physical injuries had required weeks to overcome. The emotional trauma was a bigger challenge and one which Jeff and her captain, not to mention herself, questioned.

Minutes or hours passed — her mind couldn't distinguish which — before the shuffling of footsteps reached through her stark memories and the door swung open. A large, dark silhouette appeared in the doorway, blocking the feeble light that struggled to sneak past him.

Every muscle in Chantal's body tensed, prepared to fight to the end. The figure didn't move. It was tall and stocky. He clenched his hands and held them at his sides as if he carried buckets filled with water in each fist.

Several long seconds passed as the man stood on the threshold, tension vibrating in the air. The door slammed shut, and the footsteps faded. Chantal curled into a ball and waited for the tremors to recede.

CHAPTER 20

"Have you heard from Chantal?"

Jeff hesitated a moment, his phone held to his ear, before he answered Owen. He didn't like the question or the tone of voice in which he delivered it. "She's not with you?" he asked.

"No, I phoned her, but she doesn't answer," Owen said. "Look, someone called me to a videoconference, but it was a set-up. Somebody must've hacked my email."

"Where are you now?" Jeff ran toward the exit.

"On my way to the house."

"Call me as soon as you get there." Jeff shot the words at Owen like bullets from a gun.

Jeff's heart thumped in his chest. The only reason someone would set up a fake videoconference was to separate Owen from Chantal. They were after her. The fact she hadn't answered Owen's call didn't reassure him.

He punched the button on his phone to speed dial her number and waited through the ominous ringing until her voice told him to leave a message. He dropped the device in his pocket as he raced to his car.

Jeff was still ten minutes away when his phone rang. It was Owen. The RCMP officer's breath was raspy, and the thud of shoes echoing on pavement reached Jeff's ears.

"She's not at the house and neither are her sneakers. I'm on my way to the park, the *'bois'* one."

"I'll meet you there," Jeff said. He closed his eyes briefly and prayed he would have the chance to blast Chantal for jogging by herself. He grabbed his radio and called for backup.

Jeff's tires squealed as he pulled into the entranceway of the park. Owen stood on the fringe, his hands on his hips, scanning the vast space. Slamming the car into park, Jeff jumped out before it came to a standstill and jogged over to the other cop.

"We'll need more people." Owen said. Worry etched his face.

"There's more on the way."

"I don't know," Owen said. "She may not be here. She may never have been here. But her sneakers are missing. She must've gone for a run."

"I agree," Jeff said. "And if she didn't answer her phone, either the battery died, she dropped it, or something happened."

The two men shared an apprehensive glance. They realized the first two possibilities were a stretch.

Jeff made a call and, in rapid French, barked orders at the unfortunate person on the other end. He hung up and turned to Owen.

"They'll triangulate her phone. I'll have an answer in a few minutes."

The men waited for Jeff's phone to ring, their stiff stances betraying their fear.

At the first sound of a chirp, Jeff lifted the phone to his ear. He exchanged a few questions and comments in French. His expression told it all. The news wasn't good.

"There's no signal. The battery could have died, but knowing Chantal, she'd never leave with a low battery. Otherwise, it's disabled on purpose or smashed by accident."

Owen's lips tightened into a grimace.

They turned as a police car pulled to the curb, and two uniformed officers stepped out. They split up throughout the park and, following Jeff's instructions, paid particular attention to wooded areas.

Owen headed east, a patch of trees in his line of vision. Jeff noticed his limp worsened and imagined his leg screamed in pain, but he gave the RCMP officer extra points for not slowing down.

Jeff took the west side, jogging along the trail, while the other two officers headed south. He was certain Chantal would have stayed on the path. If someone attacked her, it would have been on or near the trail.

Jeff gritted his teeth as he ran, fury coursing through his veins. He was angry at Owen for letting a scam meeting pull him in; angry at

Chantal for leaving the house on her own; and angry at this case that had thrown everyone in a different direction than intended. It had started as a straightforward assignment to ease Chantal back into the job. They hadn't expected bombs, murder, and disappearances.

Jeff closed in on some shrubbery and slowed to a walk, his eyes searching the area on either side of the path. Moving aside branches, he sighted overturned earth, still dark and fresh. The snapped and bent branches showed evidence of a struggle.

Jeff dug out his phone and called Owen, directing him to the spot. He radioed the other officers.

"Spread out," Jeff said. "We have to search this area. Look for anything that could belong to her."

Ten minutes later, they reunited, unsuccessful.

"We assume Chantal and whoever attacked her caused that," Jeff said, pointing to the disheveled bushes. "If she broke her phone, she would've contacted us some other way, or she would've returned to the house. Someone took her. There's no other explanation."

He spoke to one of the uniformed cops in French. The officer headed to the police cruiser.

"He'll call in the crime scene techs," Jeff explained to Owen.

"Damn." Owen ran his hands through his hair, affected in a way that was out of character. "Why the hell didn't she listen to me? Would that be so hard?"

Jeff couldn't answer the other cop. He knew Chantal better than anyone. She could be tough and stubborn. That stubbornness made her frustrating to work with. But she was a brilliant partner, and he loved her like a sister.

"Oh God," Jeff said. "She can't go through this again."

• • •

What was the plan for her? Hours had passed and there was no sign of anyone. No noises in the building, no movement of any kind. Were they going to let her starve to death? Would they come back and torture her? Would she suffer a slow and painful death? What was the purpose?

So many questions ran through Chantal's mind. There was nothing else to do but entertain uncertainty about her fate. She didn't think she could survive another episode like the one she lived through so few months ago. Physically, she would heal, but, for her mental health, it was too much to handle.

With an effort, Chantal pushed the horrible memories aside and concentrated on the present. She searched every corner and found nothing to use as a weapon or tool to help her escape. She yelled and screamed, but realized it was unlikely her captors had left her where someone could hear her.

Chantal circled the room, her thoughts whirling in her head. Part of her wanted them to stay away and leave her alone, unharmed. Another part wanted to face her aggressors, discover what they wanted, what made them tick, so she could find a way to escape. She knew it wouldn't be easy, but the waiting and worrying drove her crazy.

Despite months of fifty-minute therapy sessions, nothing prepared her for going through this again.

A noise caught her attention. It was faint, but she thought it sounded like a car. Had it passed by the building or had it pulled up beside it? The distinct slamming of two doors confirmed the latter. Chantal positioned herself against the wall facing the door, her feet set shoulder-width apart. Her breathing quickened. The time had come.

Loud footsteps pounded overhead. Two heavyset people, probably men. Perhaps the same two men who had brought her here, she surmised. One would be the bully who stood in the doorway and tried to intimidate her.

Chantal wouldn't recognize them, at any rate. She hadn't seen their faces and assumed men had attacked her in the park, considering their size and strength.

A key scraped in the lock, and the door swung open. The dim glow in the hallway backlit two large silhouettes. Chantal tried to take in their features and the area behind them; anything to give her a sprinkling of useful knowledge.

"Do ya enjoy your new home?" It was the larger of the two. Judging by his shape, she believed he was the man who had visited earlier.

Chantal didn't respond. Silence was her friend.

They stepped further into the room, stopping four feet away from where she stood with her arms braced by her side, ready to defend herself.

"Cat got your tongue, has it?" The same man guffawed as the other snickered beside him.

Something seemed off, but Chantal couldn't pinpoint it. They had tough-guy stances, one of them with his arms crisscrossed over his chest. The other had his hands poised beside his hips like someone from an old western movie, ready to draw a gun.

The man who spoke circled to her side, keeping his distance while he looked her over. His features remained unclear; the only light came from the hallway. Chantal tried to watch them both at the same time. She needed to react to a potential attack.

Many times, Chantal relived her previous experience in her head, with a lot of what-ifs. What if she had taken out the big guy at the knees? What if she had freed an arm and given one a neck chop? She didn't want what-ifs this time. It needed to work.

"I bet you're wondering what you're doing here, aren't ya? Maybe you should've kept your nose out of our boss' business. You should've left well enough alone. What do ya think?"

The other man moved fast, much quicker than expected. He took one large stride forward. His hand snaked out and struck her across the face. Not hard enough to knock her down, but it stung and made her widen her stance. She'd duck next time, Chantal decided.

"Answer him," he said.

Chantal glanced at the man beside her and caught the look of annoyance he shot his friend. Was he irritated because he hit her, or had he wanted to be the first to do so? Either way, she would keep up her guard.

It wasn't easy. Her head swiveled from left to right; she couldn't keep both of them in her field of vision.

A large hand gripped her forearm and spun her around. Arms like steel bands wrapped around her from behind. She struggled to free herself, but her legs flailed as he leaned back and lifted her off the floor.

Chantal let out a roar of fury, squirming and kicking with every ounce of energy she possessed. A grating shriek of laughter made her stop and stare at the man through the veil of hair falling across her face. Her chest heaved from exertion and frustration.

"What're you doing? You think a little bitty thing like you can take us on?"

"I think a child could take you on and win." Venom dripped from her words.

The hoodlum's eyes widened in surprise.

That had been her goal. Chantal wanted to throw them off their stride. Angering the man may have seemed dangerous, but anger was a powerful emotion, and it could trigger a mistake on his part. It was worth the gamble.

"You don't realize who you're dealing with." His eyes flashed as color rose high in his face.

"I think I do. I'm dealing with amateurs trying to be tough guys."

The thug took a step closer and loomed over her, his face inches from hers, blue eyes sparking fire. A clean-shaven, round face twisted from side to side in an exaggerated impression of a boxer preparing for a fight. "We're tougher than you think, and there are more of us you haven't met. You better watch your mouth."

"I'm not afraid of you." Chantal glared at him, digging within herself for the anger to mask her fear.

A palm connected with her cheek and stars danced before her eyes. She slumped forward, her limbs loose and dangling. The arms around her waist slackened. Chantal reacted. With all the strength in her right arm, she drove her elbow into the ribs of the man holding her. His shout of pain rang in her ears as her foot delivered a blow between the legs of the bigger man in front of her.

He bent over double while she ran to the door and freedom. Her hand closed around the doorknob as a body tackled her from behind. Chantal didn't know which man recovered first, but he moved fast. She wanted to scream with frustration, but she landed on the floor and the wind flew from her lungs, squelching any sound she could have mustered.

The man spewed an impressive stream of curse words as muscular arms picked her up by the waist and tossed her on the mattress in the corner. Chantal's head rang with pain as it bounced off the wall.

The larger man hovered over her with fists clenched by his sides, as if he would love to rip her apart. The other one's hand clutched his ribs as he glanced from Chantal to his partner, perhaps hoping for permission to give it back to her.

"You're very lucky, little lady." The leader pointed a large finger in her direction. "I could beat you to a pulp, but I won't. You think on that for a bit. We'll be back." He gave his lackey a dark look before they left the room, the key clanging in the lock.

Chantal released a breath. Her escape attempt had failed, but they understood she wasn't a pushover. That could work against her. The single thing to come out of the encounter was that something in their behavior hit her as strange.

With a groan, she lay flat on the mattress, hoping to figure out what it was.

CHAPTER 21

"Chantal's gone." Jeff had prayed to never say those words again. But he uttered them over the phone to Captain Bouchard. He dreaded telling Tori even more.

Bouchard demanded a full account of the incident and set out to mobilize as many people as possible.

Maps covered the tables in the conference room, along with Styrofoam coffee cups, cell phones, and pads of paper. With the manhunt in the planning stages, the physical location of where to focus the search remained elusive.

A bystander had noted two men helping an apparently intoxicated woman into a black SUV. They invited the witness to the police station to give a statement. Jeff questioned her in French as Owen stood over her, his face drawn tight into a scowl. The woman's glance jumped from one to the other, her voice rising in panic.

"Stand down, Owen. You're making her nervous. She's a witness, not a suspect."

"I don't understand anything you're saying." Owen's voice was almost a shout, making the woman jump in her seat and wrench her fingers.

Jeff inhaled a deep breath before he spoke. "Why don't you wait outside until I'm done? I'll be out soon."

Owen growled deep in his throat and left, the door slamming behind him.

Ten minutes later, Jeff joined Owen by the coffee machine. "She didn't get a good look at them, nothing to give a positive ID. But she noticed the woman had blond hair pulled into a ponytail and wore jogging clothes. She suspected the vehicle was a Jeep Cherokee because her neighbor owns one and there's a resemblance, but she's uncertain of the make or model."

"That's it?"

"Nothing more."

Cops filled the conference room. Many focused on their laptops. Several more pressed phones to their ears. Others stood awaiting instructions, their constant fidgeting a sign of their tension.

Captain Bouchard barked orders into a cell phone as he paced the length of the room. He flailed his left arm in the air to emphasize his point. Jeff stayed silent as he watched the frenetic movements of his boss. Owen cast a quizzical glance at Jeff.

"He's calling for roadblocks," Jeff said in explanation. With a frown etched on his face, his hands clenched and unclenched at his sides.

Jeff's gaze connected with a tall, scruff-faced man on the opposite side of the room, and his eyes narrowed. "What's he doing here?" he muttered.

"Who?" Owen asked.

Jeff ignored the question as Paul Morrisette met his gaze and the two men exchanged hard, lethal stares for a long moment. The SWAT cop turned away first, speaking to a cop who stood next to him.

"I gotta get out of here. I need some air." Jeff strode from the room, taking the stairs to the lower level at a trot.

He had almost reached the exit when the sound of footsteps pierced his cloud of frustration. The uneven gait was the giveaway. A flush of anger rose in him, and Jeff swung to face the man. "I didn't ask for company."

"I'm not here to hold your hand," Owen said. "But we have to work together. If you know how to find her…"

"I have no idea. That's the problem." Jeff shoved his hands into his pockets. He didn't trust himself not to take a swing at the other cop.

Owen narrowed his eyes. "Hey, why are you angry at me? I'm trying to help."

"Help? It's your fault she's gone. Why the hell did you leave her alone?"

"She's a cop and a grown woman. But, for the record, I told her to stay put."

"That's like waving a red flag at a bull. You should understand that by now." Jeff glared at the other man until Owen looked away, wearing a pained expression.

"I know. Or I should have known. I admit it."

Owen had transformed into a version of himself that wasn't buttoned up tight. His shoulders slumped, and he riveted his gaze on the cement stairs before them. The RCMP officer raised his head and darted a glance at Jeff before turning away to return inside.

"All right, forget I said anything. Things go wrong." Jeff reminded himself that the last time someone abducted Chantal, she had been working with him. Crippling guilt had torn him apart. He had no right to act superior.

"I feel useless." Owen looked up and down the street.

"I'm with you there. There's nothing we can do unless the roadblocks give us something, or a witness gives us a lead. For now, we sit and wait."

"Not my strong point."

Jeff cracked a slight smile and slapped the other cop on the shoulder. "You do a better job of it than our friend Chantal."

Chapter 22

By her calculations, they had held her captive for at least a day. Chantal was not sure how long she had remained unconscious, but, in her limited experience, chemical anesthetics lasted only a few hours.

Nothing heart-stopping had happened since the last violent incident. A grudging thug delivered food. His expression told her he would love to throw the unappetizing meal in her face, but he restrained himself.

Their behavior bothered Chantal. Why did they hold themselves back? They wanted to beat her, and perhaps worse. Who did they report to who had scruples? Was there another reason they spared her? Ransom? They'd have to return her in an unharmed condition, wouldn't they?

Chantal wasn't flush with money, nor did she come from a rich family. And the government wouldn't pay ransom for an employee. It had to be something else.

She didn't have a watch, but she guessed, by the angle of the sun and the emptiness of her stomach, she could expect another visit soon. The men didn't spend time in the house apart from their trips to deliver food, always arriving by car or truck.

As if on cue, the crunch of tires on gravel told her they had arrived. The familiar sound of footsteps moving around in the kitchen overhead reached her ears; they were preparing her meal.

Another noise intruded. Chantal tensed. Heavy boots on the floor overhead. Shouting, but the words were unintelligible. Scuffling noises. Something landed on the floor with a loud bang. A chair? A person? Several more bangs, followed by a few seconds of silence. Chantal's heart pounded in her chest. What had happened? Were the cops here?

Boots thudded on the stairs, accompanied by groans and loud swearing. Chantal stood and pressed her back against the wall. The door opened, and they hurled a large shape onto the floor.

"There. You have company now." The bigger of her captors wore a sly smile. The door slammed behind them, and the lock squeaked.

Chantal waited until the thump of footsteps was overhead before she turned her attention to the man at her feet. He had a tall, broad build, and in the dim light from the small window, his hair appeared to be a sandy blond color.

With a moan, he struggled to his feet. Chantal grabbed his arm to help steady him.

"Are you hurt?" she asked. At first glance, he didn't seem to have any broken bones. A trickle of blood ran from the edge of his mouth and dripped onto his pale blue t-shirt. His jeans had a small rip on one knee.

"No, I'll be okay." He wiped his hand across his mouth and looked her up and down. "Are you?"

"I'm all right. Who are you?"

A crooked grin spread across his face, and his blue eyes twinkled. "I would've preferred to meet you under better circumstances, but we'll make do with this." He drew her hand into his warm clasp. "I'm Eric, Owen's partner."

Chantal's eyes widened. "You're Eric? What are you doing here?"

"I came to Quebec to give him a hand with the search."

"You were talking to Owen? He asked you to come?" Chantal didn't know why, but it surprised her that Owen would reach out to his partner for help to search for her. She was even more surprised by the frisson of pleasure the thought gave her.

"Yes, and no. Someone hacked us. They broke into our emails and set up a teleconference meeting with myself, Owen, and a couple of other people. It was a ruse to get him away from you."

The news stunned Chantal. She flopped onto the mattress and leaned her head against the wall. "That's how they did it. I never suspected."

"Neither did Owen." He lowered himself onto the mattress and faced her. "They know what they're doing. It was seamless."

"How did they know I'd go to the park?"

Eric shrugged. "Maybe they studied your habits, or you played into their hands, and they took advantage of it. I don't know. If we ever catch the people responsible, we may find out."

"Where's Owen? And Jeff? Why aren't they with you?" Chantal sat cross-legged and leaned forward.

Eric differed from how Chantal had imagined him. Younger, for one thing. She pegged him for around thirty years old, up to five years younger than Owen. He was quite handsome, with blond hair, blue eyes, and a square jaw. This wasn't a bad thing, she thought, but he lacked the tough look she expected in a cop.

"We split up to cover as much territory as possible. Jeff was pretty frantic. Owen, too, come to think of it. But I'm not worried. I'm sure they'll find us soon."

"I don't suppose you have your phone, do you?"

"Nah. They took it. I'm sure they've disabled it by now."

Chantal nodded. It was too much to wish for. "Where are we?"

"I've never been to Quebec, but Jeff said something about St-Raymond. Is that possible? Do you know it?"

"Yes, of course. It's north of the city. There's a lot of forest area, hunting and fishing camps, isolated spots. I take it we're far from civilization?"

"There's no doubt it's off the beaten path. We're lucky to have found you at all."

"How did Jeff think to look here?"

The big man shrugged. "He got a tip from somewhere. They said a lot of stuff in French. Mine's a little rusty."

Chantal caught his wry smile. But she needed to focus on escape. "You've seen the place. You know our surroundings. Do you have a plan?"

"I don't think you want to call it a plan, but we've evened the odds. It's two against two, and we are highly trained police officers." A huge grin split his face.

At another time, Chantal may have responded to his charm, but now was not that time. She realized they were dealing with criminals, perhaps enforcers, also highly trained, employed by the Mafia. The odds might not be that even.

"What are they driving?" she asked.

"A pickup truck. I took a peek at it. They left the keys in the ignition. If that's a habit of theirs, we're in luck. We'll overpower them and get away."

Chantal frowned. Eric had more confidence than she did in their ability to overpower those men.

"How often do you see them?" Eric interrupted her thoughts.

"Twice a day. They bring food at noon and again in the evening."

He grimaced. "I guess I screwed up your noontime meal. They're gone."

"The question is whether they'll come back."

Eric's face creased into a frown before a grin, once more, lit his face. "Let's think positive."

• • • •

With the help of Eric's watch, which they hadn't confiscated, they noted the arrival time of their captors–six o'clock. Chantal listened to the sound of truck doors slamming and footsteps treading overhead. She had worried they would bring reinforcements, but from what she figured out, they were two.

Although Eric provided some much-appreciated company for Chantal, the afternoon had dragged on. It stretched her nerves thin, as she expected the next visit from their friends. Her new roommate attempted to distract her, telling her stories of his exploits with Owen, some of which surprised her. The cop she knew as aloof had a playful side.

But, despite Eric's best efforts, nothing erased their present situation from her forethoughts.

And now the time had come. Chantal's heart rate quickened. Their plan was sketchy. They were in an empty room with no weapons and nowhere to hide. It would be hit or miss.

Boots thumped on the stairs, and keys jangled from someone's hand. She faced the door, standing six feet away from it. It creaked open, allowing a triangle of light to fall from the hallway into the dim room. The larger man stood in front, and she noticed the gun in his hand. For a split-second, her gaze slid toward the area behind the open door before swinging it back to the two men.

The first man didn't hesitate. He kicked the door with a booted foot. The bang of it hitting the wall resounded through the basement. He raised his gun, ready to take down Eric. The man behind him pinned his gun on Chantal, who stood with her arms by her side.

Eric had a second to react. He dived from the opposite corner and drove himself into the back of the larger man. They sprawled to the floor. The second man's eyes widened, and Chantal stepped in to complete the next part of the plan.

She twisted sideways and delivered a sharp kick to the side of his knee. He doubled over, and Chantal followed with a chop to his neck. He collapsed, unconscious, his gun sliding across the floor in Eric's direction.

Eric had his arms locked around the other man's throat from behind. He rolled him over and straddled him.

"Get out!" Eric shouted over his shoulder.

Chantal hesitated. They had immobilized one man, and the other nearly so. She didn't want to leave an officer alone, not if she could help him.

"I've got this. Go check for others," Eric insisted. "We can't let them outnumber us."

With another glance at the unconscious man, Chantal realized Eric had a point. She needed to leave the house, make sure they were alone, and take control of the vehicle. She grabbed the gun off the floor and ran up the stairs.

The main floor of the building revealed a 1970s home in an advanced stage of neglect. As Chantal exited through the living room, she stepped around the only furnishing, a lime-green beanbag chair.

Chantal flattened her body against the door frame and edged forward to peer through the window. Among the weeds of the front yard, sat a black pickup truck covered in rust and pocked with dents. It didn't resemble a Mafia getaway car, but it looked functional, and it was all that mattered.

No one else was visible in or around the truck, and the area within her vision was clear. That didn't mean there weren't others, but intuition told her they had arrived alone.

Chantal took a moment to check the gun for ammunition, and her eyes widened in surprise. It was empty. What was the point of carrying an empty gun? What was up with those guys? She contemplated running back downstairs, but there were no sounds of a struggle. Eric would soon be on his way, and she needed to check the truck.

Chantal opened the door and slipped out onto the cracked concrete step, moving her gaze around her. She ducked down and sprinted toward the driver's side of the truck, a spark of hope flitting through her when the handle responded to her pull, and the door groaned on its hinges.

Her relief was short-lived. Chantal pulled herself into the driver's seat to discover the ignition was empty.

"Maudit!" The expletive didn't make the keys appear. She raced toward the house, determined to wrestle them from the men inside. The burst of a gunshot stopped her in her tracks.

"Eric," she said, under her breath. Her first instinct was to help, and she took two steps forward before she remembered she was unarmed.

The second eruption of gunfire set her in motion. Chantal could help Eric by reaching a phone and calling in the troops. Getting shot helped neither of them. She would escape by foot.

Trees surrounded the house, with no sign of any other buildings in sight. The road leading to the driveway was unpaved, narrow, and rutted. It confirmed her suspicions of isolation, and she knew she'd slog through the forest for hours without coming across another sign of life.

Chantal spotted a trail behind the house, and her first thought was to use it. Her second thought told her they would expect that reaction. She swung in the opposite direction and crashed through the trees.

Branches swatted her face and snagged her clothing. She was noisy, but Chantal had a few minutes before her captors would come out of the house. Then, she would balance the need for quiet with the need to put distance between them. For now, she had to get farther away before they discovered her.

A shout came from the direction of the house. The time for balance had arrived. Chantal stopped in her tracks and listened. Her blood pounded in her ears and drowned out everything else. She drew several deep breaths into her lungs and tried to calm her pulse. There was complete silence. It worried her more than hearing two men hurtling through the trees in pursuit. Quiet made little sense.

Chantal's gaze searched the thick foliage. Nothing moved. Where were they? They hadn't left. She would've heard the truck. She didn't dare move. Any noise she made would alert them. They were listening as hard as she was.

Chantal caught her breath as a branch snapped behind her. She glanced over her shoulder but saw nothing. No sign of movement, no noise.

Another crack of a branch, closer still, and Chantal broke into a run. She dodged and swerved around trees, moving in a zig-zag pattern, hoping to avoid a bullet. Yet no gunfire followed her, only shouts. If they believed she would stop because they told her to, they were stupider than she thought.

Although she had no idea where she went, Chantal sensed she put distance between them. Someone was behind her, but the noise grew distant. Speed and agility were two things Chantal possessed in abundance.

But luck wasn't on her side. Chantal tripped on a stump and sprawled face-first into damp moss and leaves. Scrambling to her feet, she cursed herself for her clumsiness. Abandoning her zig-zag approach, she ran as fast as she could in a straight line. She had lost valuable time; the noise behind her confirmed it. The sound of thrashing branches and heavy breathing closed in on her.

Chantal sighted an opening up ahead. It was a road, the gray asphalt visible through the trees. Her mind raced. She would make better time running on asphalt, but so would her pursuers. Yet, she would also have a chance of getting help from a passing vehicle. What would work best?

The question was moot.

Before she reached the road, a hand wrapped around her upper left arm. Chantal used her forward momentum to swing herself around, her right arm free to deliver a blow to her assailant. Another powerful hand blocked the hit, and she slammed into the solid chest of a much larger man. Her eyes lifted to meet his.

CHAPTER 23

"Where's Jeff?"

The captain's questioning gaze scanned the occupants of the room before coming to rest on Mark's concerned face.

"He left with Owen a while ago," the young RCMP officer said. "I don't know where they went. I assumed they had a plan."

Bouchard shook his head. "I need him here. I don't trust him not to do something impulsive."

"Jeff didn't strike me as that kind of guy. He seems pretty level-headed."

"Normally, yes. But he's worried about Chantal. I don't want him to search for her on his own."

"Owen's with him. I'm sure he'll keep Jeff on the straight and narrow."

Bouchard tossed a skeptical look in Mark's direction. Retrieving his cell phone from his jacket pocket, he punched in a number as his lips curled in displeasure. "He's not answering. *Merde.*"

An officer stationed in front of a laptop computer straightened in his chair. In French, he spoke to the room, his tone urgent. Bouchard responded, barking out orders that launched several men into action. The room almost emptied before Mark's eyes.

"What's going on?" He stood and grabbed his jacket, not knowing whether he should leave or where he would go if he did.

"There was a sighting near St-Raymond, but they lost track of it. We'll move more people to the area."

"Is it far?"

"About an hour north. There's a lot of wilderness. They could hide her anywhere." Bouchard's voice took on a note of despair as his words sank in.

"What can I do?"

"I need you to work with our team here. We'll need aerial views, with buildings where they could hold her. It may be isolated and hard to reach by car."

"I'm on it."

The captain nodded and reached into his pocket when a muted jangle sounded. He answered the call, his face taking on a red hue. His left arm beat the air as he yelled into the device. Mark didn't understand a word he said, but he didn't have to speak French to not envy the person on the receiving end.

"At least I know where he is, even if I'd rather he keeps me informed," Bouchard said, ending the call with a fierce scowl.

"That was Jeff?"

"Yes, he and Owen heard of the spotting in St-Raymond. They're on their way there."

Mark wished he had followed the two cops outside. He had missed an opportunity to ride along with them.

He shrugged and turned back to his computer. Mark knew another way to follow along.

• • •

"Eric!" His name burst from her mouth amid deep gulps of air, filling her burning lungs. Fear and urgency had pushed her to her limits.

"Why did you run? Why didn't you stop when I called you?" Confusion swirled across his sweat-sheened face.

"I didn't think it was you." Chantal looked him up and down, searching for a sign of injury. "I heard shots. I worried they'd killed you."

Eric rolled his eyes and released his grip on her elbow, his chest heaving. "They tried, but I got the upper hand. I got one of their guns and killed them."

"You shot them? Were they armed? The gun I took wasn't even loaded."

"I don't understand what's up with them. My guy had two guns. One of them was my own. I got ahold of mine, and he pulled the other one on me. I reacted and killed them." He looked at the ground and shook his head. "I checked his gun. It wasn't loaded either."

Chantal's mouth dropped open. Why were they carrying unloaded guns?

"I know. I don't get it either," Eric said, reading her thoughts. He looked like a dog that someone had kicked into submission. There would be hours of explanations, made longer because a police officer killed two suspects, even if it was in self-defense. It wouldn't be easy for Eric.

Chantal's shoulders slumped, and she rested her forehead against his chest as the surge of adrenaline eased. She took several deep breaths. If she had known it was him, they could have avoided a lot of fear and stress.

Raising her head and straightening her shoulders, she lifted her gaze to his again. Away from the murkiness of the basement, his hair glimmered with reddish blond tones and she noticed a two-inch scar that traced the hairline on his temple. "Okay. We'll go back and use one of their phones to call it in."

"We can't go back, not yet."

Chantal's eyes widened. "What are you saying? We have to go back. We need a phone."

"Our priority is getting away from here. Their friends are on their way." Eric's gaze swiveled around them, as if he expected a vehicle to appear. They had stood there for several minutes, and Chantal had yet to hear a car pass on the nearby road. She suspected they were still deep in the middle of nowhere.

"How do you know that? It could be hours before anyone suspects something has happened to them."

"Because I was there. One of them had a radio. When they didn't answer, someone said they were on their way. Their Mafia friends will storm this place within minutes. They won't stop until they find us."

Gone was the laid-back, confident cop, convinced Jeff and Owen would find them soon. Instead, Chantal faced a worried RCMP officer. His fears were contagious.

"Do you still have the gun? You didn't grab a phone?" She looked at his hands, as if something would appear out of thin air.

"No, neither. I emptied the gun, and I couldn't find any ammunition. No phones either. Maybe they left them in the truck."

"We have to get to the truck. It's our way out." Chantal scanned the area, eager to head back.

Eric seemed to consider the idea. "We can try," he said. "We ran a long way. I'm worried we won't make it there before the others arrive."

"We have no choice. We can't hide in the woods forever. The road could be more dangerous. They'll see us."

"You're right." He hesitated. "We'll head back."

Eric led the way. Chantal kept her gaze on the ground and pondered their predicament. They needed to reach civilization and contact Jeff and Owen. Not to mention reporting the shooting, she reasoned. But Eric was right. They might place themselves in a dangerous spot.

Ten minutes later, with nothing in sight except trees and more trees, Chantal was on the verge of asking if they headed in the right direction. Before she could say a word, Eric rotated and dived toward her. She registered his stricken expression the moment before the force of his body slammed into hers and drove them both to the ground, crushing her beneath his weight. His hand covered her mouth and muffled her screech of protest.

"Shh, don't make a sound and don't move." Urgency resonated in his tone and she did as he said, although the possibility of moving was impossible. She had to trust his judgment and assume he had seen movement ahead of them.

They remained in that position for several minutes, his breath raspy in her ear, drowning out any other sounds.

"I think it's gone, but we need to be careful," Eric said as he raised himself to his hands and knees, straddling her body.

"Who was it? Where are they?" Chantal jerked her head from side to side, searching for the source of danger.

"It's not a 'they.' It's an 'it.' I saw a drone. You didn't hear it? They're looking for us."

Chantal examined the sky. Technology had made strides that helped the criminals as much as law enforcement, but until now, she hadn't dealt with it.

"What do we do?" She propped herself on her elbows as Eric stood.

"I don't know. We can't go back. They're on to us now. We'll find shelter until they give up or we escape." He grasped her hand and pulled her to her feet. She brushed damp leaves off her pants.

"Shelter? We're in the middle of a forest. There's nothing around here."

"We were in a house. There could be more."

"How long until we find one?"

"We can't give up. Let's go. I'll keep an eye out for that drone."

Their search continued for another half hour until Chantal felt weak with hunger and fatigue. Eric was tireless. He led her through the forest, his gaze moving from the never-ending vista of trees to the sky above. Chantal also scanned the gray sky that had filled with menacing clouds, searching for any sign of a drone that could spell danger.

"We're in luck," Eric said over his shoulder. "Look, up ahead."

Chantal narrowed her eyes. "What? I don't see anything."

"There's a cabin. It's hard to see. It kinda blends in." Excitement lifted his voice. "You stay here. I'll go check it out."

Eric increased his pace, intending to leave her behind, but Chantal wasn't having it. She wouldn't let them separate again. Her fatigue driven away by hope, she kept pace with him. As they got closer, the outline of a small cabin appeared. Closer still, she saw a more rustic, much smaller version of the building they had left.

No vehicle, no sign of life. The unlocked door creaked open on rusty hinges, revealing a neat, barren interior. A wood stove occupied a corner of the main room, and a small stack of wood rested beside it. A plaid couch and beat-up coffee table were the only furniture to their left. On the right, hand painted wooden cabinets and a laminate counter, along with a chipped porcelain sink, created a kitchen. A metal table and two chairs completed the space. Chantal presumed the two doors at the back led to a bedroom and, perhaps, a bathroom.

It wasn't the Queen Elizabeth Hotel, she mused, but it would give them shelter while they needed it.

Chantal preferred to get back to civilization tonight. As far as she was concerned, she had overstayed her welcome in this neck of the woods.

"This is great," Eric said, his level of enthusiasm much higher than Chantal's. He opened cabinet doors and seemed delighted with what he discovered. "It has everything we need. There's canned food, some coffee, even bottled water."

Chantal was skeptical of how long those items had lived in the cabin, but her stomach reminded her that beggars couldn't be choosers. Eric's zeal was infectious. His beaming smile lit up his face, like a young boy on an adventure.

She realized opposites worked well together, but Chantal couldn't imagine Eric and Owen as a good fit. The boyish optimism and charm of her current cohort was at the alternative end of the spectrum from Owen's quiet and serious demeanor.

Eric opened one of the doors at the back and peered in through the crack before thrusting it open. "Two beds. It's perfect. Everything looks clean." He stepped into the room, pulled back the covers, and checked underneath.

Behind the other door, Chantal discovered a rudimentary chemical toilet and a sink with no taps. It would do for now, she reminded herself.

Minutes later, the pinging of raindrops on the tin roof made Chantal thankful for shelter, more so when it morphed into a steady, drumming beat. The deepening gloom inside the cabin sent them in search of flashlights, candles, and matches. Their hunt proved fruitful. The glow of the candlelight softened the starkness of their refuge. Chantal shook out a threadbare blanket and wrapped it around her shoulders.

"It doesn't sound like it'll let up soon." Eric looked at the ceiling as if he saw black clouds and pouring rain. Chantal didn't detect any disappointment in his tone.

"Don't you love the sound of rain on a tin roof? It's so relaxing," he said.

"Hmm. Yeah, it's very nice." Chantal preferred the whir of a microwave oven. Or, even better, the jingle of a cell phone.

In her opinion, they wasted time better spent finding the police. She stood before the small window over the sink, clutching the blanket around her shoulders, and scanning the dark forest for signs of movement, either friend or foe.

"We need to contact someone. Jeff and Owen are looking for us." She knew Eric couldn't present her with a solution, but she wanted to vent her frustrations.

Eric's voice came from close behind her left shoulder. "I have bad news for you, Chantal."

His ominous tone made her breath catch. She turned to face him, her heart thumping. His shoulders slumped.

"What is it?" she said, her voice barely above a whisper. Nothing about his appearance was reassuring.

"I overheard those guys talking." His voice broke. "Before I shot them. I hope it's not true."

"What?" Chantal wanted to shake him.

"They… they said Jeff and Owen are… dead."

"No." Her hand covered her mouth, and her eyes widened. "It can't be." Her gut corkscrewed in pain. Chantal looked deep into Eric's eyes, praying he was lying or joking. It was a terrible joke, but it was better than the truth.

"I heard them on the radio. They were updating someone, telling them about the drones… and killing Jeff and Owen." He lifted his hands and rested them on her shoulders. "I'm sorry. I know you were close to Jeff, as I was to Owen."

Chantal witnessed the sorrow in his eyes, even with her own stunned reaction.

It was more of a non-reaction. Her body went cold, her brain numbed. Jeff, by her side through the best and worst, was gone. He had been like a treasured brother to her.

"Oh my God, Tori,… how will she… this is horrible." Thoughts of her friend, expecting their first child, flashed through her mind. A tiny baby who would never know the love of her wonderful father. Sobs broke through her dam, and the sound echoed off the drab gray walls.

Strong arms enfolded her. A hand rubbed her back. Soft words reached her ears, but their meaning was lost to her. She had no room for anything other than pain.

When Chantal's tears subsided, she folded onto the couch, uncaring of the musty smell or the cloud of dust that escaped.

Her thoughts moved to Owen, the man she had known for mere weeks. He had infuriated and frustrated her, but she grew to respect him and his judgment. She suspected she could have developed more than a professional liking for him, but that was something she would never have the chance to explore.

Chantal's gaze shifted to Eric. He sat on one of the kitchen chairs, facing her, but his bleak, empty gaze stayed fixed on the floor. She wasn't sure how his pain compared to hers, but she knew he and Owen had been friends and co-workers for a long time. Owen had spoken of him with respect and fondness.

She forced herself to picture the mobsters as they talked about the killing of the two police officers. Imagining herself present in the room at that moment, she felt the wrenching pain. Chantal would want to kill them. Is that what happened? Had Eric lost his judgment as an officer of the law and killed them out of revenge? Perhaps. Did she blame him? At this moment, no.

CHAPTER 24

Hours passed. Eric lit a fire in the wood stove and prepared a simple meal of canned beans while Chantal slumped on the couch, empty and exhausted.

"It's horrible, and you think you'll never get over it. Don't feel guilty for dragging Jeff into this case."

Until this point, guilt hadn't played a part in her emotions. Jeff's addition to the operation had pleased her. Captain Bouchard decided the plan, and she never questioned it. Deep down, she had wanted Jeff's skills and knowledge alongside theirs. But she had put him in danger. A ball of despair wedged in the pit of her stomach.

"This is hard, but you, of all people, should understand how to bounce back from hardship, after what you've been through."

Chantal looked at Eric with a question in her eyes. *How did he know about her past?*

It was as if she spoke out loud. "I know a lot about you. Owen told me your story. He felt sorry for you. He didn't show off his soft heart, but it was there." A distant look shadowed his face. "That was a big part of what I liked about him."

Chantal had never wanted or appreciated pity, and it hurt to know Owen had thought of her that way.

Eric shook himself. "Anyway, I have to say you're a very brave woman. To live through that experience and return to police work, I take my hat off to you. It can't be easy. You must still have nightmares."

Chantal's thoughts drifted to the endless nights spent reliving the torment she had suffered, both physical and psychological, in that other cabin near another lake and another town. She slid her hands underneath her legs to still the trembling.

She thought of all she had lost, both today and six months ago: her best friend and partner, her dignity, her optimism, and her confidence. Chantal wondered how to find the strength to go on. There seemed little left worth living for.

"We should try to get some sleep. It's late now. In the morning, we'll feel better, and we can work on a plan." Eric seemed oblivious to Chantal's depressed state. He shuffled around the room, lighting another candle for the bedroom. He hesitated beside the couch and laid a gentle hand on her shoulder.

"Are you coming? You're shivering. You'll be warmer underneath the blankets. We can even sleep in the same bed and share our body heat, if you like."

Chantal shook her head, not sure which question she answered. Perhaps both of them. Eric rustled around in the next room. She assumed he settled in for the night.

Several minutes later, she lay on her side, pulled the blanket over her, and stared at the candle that flickered on the scarred table beside her. A blur of images passed through her thoughts—memories from good and bad times—and her spirit spiraled to a new depth.

Hours passed with no sleep and no abating of the images until Chantal drifted into a restless slumber.

• • • •

Chantal's eyes shot open as footsteps trod near her head. She sprang to an upright position, fighting off a sudden wave of dizziness. Eric peered at her with concern.

"You slept here last night? Why didn't you come into the bedroom?"

She shrugged. "I fell asleep here and didn't bother getting up." Chantal couldn't tell him the truth–she wanted to be alone in her misery.

He sat on the coffee table, his knees brushing hers.

"Look, I realize you're having a hard time dealing with this, so close on the heels of your own trauma. But you have to put it aside and be strong. That's what it takes to be a good cop. You don't want to find yourself back behind a desk, do you?"

Chantal thought of the mindless hours she had put in over the past several months and wondered if it was where she belonged. It was safe. She would harm no one while she was there, not her or anyone else she cared for.

Eric leaned forward and took her limp hands between his, massaging her knuckles.

"You may think I'm unfeeling, but I'm not. The thought of never seeing Owen again cuts me to the bone." His voice wavered. "We've been together for years, first as partners, but we became friends in no time. I'm telling you, when he was shot six months ago, I would've taken that bullet for him, just to spare him the pain. That's how I feel about him, and I know that's how you feel about Jeff. If you could've saved his life yesterday, you would've done it. Some things are out of our control."

Chantal's lungs tightened, as if the air couldn't go in or out. Memories tumbled over each other before they fell into slots in her mind. She thought of Jeff and Owen and their horrible fate. She thought of Tori and hoped she would see her again.

That final thought drove her. She straightened her shoulders and pushed herself to her feet.

"I'm strong. I can get through this," she said. "But first, we have to get out of here."

"You're right." Eric seemed bolstered by her new attitude. "Let's discuss a plan."

"I can't sit around any longer. I'll make us something to eat and then we'll make some decisions." She brushed past him and crossed the room to the kitchen cupboards.

"That's the spirit. I'm glad to see you've come out of your funk." A smile animated his face as his gaze followed her.

"That's the way I am. I have to keep busy."

"Good for you. We'll get through this together. We have to stay focused."

Chantal opened cupboards until she found what she needed. She discovered a can opener in a drawer. Within a few minutes, she had a pot of canned chicken noodle soup warming on the two-burner stovetop. It was a strange offering for breakfast, but it was fast and would serve the purpose. She paused and stared out the window, drawing deep breaths and getting herself on an even keel.

When the soup bubbled, she swiveled toward Eric. "It's ready. Why don't you have a seat?"

He flashed her a smile as he pulled out a chair and sat down. Chantal tugged her sleeves over her hands to carry the bowl to the table.

"That looks pretty hot," Eric said.

"Be careful."

Chantal lowered the bowl toward the table. When it was an inch from the surface, she flung the steaming liquid into Eric's face. A howling scream burst from his throat. His frantic hands swiped at the hot, clinging noodles.

Chantal tossed the bowl aside, the sound of breaking glass ringing through the cabin. She raised her foot and thrust it into his stomach. The chair toppled backwards. Eric followed it onto the floor, his eyes wide with shock.

Another solid push with her foot sent him onto his side. He attempted to get onto his knees, but Chantal seized the chair and broke it over his back. The twisted remains followed the path of the shattered bowl.

The force flattened him. Chantal pounced. Her knee against his kidney kept him there long enough for her to yank his arms behind his back. From the pocket of her jeans, she retrieved a thin cord she had found in the kitchen drawer.

She tied the best knot she could, jerking it several times to be certain it was secure, before rolling him over. Chantal stood and glared at him from her full height. Her pounding heart and raspy breath muffled Eric's words, but she didn't miss the meaning.

"What the hell? Have you lost your mind? Let me go!"

Exertion and burns reddened Eric's face. Blisters appeared on his skin. Chantal's heart held no sympathy for him.

CHAPTER 25

"And?"

"You weren't kidding about the wilderness, were you?"

"Are you saying you didn't make any progress?"

Mark glanced at Marcel Dubois, the technician assigned to work on the aerial views with him, before turning back to Bouchard. "We did our best, but there's not much there. A lot of trees, clusters of fishing camps, some isolated houses and cottages, but they're widely spaced. It'll take time to reach them all and check them out. If we had something to narrow it down, a ping from a cell phone, a sign…"

The captain nodded as his brow furrowed.

"Any news from Jeff or Owen?" Mark hesitated to ask, afraid of provoking another rant from the captain.

"Nothing. They've gone silent again."

It was Mark's turn to frown. "Should we worry about them?"

Bouchard shoved his fists in his pants pockets and strode to the window, his shoulders tense. "Cell phone signals are bad out there. Too many trees, hills, and valleys, and not enough towers. We'll hear from them, at some point."

Mark sensed, like him, the captain wished he worked in the thick of the action, instead of holed up at headquarters, waiting for news.

On the heels of that thought, a cell phone jingled. Three sets of eyes turned to the lit screen of the device. Bouchard reached for it and snapped a greeting.

His face registered shock, and Mark's gut clenched.

The captain mumbled a few more words in French before he laid the phone on the table, his gaze lowered.

"They found two bodies. Men. No identification yet."

"You think…"

Bouchard raised his head and pinned Mark with a tortured gaze. "I don't think anything. Not until I have positive ID. They'll send us the coordinates as soon as they can. We'll zero in on the area, see what we find."

Mark's mouth went dry. He craved a drink of water, or something stronger. Things had come to a head.

• • • •

"How did you know?"

"You're good. Very good, but you screwed up."

"How?" He spoke through gritted teeth.

"I saw Owen's scar. It wasn't a bullet wound. It was a knife."

Eric's head fell back against the floor with a thud. His eyes closed, but a wry smile formed on his lips. "Damn. You got me there." He opened his eyes and met her gaze. "I'm normally pretty thorough in my research. I guess I got so caught up in your history I didn't look into Owen's deeply enough."

Chantal ignored his dig. "Who are you?" She didn't suppress her fury as she towered over him.

"Eric. I already told you."

Chantal nudged his arm with her foot. He didn't flinch. "You're not Eric. You just admitted you don't know Owen."

He shrugged and shifted his gaze to the ceiling. "In my mind, I'll always be Eric." His tone was melodramatic. He seemed serious, and Chantal wondered if she was in the company of a sociopath.

She nudged him again, and it took every ounce of her willpower not to deliver a kick where it hurt.

"What's your connection to the Mafia? It's obvious the whole set-up involved you."

His gaze returned to hers. "No connection at all. I wanted to join in the fun. And make a little money at the same time." The smirk on his face confirmed her suspicions about his mental health.

Chantal drew a deep breath. "What about Jeff and Owen? They're not dead, are they?"

Eric shook his head and made a tsk-tsk sound. "Alas, I never lie about death. Poor Owen will never reap what he sowed. For instance, I admit I killed those two imbeciles at the house yesterday. However, it wasn't in self-defense." His ghoulish grin sent a chill up her spine. "Unfortunately, I didn't have the pleasure of disposing of your sidekicks, but I have first-hand evidence the deed is done. So sorry for your loss."

His expression belied his words. Chantal's heart coiled. She didn't want to believe him, and she wouldn't, until she saw proof. Her most urgent need at the moment was to contact the police. The rest of the story would come out in due time.

Hurrying into the bedroom, she threw back the blankets on the bed he had slept in. She tossed aside the pillows. Nothing. Chantal dropped to the floor, peered under the bed, and found what she wanted: a gun and a cell phone.

A quick check revealed the weapon was loaded. As for the phone, her lips curved upward when she pressed the button on the device. The good news was that it had 64% power. The bad news was there was no service. That wasn't surprising.

Chantal had to venture outside to get a signal. She suspected Eric's drone-sighting had been fake, but she also knew it was likely someone searched for their dead comrades and the person who killed them. Hiding in a cabin didn't mean someone, whoever they were, wouldn't find them, but she'd take care not to expose herself to danger.

Chantal rifled through the kitchen drawers and found more twine. She secured her erstwhile friend's feet, tying them to the table for good measure.

"You won't win, you know," he said as she concentrated on her knots.

"This isn't a game."

"It isn't? How disappointing. I love games."

Chantal glanced at his face and witnessed the look of a true madman. He bared his teeth in a dreadful grin, and his eyes sparkled with something that resembled glee. She gritted her teeth and fought to ignore him.

"Poor Chantal. You've forgotten how to have fun, what with your terrible past." He seemed oblivious to the fact that he lay on the floor, bound, and stripped of his weapons. "Does this cabin remind you of the one where they held you captive? Is that why you wouldn't come into the bedroom last night? Afraid I would overpower and torture you?"

Chantal got to her feet and pulled on her jacket to protect herself from the drizzle.

"Maybe you're tougher than I gave you credit for. Our lady of victories." He threw his head back and gave a diabolical laugh. He followed it with a grin and a wink as Chantal cast a last disdainful glance at him.

She left the building with the gun and cell phone.

Chantal needed to move upward to find a signal, but with no visible trails through the thick forest, she had no idea which direction to take. Shrugging her shoulders, she turned to the right and climbed the nearest hill, using the trees to drag herself up. She watched for any movement, either human or animal. It wasn't unusual to meet a black bear or wolf, not in this area.

By the time she reached the top, her strained breathing drowned out the sound of her pounding heart. It had been farther and steeper than she expected.

Chantal pulled the phone from her pocket and checked the signal. One bar appeared in the top left-hand corner of the device. She hoped it was enough. The phone was, of course, locked with a pass code, but it accepted an emergency call.

The 9-1-1 operator answered on the first ring. Despite a wavering signal, she knew someone was there. Chantal yelled into the phone and identified herself as a police officer and requested backup. She reported having a captive and said the police needed to exercise extreme caution in the area.

The woman responded. A few words made it to Chantal's ears, and they were enough to understand the operator wanted a specific address, something Chantal couldn't offer. The system would have to use the phone's GPS coordinates to locate her. All Chantal could provide was the general area of St-Raymond.

She stayed in the same spot for several long minutes, waiting for confirmation that the operator had pinned down her location. Chantal couldn't risk moving. The signal was sketchy, and she could lose it. At last, the magic words reached her. Help was on the way.

Chantal pocketed the phone, removed the gun, and moved down the hill, watching her step and casting uneasy glances around her. She couldn't make too much noise. Armed or not, she was easy prey.

Shoving open the door of the cabin, Chantal's gaze moved to the floor beside the kitchen table. Her heart clenched. Eric wasn't there.

She backed up against the door and held the gun in front of her. A quick glance told her he wasn't in this room. He was in one of the back rooms or had escaped into the woods. The latter was the most likely, but she couldn't chance a surprise attack.

Keeping her gun trained on the opposite wall, Chantal circled the room and sidled up to the back wall. Her gaze wavered between the two rooms, unsure where he could be. Were the doors closed when she left? She couldn't remember.

Her foot came up and smashed the bathroom door open. She followed through, ready to shoot if needed. There was nowhere to hide. Chantal spun around and used the same procedure to enter the bedroom. It took seconds longer to search, but with the same result. Eric, or whatever his true name, had escaped.

Chantal kicked the doorframe in frustration. Who was he? Houdini? Her knots had been solid.

She noticed the table's position. Eric had heaved it a few feet across the room. The weight of it hadn't deterred him. Lying on the floor was a shard of the soup bowl that helped set her plan in motion. It had served his purpose also, cutting the cord that bound him.

Chantal exhaled a groan of exasperation.

Was he lurking outside, waiting for her to come out? Had he joined his buddies? Or did he work alone?

Chantal wedged a chair under the doorknob. It would give her added protection until the cops got here. She glanced at the two windows in the main room. Eric could reach her through them, but she had a weapon, and she wouldn't let down her guard.

Chantal checked the time on the phone every few minutes. She shifted from one window to the other, peering through the space between the curtain and the frame, watching for movement. She wondered if the 9-1-1 operator had correctly read the coordinates. *What was taking so long? Why didn't she hear sirens or see armed officers? Would they find her before Eric got to her?*

Forty minutes passed, and Chantal worried Eric would come back with his friends, and they'd outnumber her. How long could she hold them off in the flimsy cabin? A powerful weapon could pierce the walls. If they set fire to it, it would light up like a torch. Her mind raced from one possibility to the next.

From the bedroom window, she detected movement in the trees. It was distant and difficult to tell whether it was human or animal. Chantal kept her gaze pinned on the shape, afraid to lose track of it if she looked elsewhere. It scuttled from behind one tree to another. It was a person, but their identity remained unclear.

Were there others? Was a team advancing on her?

She swung around as a voice boomed through a bullhorn in French. It instructed the occupants of the building to come out with their arms raised. Chantal's shoulders slumped, the tension easing. It was the police. She was safe.

Laying her weapon on the kitchen table, she opened the door and raised her arms. Chantal took in the sight before her, and her knees buckled.

CHAPTER 26

She babbled in French, voicing her disbelief. A heavy arm circled her shoulders, and a deep voice mumbled comforting words in her ear.

Chantal raised her head and caught Jeff and Owen exchanging concerned glances. She sounded like a crazed woman, but the relief she had felt as they stood side-by-side among the other police officers had shaken her to her bones.

Jeff asked her several times if she was unharmed, to which she answered yes, but his anxious expression told her she hadn't convinced him.

At last, Chantal drew herself upright and took a deep steadying breath. Eric was still at large, and she needed to help find him and his accomplices, if they existed.

When she fell to her knees in front of the cabin, a SWAT officer had approached and grasped her elbow.

"Come with me. You're safe now."

The voice was familiar to Chantal, yet it seemed so far away. It was as if she was in a bubble where sound was distorted, and reality lay just beyond her reach.

The officer wrapped his free arm around her waist and rushed her out of harm's way while they searched the building and the perimeter for suspects. It was only as she reached Jeff's side that she realized the voice belonged to Paul Morrisette.

She now sat in the back of a police van, accompanied by her two colleagues and two other officers, eager to hear her story.

Chantal explained about being captured and taken to the house in St-Raymond.

"I'm not sure how long I was alone. I lost track of time. Then they threw Eric into the room." Her gaze locked on Owen's.

Owen's expression morphed from a frown to a bewildered scowl. "What? My partner Eric? He's here?"

"I thought he was Eric at first. He claimed to be your partner. He knew a lot about you. I had no reason to doubt him. But that changed. I'll explain how later. We came up with a plan to overpower the men. In reality, Eric came up with the plan, and I followed along."

She sent an apologetic look in Owen's direction. She didn't know what name to give the man. The RCMP officer nodded and waved his hand to encourage her to go on.

Chantal described the resulting scuffle with the two men and how Eric ordered her to leave the house. The police officers exchanged glances when she told them she heard shots and how Eric gave his version of what happened.

Jeff met her questioning look. "We found the bodies in the house. Not long after, we got news of your location."

"He killed them. They carried unloaded guns. Don't ask me why. I don't understand it, but I suspect Eric knew. I'm sure he killed them in cold blood."

Chantal gestured toward the cabin. "He found this place, or he pretended to find it. He told me... he told me they had killed you both." She took a shaky breath. "It upset me. No, it horrified me. I couldn't think of anything else."

Jeff reached over and squeezed her hand. "He played mind games with you."

"Yes, and he succeeded." Chantal turned to Owen. "He screwed up when we were in there." Chantal nodded in the cabin's direction, "I realized he wasn't who he claimed to be. I threw hot soup on him and tied him up. Apparently, not very well."

"You threw soup on him?" Jeff's expression hovered between disbelief and amusement.

"Boiling hot soup. He'll have scars."

A proud grin appeared on Jeff's face.

"Did he say anything that could help us?" Owen said.

"Nothing solid. He claimed he's not involved with the Mafia. He said he joined in for the fun of it and to make some money. I'm not sure I believe him. The guy convinced me he was a cop and a good friend of yours. He's a born liar, maybe a psychopath."

Owen pulled his phone from his jacket pocket, tapped a few buttons, and turned it to face her. "This is Eric," he said.

It was a photo of two men, one of them Owen. The other was shorter, on the heavy side, with dark hair and a goofy grin.

She shook her head. "It's not him."

"It couldn't be. He's the farthest thing from a psychopath you'd ever meet." Despite the confidence in his voice, a flash of relief crossed his face.

"But he knew so much about you... and me. He did his homework."

Jeff frowned. "It's too much of a coincidence that this guy takes you while all this other stuff is happening. There has to be a connection."

"I agree it's far-fetched," she said. "I'm telling you what he told me."

"There were no clues of where he was from or where he'd go?" Owen wore a perplexed frown.

Chantal had already answered that question. She shrugged her shoulders, unable to give him anything more.

Movement outside the van caught her attention. Paul hovered nearby. He had removed his headgear, and his concerned expression puzzled Chantal. Jeff noticed her distraction and followed her gaze. His brows drew together when he spotted the other cop.

"What's he doing here?" Jeff's voice came out as a low growl.

"It's his shift, I guess. He brought me from the house to you."

Jeff seemed on the brink of answering with a churlish remark, but two K-9 officers appeared with German Shepherd dogs and asked him a question.

Chantal realized the search would intensify. She hoped she was wrong, but something told her their attempts to find 'Eric' would be futile.

Another van pulled up. The lettering on the side heralded the crime scene technicians. They would scour the cabin for fingerprints and evidence, as they would the house where the two men held her captive.

Jeff stood. "Let's get out of here. I'll take you back to your place. You must be dying for a shower and a change of clothes." He turned to Owen. "We'll meet up at headquarters in two hours."

The RCMP cop shot an uncertain glance at Chantal before nodding his head.

Chantal climbed into the passenger seat of Jeff's car. "Why do you want to talk to me alone?"

Jeff didn't answer as he focused on getting the car out from among the other police vehicles on the rough gravel lane. When they hit the main road, he glanced at her. "What makes you say that?"

"You excluded Owen. Did something happen I should know?"

"No, but I'm concerned that the guy who abducted you claimed to be a friend of his. And he had a lot of information only someone close to him would have. It raises two possibilities: Owen has direct involvement, or he fed information to someone by accident."

"I disagree," Chantal said. "He's too professional to feed anything to anyone, accidental or not."

"Which leaves the possibility he's directly involved."

"I don't believe it."

"You hardly know him."

"He's a cop, and I believe he's a good one. There are other explanations. Eric could've gotten information from a lot of sources. We could just as easily point the finger at Mark. After all, he lived in the Quebec City area for years. And he's tech savvy."

Jeff nodded his head. "Okay. But I don't think he has the connections or the know-how Owen has."

"You hardly know him." Chantal threw his own words back at him.

Jeff sent her a look that said he didn't buy it.

Neither did she, so she countered with another argument in Owen's favor. "I'm a good judge of character."

"You fell for Eric's story."

Chantal grimaced. "You weren't there. He's very convincing."

"Owen could be the same."

Chantal fell silent. Jeff was right. Had both men taken her in? It was a humbling thought. She prided herself on her astuteness. Yet Eric reeled her in with his charm. She had felt comfortable and safe with him.

Owen wouldn't win prizes for his charming manner, but he appeared solid and trustworthy. Had that been his goal? Had he known she needed something solid in her life and played her with it?

She shoved those troubling thoughts aside. "What do we do?" she said.

"We'll start by finding out if Owen is who he says he is."

CHAPTER 27

"You can't work undercover anymore. They're onto you," Jeff said.

"Owen too," Chantal added, feeling like a troublesome child wanting to take her sibling down with her.

An order from Captain Bouchard to convene at police headquarters had waylaid their trip to Chantal's apartment.

"And Jeff," she said, turning to face Bouchard. "Eric told me both Jeff and Owen were dead. He may not have a lot of details about him, but he knows he exists and we're close."

Chantal didn't want her boss to send Jeff into an undercover situation where his identity was compromised.

"Owen could've told Eric about me."

The captain leaned back in his armchair and laced his fingers over his stomach. His gaze pierced Jeff's. "What makes you so sure Owen is in on this?"

Chantal's head swiveled toward her friend. His answer interested her.

"I didn't say I was sure. I'm suspicious. This Eric guy knew too much." He shot a quick glance at Mark Pratt. The RCMP officer sat to the side, his gaze fixed on Jeff, but his face was impassive.

"He wasn't aware of how Owen got his injury. He couldn't know him well." Chantal folded her arms across her body as she spoke. "Owen could be as much a target as I am."

"You have a point." Jeff shifted his gaze from Chantal to encompass the other two cops. "Maybe it's the real Eric that's in on the scheme, and he's the one feeding this other guy information. He could've left something out. I'm not saying with certainty that Owen's involved. I just want to be careful."

Bouchard stood and turned his attention toward Mark. "What do you think? We're speaking in front of you. I assume I can trust you to keep this conversation to yourself. We need your input."

"I don't know Owen any better than you do. Only by reputation, which is excellent. It'd surprise me if he's corrupt. Same goes for his partner."

From the corner of her eye, Chantal caught the suspicious look Jeff threw in Mark's direction.

"I agree with Mark." Captain Bouchard turned to Jeff. "I've spoken to Owen's supervisor at the RCMP. He had nothing but good things to say."

Owen chose that moment to arrive. Chantal witnessed the surprise on his face when his gaze moved over the four of them, no doubt wondering why he hadn't received an invitation. Whatever his opinion, he kept it to himself.

"We have to move out of the house and end the rental." Chantal stood and faced him. "For obvious reasons, we have to shut down the undercover operation."

He sent her a grim-faced nod.

Bouchard's tone of voice was neutral, but the concern he directed toward Chantal was clear. "I'll take care of it. Why don't you go home and get some rest?"

"I will." Rest would be elusive. Chantal needed to know where Eric was and would feel better if he stood on the unpleasant side of jailhouse bars.

Her ex-partner read her mind. "Why don't you stay with Tori and I for a few days?"

"No." Chantal's response was emphatic. "I'm staying as far away from you two as possible. If Eric is going to come after me, I don't want anyone else in danger."

"That's why you shouldn't be alone," Bouchard said. He turned his gaze to Owen. "Neither of you should. We can arrange for a safe house for both of you."

"For tonight at least, we can stay at my apartment. I have an extra room."

Bouchard considered the offer for a few seconds. "That would be best. I'll have a car stationed outside the building. We'll send someone to pick up your belongings from the hotel."

"Perfect," Chantal said, after seeing a nod of acquiescence from Owen.

Jeff directed a hard look at Chantal, but she shrugged off her friend's concern.

"Let's go," she said to Owen. Chantal wanted to get home with no further arguments with Jeff.

A patrol car dropped them off at her apartment and circled the block before taking up a position across the street. Chantal stood on the sidewalk and looked up at the building. When she caught Owen's quizzical stare, she gave him a dry smile.

"I'm so happy to be here. A few times over the past couple of days, I wondered if I'd ever see it again." She held up her hand as if to ward off an attack. "Don't say it. As a cop, we never know if we'll make it home at night. I'm just saying, I'm glad to be here."

"I'm not arguing with you. I understand how you feel. And I appreciate you letting me stay here."

Owen had never spent more than a few minutes in her apartment, so Chantal escorted him to the spare bedroom. As he stood in the doorway with his hands in his pockets, she grabbed a box of books off the bed and slid it under a small desk. She then retrieved a pile of folded laundry and clutched it to her chest.

"The sheets are clean. I don't have guests often." Chantal studied the room, worried about leaving something too personal for him to find. She wondered if it was just her who felt the awkwardness of the arrangement.

"This is fine. All I need is a bed. No need to fuss."

"The bathroom is across the hall. You'll find towels in the closet. Let me know if you need anything."

He nodded and moved aside as she brushed past him and headed to her own room. She deposited the laundry on a chair and drove her hands through her hair, giving herself a mental head shake. *Get a grip, Chantal,* she thought. *It was your idea to invite him here. If you can't handle it, keep your mouth shut.*

Chantal took a calming breath and headed for the kitchen. She sifted through her fridge and put together a simple meal of steak and a salad.

"I hope you're not expecting a gourmet meal. Cooking isn't my strong point," she said as Owen entered the room.

"I can help."

Chantal handed Owen a knife and a green pepper as he steered the conversation to the meeting he interrupted.

"I missed the second part of the debriefing. Is there something you're not telling me?"

"No. I went over everything again for Captain Bouchard. Nothing new." She took her time emptying vegetable remnants into the garbage bin.

"I would have liked to be included." His tone was mild, but Chantal detected the effort it took to keep it so.

"You didn't miss anything." She concentrated on an onion as she peeled off the skin.

"Jeff blames me for your abduction."

Chantal's head shot up at his straightforward statement. "What?"

"He was angry because I left you alone."

Her eyes flashed. "He has no right to be mad at you. I'm a big girl, and it was my decision to go for a run."

"I told you not to leave."

"You have no right to tell me what to do either."

Owen held up his palms in defense. "I'm just saying we can't take any chances. Neither of us can."

Chantal pulled in a deep breath and braced her hands on the counter. "What's your theory? You must have one."

"He killed the guys who caught you, right? Why would he do that if he worked with them? What did he have to gain?"

Chantal shook her head and waited for him to continue.

"If those guys were Mafia gangsters, he took a big chance killing them. Their boss might not take to losing his employees."

"Unless Eric followed his instructions."

Owen nodded in agreement. "But was it set up? An act? Or did the guys think Eric was on your side?"

"Those are all questions I can't answer, not yet."

"That makes two of us." He leaned back against the kitchen counter and crossed his arms over his chest. "How did you figure out he wasn't my real partner?"

She smiled. "He said he would've taken the bullet for you to spare you the injury."

"How did you know it wasn't a bullet?"

Heat rose in Chantal's face. She turned her back to him as she wiped the kitchen counter. "The night in Montreal…at the hotel… you came out of the shower with… a towel."

His chuckle rose from deep within his chest. "Yes, I remember. I didn't realize you got that close a look."

Her mortified gaze met his amused one. "I didn't look, not on purpose. I noticed it, that's all."

"Fair enough." He glanced at the pan on the stove. "I think those are done."

Chantal's eyes widened at the sight of the blackened steaks. She yanked the pan off the burner. "Sorry about that. I hope they're edible."

"Don't worry about it. They'll be fine. I like mine well done."

Chantal seemed to remember him ordering a medium rare steak at a restaurant in Montreal, but she didn't comment.

"How did you find me?" Chantal asked as she sawed at the charred piece of meat.

"Jeff and I left on our own." He paused and considered his words. "Actually, Jeff took off on his own, and I forced my company on him."

Yes, Chantal thought, that made more sense.

"We didn't have a destination in mind until we heard they spotted a vehicle matching the description in St-Raymond. We headed in that direction."

"Did you keep the captain in the loop?"

Owen's mouth twisted into a grimace. "No. I followed Jeff's lead. He didn't seem to want to contact his boss. I think he's more the type of guy who'd rather beg for forgiveness than ask for permission."

Chantal snorted a laugh. Owen had summed up Jeff's character in one sentence.

"Anyway," Owen continued. "I can confirm the cell phone service is terrible in St-Raymond, at least in the area you were in. Once we got there, we couldn't phone anyone even if we wanted to."

"I was lucky to get through to 9-1-1."

"That's what led us to you."

With the dirty dishes in the dishwasher and the kitchen returned to its normal clean state, the awkwardness returned. This time, it was obvious Owen felt it too.

"I think I'll make it an early night," he said as he glanced at his watch.

"Yeah, me too. Tell me if you need anything."

Owen paused and faced her.

"I need to know I'm not stabbed in the back by my partner."

As the bedroom door closed behind him, Chantal wondered whether he referred to his partner Eric, or whether he pointed the finger at her.

• • •

The next morning, Chantal felt the need to make it up to Owen. She prepared a breakfast of bacon, eggs, toast, and hash browns. The activity also helped to work off some of her anxiety. She hadn't taken a morning run in several days, and it got to her.

Owen seemed surprised by her magnanimous offering, but he didn't make any comments. He thanked her and dug into his meal.

"I'll look at mug shots today since I'm the only person who's seen this guy." Chantal rose from her chair and emptied another uneaten meal into the garbage bin. "I'll get ready and go down to the station."

"Fine. I have a couple of things to do this morning," Owen said, gesturing toward his computer. "I'll call a taxi and meet you there later."

Chantal didn't dig any further. They may be temporary roommates, but she didn't think that gave her the right to pry into his personal business–if it was personal.

154

CHAPTER 28

Jeff's gaze swept the conference room as he entered and stood with his fists on his hips. "Where's Owen?"

Mark glanced up from his laptop and shrugged. "Haven't seen him."

"He told me he had something to do this morning. He'll be here later," Chantal said, turning from the notes on her laptop.

Jeff's lips tightened, but he kept his comments to himself.

"I thought they'd send me mugshots." Chantal had spent a couple of hours with the department's police sketch artist, putting together a likeness of the man who had 'saved' her from the kidnappers. Although the sketch was precise, she needed to sort through mug shots to see if she could identify the man known as Eric.

All heads turned as the captain strode in. "We'll have access in a minute," he said.

Jeff turned back to his computer. "Good. Our friend is getting impatient."

"Really? I don't believe you." The older man aimed an indulgent smile in Chantal's direction.

"Here it is." Jeff slid the computer over to Chantal. "I'll get you a large coffee to go with that."

. . .

"I'm going crazy."

"It's only been an hour."

"You spend an hour staring at pictures of criminals, one after another, and see if it doesn't drive you crazy."

"Now you understand how witnesses feel."

"I do. I'll never ask anyone to do this ever again."

Jeff laughed. "No luck?"

"No. And I've worked my way through Mafia connections in Quebec, Ontario, even the Atlantic provinces."

"Head west now."

Chantal leaned back in the chair. "I have a feeling he's never been booked. He's too slick to get caught."

"Yet."

"Right. Yet." She took a sip of her coffee and grimaced. "Any news from Owen?"

"Nothing."

She looked at the other RCMP officer. "Mark, have you heard from him?"

"Not a thing."

Chantal grabbed her phone and tapped in a text message.

"You getting lonesome? It's only been a couple of hours since you last saw him."

Chantal ignored her partner's snideness. "I've got a bad feeling. Why isn't he here by now?"

"He's an experienced police officer. He can take care of himself."

Chantal set down her phone with more force than she would under normal circumstances and shifted her attention to Jeff. "How come you're not so relaxed when I say that about myself?"

Jeff studied the bottom of his coffee cup with unusual intensity. "What? You're a great cop."

"It seems like you don't have any confidence in me. You treat me like a little sister. I think that's your problem. You're sexist."

Jeff's head shot up. "I am not. I consider you an equal."

"You consider me a helpless female." Chantal's voice rose. "But Owen's an experienced cop and doesn't need any help. Because he's a man."

"That's not it at all." Jeff looked at Mark in desperation, as if the other cop would help him. Mark shrank further into his chair and showed no sign of coming to Jeff's rescue.

Chantal's eyes narrowed on her prey, ready to come at him with a knock-out punch. "Or is it because of what happened in Trois-Rivières?"

Jeff straightened in his chair and pointed a finger at her. "Don't even go there. I never judged you because of that. I…"

"Okay, children, you can stop fighting and get back to work." Bouchard said as he joined them. When Chantal opened her mouth to argue, he held up a hand. "Save it for later. You can fight as much as you like on your own time."

When the captain turned his back to her, she caught Jeff's gaze and stuck out her tongue at him. He sent her a wide grin.

She loved the big goof, she thought. *What would she do if he had died?*

"No one else is wondering about Owen?" She already knew Jeff's opinion, so she focused her attention on Mark and the captain. When they shrugged without showing much interest in the topic, Chantal returned to the tedious task of scrolling through mug shots.

An hour later, she still fretted. "How come he hasn't answered me?"

"Maybe he's busy." Mark's words sounded casual, but he looked at his watch with a trace of unease.

"Too busy to send me a quick text?"

"It's possible." Jeff strode into the room with a tray of cardboard coffee cups. He set one in front of Chantal.

"I can't drink more coffee, Jeff. My nerves are hyped enough. Thanks anyway." She turned to face Mark again. "If he saw one of us trying to get in touch with him, he would've answered. It could be an emergency. He knows that."

Everyone fell silent as Chantal moved her gaze between them.

"Maybe he's meeting with his Mafia connections," Jeff said.

"Will you stop with that? This isn't a time for jokes." Chantal checked her phone again as she tapped her fingertips on the desktop.

"Who said I was joking?" Jeff flashed her a smile. If he hoped to ease the tension, he didn't succeed.

Chantal jumped out of her chair and paced to the window. She wrapped her arms around her waist as she watched for a taxi with a tall, dark-haired man as a passenger.

"To make you feel better, I'll get someone on it." Jeff pulled out his phone and placed a call. He instructed the tech team to track Owen's cell phone. When he hung up, he captured Chantal's gaze as she faced him. Mark no longer rattled on his keyboard, and Chantal, for once, remained still. Thinking one of their own could be in danger was a grim moment.

The sound of footsteps shook them out of their daze. Bouchard strode into the room and came to an abrupt stop when he saw them.

"What's wrong?" His frown was deep and suspicious.

"We think Owen's missing," Jeff said.

Chantal repeated their brief conversation that morning, how he still hadn't shown up at HQ, and wasn't available by phone.

"He gave no hint about what he had to do?" Captain Bouchard asked.

"No, and I didn't question him either. I thought he had work to do on his computer." A wave of guilt flowed over her. If she had been more insistent, they might know where to look.

"We'll check camera surveillance in the area," Jeff said. "I've already asked to triangulate his phone."

Bouchard nodded. "He'll turn up."

His words were optimistic, but his tone said otherwise.

• • •

Chantal abandoned the mug shots and went for a walk outside. She hoped the much-appreciated warm air would help her center her thoughts on Owen and where he could be. She was more worried than she let the others see. Irresponsibility was not Owen's style.

She felt the need for a run, but that wasn't possible. Not only did she not have her gear, but she wanted to stay close to the station in case a call came through about Owen. Chantal would love the chance to give him a piece of her mind about taking off and not telling them where he was.

As that thought formed in her head, her phone vibrated in her back pocket. Chantal's brow creased when she read the text. She spun around and struck off toward HQ, her heels clicking on the sidewalk.

Inside the building, she hiked up her skirt and took the stairs two at a time. She swung around the corner toward the conference room and stifled a squeak when a hand reached out and wrapped around her elbow.

"What are you doing? Trying to scare the life out of me?" Chantal wrenched her arm out of Jeff's grasp.

"Follow me."

Chantal trotted beside him as he marched down the corridor. "What's going on?"

"Wait."

It was frustration more than anger that made Chantal grit her teeth. The cloak and dagger game didn't appeal to her.

Jeff pulled open the door to another, smaller conference room and waved her in. Captain Bouchard and Mark sat at the round table, their expressions grim.

"What's going on?" She directed the question to her boss this time, hoping for an answer.

"We received a file. Anonymously."

Chantal's gaze shifted between the three men. "What kind of file?"

Jeff sat at the laptop and jiggled the mouse. "You'll understand once you see it."

They focused their attention on the large TV screen on the opposite wall.

Jeff opened an email and clicked on an attachment. A video popped up on the screen. Someone appeared to have filmed it with a camera installed near the ceiling in a dark room, furnished with a chair, a cot, and a toilet. If there was anything else in the room, it wasn't within camera range.

Chantal's attention zeroed in on the people in the video. There were three men, one sitting, one standing, and the other pacing. Her gut clenched when the camera focused on the man in the chair, his hands tied behind him. Plastic tie wraps attached his ankles to the chair legs.

The left side of his face was swollen to twice its size. Dried blood was smeared beside his mouth. If there was further damage, the poor lighting masked it. Despite the obvious roughness with which they had treated him, the man's expression was alert; his gaze followed the pacing man with interest.

Chantal's gut roiled. She had been right to fear for him. At least, he was alive, she told herself. "Where did this come from? Do we know?"

"No. Not yet, anyway. Whoever sent it is too smart to make it easy for us," Jeff said.

"We'll have it analyzed," Bouchard added. "We might come up with something." His voice held little conviction. "Do you recognize the men?"

Chantal approached the screen. Being closer didn't make it clearer. The men were visible from the neck down and had their backs toward the camera. Their shapes and sizes did nothing to help identify them.

"No," she said.

The camera zoomed in for a close-up of Owen's face. The intent was to show the viewers his suffering. Instead, what Chantal witnessed was almost total indifference. Owen was a true master at hiding his emotions.

"This happens when people snoop into our business." The voice originated from behind the camera. Whether he intended the message for Owen or the police was unclear. The only person who could respond was Owen. He sent the man an icy glare. If he felt threatened by the comment, he gave nothing away.

A second later, the video ended. Chantal stared at the blank screen, a hundred thoughts running through her mind. Her teammates' faces mirrored those thoughts.

Bouchard directed his question to Chantal. "Did you recognize the voice?"

"No. I'll listen to it again, but it didn't sound familiar."

"What about the men? Do they resemble any of those hanging around Dion or Griggs?"

Chantal threw her hands in the air. "They could've been. All I saw were their backs. Not even their heads." Frustration tore through her. "I guess there's no point in asking if they found Owen's cell phone."

Jeff winced. "No signal. We have to assume they destroyed it."

"We'll stay hopeful they'll trace the email."

Chantal didn't respond to her supervisor's remark. The science behind creating untraceable emails had been in the hands of criminals for a while. These guys would be no different.

"I don't understand," she said. "What are they trying to prove? First someone captures me. Eric gets me out and kills the two guys. Now, someone goes after Owen. Is it the same person?"

"It could be," Jeff said. "It's not likely to be random."

"But what's the point? What do they hope to achieve?"

Mark spoke up. "I agree with Chantal. I may not be a Mafia expert, but this doesn't seem like typical behavior. They're beating around the bush."

"I don't understand it either." Captain Bouchard shoved his hands deep in his pockets as he spoke, his head bowed in thought. "But everything we have so far leads us to OC. It started with the fraud, which went through Griggs, who was connected. And the car bomb had a Mafia signature on it. I don't think it's a good idea to abandon that theory yet."

"Something's not right," Chantal said. "It's the same feeling I had in that house. There was something strange about those men. Like these."

"We're talking about criminals," Mark said. "They aren't people you'd hang out with."

"I know that. I've seen a lot of criminals in my time." Her tone came out harsher than she would normally use, and she realized it. She turned to Mark. "I'm sorry. I don't have the right words, but I have a weird feeling about these guys. It's difficult to describe what I feel, to understand what it is."

"It'll come to you." Jeff laid a heavy hand on her shoulder. "You're tired and stressed. We all are. There's nothing we can do now. We'll see if the team comes up with something from the email. If not, we'll expect another message from them. They're taunting us."

Yes, Chantal thought, and Owen was the pawn this time, not her.

CHAPTER 29

A shrill ring woke Chantal at five o'clock in the morning. Nothing good happened at that hour.

"Sorry, but you need to come to the station." Jeff's voice held more dismay than sympathy.

"What happened?" Her heart thumped in her chest, and her mind veered toward the worst. "Tell me."

"It's about Owen."

"Is he…?" She couldn't say the word aloud.

"As far as I know, he's alive. Just get here."

Twenty minutes later, Chantal jogged up the steps of the SQ building. She burst into the conference room to find Jeff, Captain Bouchard, and Mark already present.

"What is it?" she asked.

Bouchard's face was grim. "We have another video. Watch."

On the large screen appeared the image of a man, presumably Owen, lying on a cot, covered by a thin blanket. Chantal frowned as another man entered the room. She gasped as the figure passed underneath the bare bulb hanging from the ceiling.

"What? How…"

"Wait," Bouchard said.

The man she knew as Eric scurried to Owen's side and got down on his knees by the bed. He shook Owen awake and spoke to him, but his words were unintelligible.

Owen rolled over to face him. His expression revealed nothing - no surprise, no recognition, no fear. Without hesitation, he pushed himself up and swung his legs out of the bed. Eric latched onto Owen's elbow and helped him to his feet. As Eric led the way to the door, Owen stumbled, righted himself, and followed. His hand wrapped around the thigh of his injured leg, dragging his foot across the floor.

Eric removed a gun from his jacket and held it in front of him as he peered through the door opening. Over his left shoulder, he glanced at Owen and nodded. They slid over the threshold and out of sight of the camera.

It stunned Chantal into silence. How could this be? Owen showed no opposition, didn't question the man, and reacted as if he trusted him. Had she been so wrong?

She turned to Bouchard. "Where did you get this? What's going on?" Her gaze shifted in disbelief to Jeff. A frown creased his face, and there was a flash of sympathy in his eyes, but he offered no response.

"It arrived by email, anonymously again, to Mark's computer." The captain gestured toward the glum-looking RCMP officer. "It came from a different address this time."

"He's trying to keep us on our toes," Mark said.

"It had to be the same camera, the same guy filming it." Chantal's gaze zeroed in on Mark, as if he had all the answers.

"I suspect it's filmed remotely. I can't explain why they want us to see this, other than to tell us Owen isn't in their hands anymore."

"Unless he is." Chantal strode to the window and back. "This Eric guy might work for them. They could've staged it. They're trying to send us off course."

"And what about Owen's reaction to Eric?" Jeff drew her attention away from Mark. "He didn't seem too worried."

"Owen doesn't show his emotions. You can't tell what's going through his mind." She waved her hands in the air as she spoke. "He wouldn't turn down an invitation to escape, no matter who made the offer."

"I know you want to believe he's innocent, Chantal," Jeff said. "But even you can admit he was comfortable with that guy. He stayed calm in the first video because he knew someone would rescue him."

"Owen would've recognized him from the police sketch," Bouchard said. "He would have known he was the same man that kidnapped you. He wouldn't have trusted him. Not unless he knew him."

Chantal wanted to argue. She wanted to convince everyone Owen acted true to form, that he had a plan.

Her shoulders sagged. There hadn't been an ounce of fear or doubt in Owen's expression. A new accomplice had joined the list of possibilities, and he was an RCMP officer. Even worse, he was one she had trusted.

Chantal slumped into a chair, her elbows on the table and her head in her hands.

"I don't understand anything. How could he? He's not like that."

"He's a player," Bouchard said, not without sympathy. "A very talented one."

Jeff pulled a chair forward and sat in front of Chantal. "We can't let this distract us. We have more information than we had, and we need to use it."

"More information, yes. But all of it's bad." She leaned back in the chair and fixed her gaze on the ceiling.

"Jeff is right," the captain said. His stern tone drew Chantal out of her daze. "We have to put together a theory based on what we know."

Chantal squared her shoulders. She needed to pull herself together. It wasn't the first time she was disillusioned, and it wouldn't be the last. She was a cop with a job to do.

If she repeated that statement often enough, it might take away the pain.

Chantal shoved herself out of the chair and strode to the window. In the distance, the outline of the upper town appeared hazy in the early morning light.

She cleared her throat. "Okay. Our alternative theory is that Owen and Eric are working as a team." As she spoke the words, a strength built inside her; a strength born of anger. They had conned her, and that was difficult to tolerate. She didn't like anyone to think her naïve, and if that was how Owen thought of her, he would pay for it.

"If we believe organized crime is behind the killings, Eric and Owen are on their payroll." Chantal turned to the other occupants of the room, her arms crossed over her chest. Her raised brows asked for confirmation.

"I agree," Jeff said. He didn't appear surprised by Chantal's change of attitude. "And he kept them informed of what we were up to."

"He set up Beaudet and Griggs." She said this last with a note of despair as it hit Chantal how far Owen's betrayal had reached. Murder. "I have to say, Owen's interaction with Dion shocked me. He took a tough stance and explained it in a way that made sense. I can look at it in a new light now. It was another act. Owen and Dion played games with me."

Jeff responded to the misery in her voice with a gentle squeeze of her shoulder.

"What was the purpose of abducting you, Chantal?" Captain Bouchard asked, his face creased. "And having you rescued by Eric, also part of the team. Why the elaborate set-up?"

His two subordinates turned their gazes to the captain, both of them considering the question with care.

"Maybe they wanted to pressure us to back off," Jeff said.

Bouchard nodded. "Perhaps."

Chantal, her forehead wrinkled, focused on her memories in the cabin. "But, at that point, I didn't suspect Owen worked with him. He pretended he was a friend of Owen's. Why pretend? He was taunting me, nothing more."

"Granted," Jeff said. "But they could've had a plan that risked exposure, and they needed a bargaining chip with the cops. You were the one. He fed you that line about being a friend of Owen's just to keep you quiet."

Chantal looked at her ex-partner with sadness in her eyes. "You could be right."

The group's attention turned as a young woman entered, hesitating just inside the room. She focused on Bouchard and spoke to him in French.

The captain stood. "Good timing. She has the results from the fingerprints lab." He took the file and opened it on the table. Chantal sent a nod of thanks to the clerk before turning her attention to her boss. A series of grunts and flickered eyebrows increased the intrigue and did little to calm Chantal's nerves.

"What is it?" Chantal felt Jeff's calming hand on her shoulder, and she reeled in her impatience.

"Our friend Eric left plenty of prints in the cabin. Wearing gloves would raise your suspicions, wouldn't it?" Bouchard said as he glanced at her. His frown deepened as he continued. "Unfortunately, they're not registered."

Chantal's kernel of hope shriveled. If they had been lucky, the fingerprint registry would have scored a hit and given them the real name of Owen's accomplice and perhaps led them to both men.

But something didn't add up in her boss's statement.

"There's more than that. The fact he's not registered doesn't merit your reaction," she said.

The captain sent her a grim smile. "You're correct. We can't identify his prints, but they have turned up at two separate crime scenes. One of them was from three years ago. They caught a young drug dealer operating a meth lab. They arrested him, no deaths at the scene." He flipped over another page in the file. "The other one was more recent. Six months ago, in Toronto, a police raid of another drug bust went wrong. There was a leak, and it botched the raid. They had guns and knives. They arrested two suspects, others escaped, and two officers were injured."

The captain's gaze met Chantal's. "Owen was one of the injured."

CHAPTER 30

Chantal's mind reeled. The evidence was disastrous, tying Owen to this case with a firmer knot.

No one spoke. Several moments passed before she shook herself out of her shock and found three sets of eyes focused on her, waiting for a reaction.

She held her hands out to her side. "What do you want me to say? I was wrong about him? I know."

"We're not pointing fingers at who was right or wrong. We just want you to be okay," Jeff said.

"I'm okay." Chantal turned to her boss. "Can I see the file, please? We've got work to do."

They split the files between the three investigators. Mark took the oldest one, while Chantal handled the more recent one where Owen suffered an injury. Jeff continued with the current one.

Each officer worked in separate offices.

The anger returned. Not only had he fooled Chantal, but Owen had strung along his colleagues for years and gotten away with it. If it killed her, she would make sure this was his last shot.

Chantal downloaded the file from the case. It resembled what Owen had told her, except he had skimmed over the details. And omitted the part where he was the leak. *Was his injury during the raid an accident, or was it deliberate to allay suspicions?*

Chantal's attention returned to the file. Owen had been the lead investigator. He was the officer credited with uncovering the whereabouts of the drugs and a significant amount of cash. As luck would have it, however, someone shared the news of their raid with the criminals, and they were packing up when the police arrived on the scene.

It caught the side of law enforcement off guard when the criminals met them with force. Someone stabbed Owen, and another officer suffered a bullet wound. After the initial confusion, the cops got the upper hand, but two suspects escaped and were never found.

Chantal turned in her chair and gazed toward the window, lost in thought. She couldn't find a connection between Owen and Eric in the file, but it was there somewhere. Eric's fingerprints had been at the scene. His association with three crimes, two of which involved Owen, was an extreme coincidence. She assumed Eric was one of the two who got away. Had Owen helped him?

Chantal pulled a pad toward her and scribbled notes and questions she wanted to run by the others. She sent a quick message to Jeff and Mark to meet her in the conference room in ten minutes. Grabbing her laptop, pad, and pen, she stopped at the coffee machine to get a caffeine jolt before entering the deserted meeting room.

Chantal watched as her screensaver appeared on the 60-inch screen on the wall. She didn't react when two sets of footsteps thumped behind her, nor did she glance up from her keyboard when they pulled out chairs and sat down, one on each side of her.

Instead, she jumped up and grabbed a roll of plastic from a counter, along with a couple of erasable markers. From the roll, she removed three sheets of plastic and placed them side-by-side on the wall. She sensed she had her colleagues' full attention.

With a black marker, Chantal numbered the top of each plastic sheet from one to three.

"Okay, let's fill in some facts from each case. I'll start." She moved to the middle sheet. "This one involved Owen," she said as she scribbled his name. "Eric's fingerprints found at scene." Another note. "Arrests made. Two people escaped. Eric was one of them." She stopped to stare at what she had written. "Okay. Last thing. Two cops injured. They stabbed Owen in the leg."

Chantal turned to face Mark, whose eyes widened under the fierce determination in her gaze. "What do you have for the first one?" Chantal pointed her finger at Mark.

He looked at his notes. "Same for the fingerprints. They resolved the case, they arrested the suspect, and he served time at CBI." To respond to Chantal's perplexed look, he explained. "Collins Bay Institution, a prison in Kingston, Ontario."

He glanced at his notes again. "Two years later, someone murdered him in the prison's laundromat while he performed his duties."

This last grabbed Chantal's attention. "What was his name?" she asked.

"John Wilson Stone."

Chantal inscribed it on the wall.

"Did they find out who killed him?" Jeff said.

Mark shook his head, prompting more notes on Chantal's part.

"Anything else?" Chantal asked.

Mark paused. "Yes. Owen was the arresting officer."

Chantal released an audible breath. This was a major find, she thought. It was now three for three.

She added it to the chart and turned to Jeff. He didn't need any prompting.

"They assigned Owen to a white-collar crime team that brings him to Quebec."

Chantal interrupted him with a raised finger. "Or he made sure they assigned him to it."

Jeff shrugged his agreement as Chantal turned to jot down an abbreviated version of Jeff's remarks. When he didn't continue, she shot a quick glance at him over her shoulder.

"Just waiting for permission, dear leader." He grinned as Chantal rolled her eyes. "Griggs had known ties to the Mafia but may have been running his own scam along with Eric and/or Owen with the email fraud. At any rate, he and Beaudet were expendable. They were both murdered after the car bomb targeted you and Owen."

"Or was it a set-up to make it seem like they targeted us?" Chantal said, as she scrawled on the board.

"To what end?" Mark interjected.

Chantal turned and looked at him as thoughts swirled through her head. "To throw us off his scent?"

"I think that's the most likely scenario," Jeff said.

"Next. I'm kidnapped, for reasons unknown. The fake Eric saves me. He kills the two kidnappers, who are strangely unarmed and strangely strange. He lies about Jeff and Owen being killed, probably lies about the drone, and conveniently finds a cabin in the woods for us to hide in."

"You outsmarted him."

"Thank you, Jeff, for the compliment, but he got away, so I wasn't that smart."

Chantal pulls off another strip of plastic to add to the wall; the sheet for the present case was already full.

"Then they kidnap Owen, send us a video, and our friend Eric frees him."

"And, evidently, his friend too," Jeff added.

Chantal stood back and wrinkled her nose at the scantiness of the notes for the first cases. Yet, it gave her fresh resolve. She arranged another sheet of plastic on the wall and scribbled two questions on it: Was Owen behind the prison hit on the perpetrator? Was his injury an accident or on purpose?

She turned to the others. "What else do we need to know?"

Jeff creased his forehead in thought. "If Eric was in on it from the beginning, does it mean he was involved in the email fraud? Is he a tech wizard? Did he intercept Mark's text and plant the cameras in your apartment?"

Chantal turned back to the wall and added the notes, but she couldn't suppress a shiver at the thought of Eric creeping through her apartment when she wasn't there.

"How was Owen chosen for this case?" He wrote the words as he spoke them aloud.

Chantal nodded. "Mark, I'd like to contact Eric Sutton. Jeff, can you dig up more on the first one? I feel like it's the link."

Neither Jeff nor Mark questioned Chantal leading the charge. They turned their attention to their laptops. Within minutes, Mark had a photo of Eric Sutton on the screen.

Chantal's eyes narrowed as she studied him. Owen had shown her a blurry photo from his phone. This was a professional shot of a balding man. What hair remained was dark brown. He was clean-shaven with blue eyes, around 45 years old.

"What do you know about him, so far?" she asked Mark.

"Not a lot. He has twenty years in the RCMP, rising to reach the undercover drug detail. He and Owen worked together five years before he was injured and moved to white-collar."

"Were they on the same two operations?"

"I'll dig deeper in the files, but they could have been. The dates line up."

"This Eric might not be clean either," Jeff said, drawing a sharp glance from Chantal.

"Let's call him," she said. "He knows Owen is missing. Bouchard has kept their supervisor informed."

The real Eric Sutton picked up the call to his cell phone on the second ring. Chantal introduced herself, told him he was on speakerphone, and rhymed off the names of her two co-workers. The man didn't seem surprised by their call.

"This is about Owen, isn't it?" he said.

"Yes. What have you heard?" Chantal asked with a quick glance in Jeff's direction. She wanted him to understand he could take the lead whenever he wanted.

"Only that a group, possibly Mafia, captured him. What happened? What went wrong?" The cop's voice was gruff. Chantal wondered if it was his habitual tone or if emotion brought on the roughness.

"That's what we're trying to find out. We hoped you could help us. We understand you've worked with him for a while."

"Yes." The cop's voice was uncertain. "How can I help?"

"We're exploring the idea that this may have been a revenge incident, perhaps unrelated to the assignment Chantal and Owen worked on. We thought you could give us some ideas," Jeff said.

"I see." The man's voice gained confidence. "If you want to know if I'm aware of anything specific, I'd say no."

"Did you work with Owen on the Stone case?"

"Stone? Yeah, that was our first one together. Why do you ask?"

Chantal shot a look at Jeff, worried he had put Sutton onto something they didn't want to reveal. Jeff gave her a reassuring smile.

"Just trying to set up a timeline. We understood you worked together for five years and the Stone job happened around then. There was nothing that made you think someone targeted Owen?"

"No. They put Stone away, but there didn't seem to be anyone who cared. He was a two-bit dealer they replaced with another. You know how it is."

"Right," Chantal said. "What about when Owen was injured? Can you give us some info on that one?"

"Yeah. That was a shit show. We thought we had it in the bag, but someone leaked the op, and it went to the dogs. Owen was lucky it was just his leg, although it was damaging enough."

"Did they catch the leak?" Jeff asked, already knowing the answer.

"Nah. We're still looking for it. But I'd like to get my hands on the guy."

They promised to keep in touch with him and signed off. The three cops looked at one another before Chantal spoke. "I don't know if that gave us anything. He could be in on it too."

"We'll dig deeper into that case."

While Jeff and Chantal questioned Eric, Mark's fingers worked on his keyboard in a fervor. By the time they ended the call, excitement animated his face.

"I searched through the file," he said. "There was a rumor Stone had a large stash of money. They never recovered it."

Chantal considered this for a moment. "I don't like the fact it was a rumor, but we'll note it anyway, if only not to forget it."

"There was something else, too. There was an inconsistency with the inventory count."

Chantal's hand stopped midair, and she turned to look at the other cop.

"The final count at HQ differed from the preliminary count at the scene by 25%," Mark said. "Lower." The last precision was unnecessary. Chantal understood the implications.

"That's a big difference," Jeff chimed in. "Along with the rumor of missing cash, it smells bad."

"Very." Chantal added the note of missing drugs to the chart. "Owen and Eric could have cashed in on this one. We need to check his finances." She added this last statement with a red marker. "Mark, I think you're the best one to look at that."

"I'll need a warrant if I want to dig deeper."

"We'll talk to Bouchard. I'm sure we'll get it." Chantal hoped she could make good on that promise. "What about the other case six months ago? Can you find anything there about missing money or contraband?"

"I'll check it out."

Jeff stood and pulled two more pieces of plastic off the roll, placing them at the far end of the wall. On the first one, he wrote: Revenge hit—was Owen rescued or abducted? On the second, he wrote: Owen and fake Eric set up the entire operation—why?

He stepped back and looked at his notes before reaching for his phone. "I'll call Bouchard."

"I'm here." The captain strode into the room and waved his hand in Mark's direction. "I've transferred another video by email."

Chantal's heart tripped. *What now?* She dropped into a chair.

The image was of the same dull, dank room, with cinderblock walls, a chair, and a cot. This time it was empty. Chantal wondered what the purpose of the video was. She didn't wonder for long.

Two men came in. They could have been the same two from the first video, but it was impossible to tell.

One thing was certain; their shock at finding the room empty was genuine. The second man almost collided with the first when he stopped dead in his tracks. With frantic expressions, they searched the room. As if a grown man could conceal himself with so little to hide behind.

The men faced each other, their mouths open in disbelief and their eyes wide. Their gazes turned toward the camera in the corner, knowing the people they worked for had captured their moment of incompetence.

The group gathered in SQ headquarters watched the video with fascination. They jolted with shock when the wall exploded, and the video went dark.

CHAPTER 31

Chantal tossed her purse onto the table, followed by her keys.

It was late, past ten o'clock, and she'd been up since five. Tomorrow, she'd be at the office early again.

Her emotions had taken a beating today. The horror of witnessing cold-blooded murder hung over her like a shroud, and she couldn't throw it off.

Chantal would never forget the stillness at SQ headquarters, the repulsion that engulfed them like a tsunami.

It was Bouchard who broke the spell with his whispered words. *"Mon Dieu."* The legs of his chair scraped across the floor as he stood, picked up his phone, and walked to a corner of the room.

Chantal's gaze met Jeff's, and his expression mirrored her shock.

"They eliminated them," he said. "Like Griggs and Beaudet, and the others."

"Yes." Chantal breathed the word, her lips barely moving, her thoughts tumbling over each other. Could Owen be a partner in this atrocity?

"It was in Trois-Rivières, twenty minutes ago."

Chantal's head swiveled to face Bouchard. Trois-Rivières. The town where her own nightmare had happened. Now it was the site of another act of violence. And a cop could be an instigator.

In her apartment, Chantal threw herself into an armchair, and not for the first time, wished someone waited at home for her; someone to listen to her problems and worries; a sounding board. Even a dog might do the trick.

Instead, images raced through her head on an unending reel with no one to distract her.

The team had gone through the motions for the rest of the day, each of them quiet but focused.

Mark didn't come up with anything wonky from the second case, as far as money or drug count went. But it didn't mean Owen and his friend hadn't gotten some funds from another source. They may have learned from their mistakes the first time around.

As for the current one, before it went down the drain, Owen may have gotten a kickback from some funds they laundered. Maybe they put him in place to make sure the criminals remained undetected, sending law enforcement on a wild goose chase. Beaudet and Griggs were human sacrifices for the benefit of lining the pockets of Owen and 'Eric.'

As she considered this possibility, her spirits plummeted even further. A bone-numbing disappointment replaced the restlessness and adrenaline. Her frustration was not only with Owen, but with herself. How had she trusted him? Was she so naïve she couldn't detect bullshit? She had always prided herself on being able to size up people.

Owen irritated and annoyed her on occasion, but she had never doubted his dedication to the job. She had sensed nothing but total commitment to finding the perpetrators, even though they considered the assignment, at the outset, to be a less-than-appealing white-collar.

Chantal peeled off her clothes and climbed into the shower, hoping to rinse away her doubts and misgivings.

• • •

Chantal was in the conference room, her second cup of coffee in her hand, when Jeff strolled in, followed by Mark.

After a clipped greeting, she grabbed the black marker and stood in front of the list of questions to explore.

"To check out the theory of a revenge killing, we'll dig into the death of this guy," she said, pointing to the name of the man killed in the prison hit. "We'll talk to his family, friends, wife, girlfriend, whatever. Mark, can you get me a list?"

The man nodded and concentrated on his laptop; the keys clicking underneath his fingertips.

"Who else could want revenge?" Chantal asked Jeff.

"Whoever expected to get the money and the drugs."

"Right," she said. "And who could that be? OC? Someone higher up?"

"That should be in the file. Stone was a peon. They weren't going after him when they organized that strike." Jeff turned to Mark, but before he could ask, the RCMP officer nodded. Duly noted.

"Is it possible all three cases involved the same group of people?" Chantal said to the room at large.

A deep voice answered from the doorway. "It could be, but it'd surprise me."

They turned to watch Bouchard stride into the room.

"Why?" Chantal said.

A wry smile lifted the corners of his mouth. "It would be too easy."

"We'll check all parties involved," she said.

Bouchard strolled along the wall, reading Chantal's neatly written notes and squinting at the few words scrawled by Jeff.

"Good work," he said. "And I see you're using Mark's excellent technical skills."

A faint blush climbed the young man's face as he looked up from the screen. "I've got some names for you. About Stone."

"Good," Jeff said. "We'll need a list of all last-known addresses and numbers of everyone. Criminal records, if they have any."

The ringing of Bouchard's phone interrupted them.

"*Oui.*" The drawing together of the captain's brows piqued Chantal's curiosity. "*Emmène-le.*"

He disconnected the call and gazed at them. "We've intercepted a call to Owen's cell phone. It seems to be from Dion."

Chantal and Jeff exchanged a curious glance. Owen wouldn't get a call from the Mafia guy if he had arranged the rescue of the cop.

A knock told her she might soon have the answer to that question. A young man entered the room carrying an electronic device in his hand. He placed the small black box on the table before leaving the room.

Bouchard reached forward and pushed a button. A voice familiar to Chantal's ears resonated over the phone.

"Mr. Danvers, I'm still waiting to hear from you. What's taking so long? Is there a problem? Get back to me, please."

A silence hovered over the group until Jeff broke it. "I guess that eliminates one of our theories."

"Not necessarily," Chantal said. "They could have set it up. Maybe it's a code."

Bouchard stroked his chin. "I have my doubts, but we can't eliminate the possibility. We'll follow up." His expression was serious as he stared at Chantal for a long moment. He came to a decision. "You'll meet with him. Jeff, you'll accompany her, as her brother. Your story can be that your husband ran off and emptied your bank accounts. It might reveal their hand."

Chantal hoped her face didn't give away the jolt she felt. She threw a glance in Jeff's direction and realized he shared her thoughts. They would work undercover as a team, but in a situation that may be compromised.

"I realize what you're thinking," Bouchard said. "We'll take every precaution. You'll meet in a public place in broad daylight. If they suspect you're cops, they'll play their cards close to their vest. If they don't, you'll use the time to move the case forward. At least, we'll come out with a feeling of where they stand."

Chantal nodded. Yes, they were in a dangerous position. That was part of being a cop. And Owen still hung in the balance. They didn't have time to waste.

"I'll call him and set up a meeting." Chantal's mind reeled with the thought of facing the Mafia boss and how they would pull it off. Her gaze slid to Jeff, and she knew the wheels turned in his head.

• • •

This time, the police department dug into their pockets and paid for a flight to Montreal. Within two hours of their arrival at the Quebec City airport, they were outside the designated meeting spot in the other city. Chantal hoped the efficiency of the journey carried over into the encounter.

The building was nondescript to the point of being invisible amongst the others on each side. Jeff and Chantal were told it was a restaurant, but there was no indication someone conducted legitimate business inside.

"Are we in the right place?" Chantal checked the address on her phone, her nerves frayed and jumpy. They had planned a public place for the meet.

"This is where the GPS led us." The words escaped Jeff's mouth as the door opened and a man in a black suit stepped onto the sidewalk beside them.

He was an inch or two shorter than Jeff, but the stomach that hung over his belt rendered him much wider. His gaze flashed over Jeff, but a gleam appeared in his eyes as he took his time checking out Chantal. Her heart thumped, but she stiffened her spine and raised her eyebrows with a glare in her eyes.

A sneer lifted the corner of his lips as he nodded toward the door. "This way."

Once inside, two other men, similarly dressed but more muscular, met them. With serious expressions, the thugs searched the cops and rifled through Chantal's purse. They had expected this. Neither of them was armed or set up with a wire.

The first man stayed out front while they trudged up a steep set of stairs to the second floor. From there, the men escorted them to a dining area that contained a handful of round tables with a larger rectangular one against the farthest wall. At the end, sat Martin Dion, an array of platters positioned on the table, including an immense bowl of mussels with shrimp, fried prawns, and calamari surrounding it.

He didn't speak as he stood to greet his visitors, but his dark, suspicious gaze narrowed on the man beside Chantal.

Jeff held out his hand to him. "My name is Jean-François. I'm Michelle's brother." He added a slight French accent to his speech to imitate Chantal's. The other man looked at his hand with distaste, prompting Jeff to withdraw it, along with his smile. Dion gestured toward the chairs to his right, his invitation to join him.

Waves of irritation radiated from the man. His piercing gaze moved from Jeff to rest on Chantal. "I don't like people who play games with me. Not unless I'm the one calling the plays."

"Neither do I." Chantal forced her hands to rest in her lap and to keep a relaxed posture, but her expression remained hard and unsmiling.

"What is he doing here? Where is your husband?"

The man's anger appeared sincere. But it could be a role he played, Chantal thought, just as they did.

Chantal stayed in character. "I don't know. I hoped you could tell me."

The flat of his hand slammed the table, making the cops flinch. "What are you accusing me of?"

Chantal's tone stayed even, despite the jumping of her nerves. "Nothing. I'd like to find out where he disappeared to after emptying our bank accounts. I thought he may have tried to do business with you without my knowledge."

The man's angry stare was locked with hers until he broke the silence. "I contacted him a week ago, and he never answered me. He's very disrespectful. I don't handle that very well."

Chantal's thoughts swirled in confusion. "He got your message. We met with your two minions, Walsh and Trenton. We're waiting on them to get back to us."

Dion gave her a long, hard stare before he responded. "I don't know who you're referring to. It seems someone stirred the pot and made it look like we are the cooks."

His expression made it very clear he wasn't happy with this development.

"I was interested in your husband's proposal," he continued. "I wouldn't hand it over to anyone else. I'm the one with the expertise in these matters."

Chantal fought the urge to glance at Jeff, to gauge his reaction to Dion's comments.

"At any rate," Dion said. "When you find him, tell him he can look elsewhere for a business partner. He's not an honorable man."

"No, he isn't. And he has a dishonorable friend, someone I don't like," Chantal said. "He said his name is Eric, but I think it's a fake name. Perhaps you know him. He's about 6 feet tall, has reddish blond hair, a small scar on his temple. We suspect he may be an expert in computers, particularly in getting around cybersecurity."

The man's expression didn't change, but Chantal thought she detected a flash in his eyes. "No, I don't know him." He intertwined his fingers and rested them on his stomach. "What happens to our business deal? Will I now be working with you and your brother?"

"I no longer have the means to support the deal. I have to regroup." She twisted her mouth into an angry scowl. "And, in the meantime, I need to find my husband and his partner. I don't like being lied to and stolen from."

A wry smile transformed his face. "On that, we agree. If there is something I can do, I'd be happy to help."

Chantal held his gaze for a few seconds before she spoke. "Of course, if you hear something within your network of friends that concerns my husband or the man who calls himself Eric, I would love to hear from you." She removed a business card from her purse, one created for the Danvers' fake company, and slid it across the table toward Dion. "I wrote my cell phone number on the back. You can contact me with that."

The man didn't touch the card or move his gaze from Chantal's. "I'll be in touch if I have anything for you."

Chantal accepted his words as the dismissal he meant them to be. She pushed her chair back and stood as Jeff rose to his feet beside her.

She gave Dion a faint smile as a burly man appeared by her side, ready to escort them from the building.

CHAPTER 32

Chantal laid her head against the rear of the seat and closed her eyes. The engines whined as the plane lifted off the tarmac and headed east. They had left Quebec City only a matter of hours earlier, but the trip had already exhausted her emotions. Or rather, the stress of the entire case had caught up to her.

It would be a lie if she said the experience in that building today hadn't frightened her. They were unarmed and at the mercy of a known criminal. Not only that, but she had to keep her perfect stage face on; otherwise, their story wouldn't work. The anger she felt toward Owen carried her through, and she channeled a scorned woman with authenticity.

"No matter how well he conceals his thoughts, I don't believe he has knowledge of Owen and Eric."

Chantal opened her eyes and turned her head toward Jeff. "I agree in part. Owen isn't on his radar, but I feel something about Eric rang a bell with him."

Jeff shrugged. "You could be right. You're better at reading people than I am."

Chantal's laugh was abrupt and without humor. "Sure. I read Owen well."

"You can't always be perfect," he said. "You are a girl, after all."

Her hand snaked out and swatted his leg. "Behave yourself. Or I'll tell Tori."

His chuckle came from deep inside. "I'm not worried. Tori can't resist my charm."

The smile lifted the corners of Chantal's lips. She closed her eyes and tried to relax for the last leg of the trip.

• • •

The three of them faced the wall, staring at information scrawled on the plastic sheets.

"Okay, let's complete this chart." Jeff grabbed the black marker and advanced toward a fresh sheet entitled 'John Stone'. "We'll start with his mother."

Mark consulted the paper he held in his hand. "She was a prostitute until after her third child was born. Then she gave up the job to rent her bedroom by the hour for other hookers to use. The three kids, two boys and a girl, roomed together in one bedroom, while Mom waited in the living room, drinking vodka and doing drugs."

Chantal stared at him with an incredulous look. "Are you serious? That's horrible. Where is she now?"

"Dead. OD'd about five years ago."

"It looks like John came from a great background. I guess it's no surprise he ended up in prison." Jeff shook his head. "And someone murdered him there."

"You can't always base it on your roots, but in this instance, there's a good argument for it," Chantal said with a grimace.

Jeff continued his line of questioning. "Where did John fall in the pecking order?"

"Oldest child. Had a younger brother and sister. They all ended up in the foster care system."

"How old would he have been by now?"

"He'd be about thirty-five. The brother would be thirty-three, and his sister is thirty."

"Next. Dad?"

"None on record. There were semi-steady boyfriends, but no one hung around."

Chantal spoke up. "Younger brother?"

"His name is William, or rather it was. He's deceased. Killed in a car accident three years ago. He looked clean."

"Did anyone visit John while he was in prison?"

"Yeah, the sister did. Amelia. She's also having problems, heading down the same path as her mother."

"Any other relatives? Aunts? Uncles? Cousins?" Jeff asked.

"None that I could find."

"Friends?"

"Nobody that gave a damn. No one even claimed the body. The government took care of it."

"Do we know the reason behind the murder?" Chantal asked.

"The official reason amounted to the usual petty stuff that comes up in prisons. He annoyed someone too many times, and they got rid of him. They never prosecuted anyone."

"And no one cared," she said.

Jeff stepped back to scrutinize his notes. "It looks like a dead end to me."

There were nods all around.

"All the same, let's get some photo ID to match with names," Jeff said.

"We still have our two theories: OC, or Eric and Owen working on their own."

Jeff turned to Chantal. "You're not ready to write off Eric being connected with the Mafia?"

"Not yet. I have to figure out how to find that info. Dion was stone-faced, but he might be a talented actor."

"You know, this isn't easy for me," Mark said. "Owen and I both work for the RCMP, and there's nothing I hate more than a dirty cop. But I'm thinking it's a partnership between him and Eric."

Chantal sent him a sympathetic glance. "There's another possibility."

Jeff and Mark looked at her with identical expressions of expectation.

"Owen is innocent, and he's a pawn, captured by Eric, either on his own or with help from someone else."

Jeff's brows lifted. "I'm surprised you're still hanging onto that idea. I thought you'd given it up."

Chantal thought so too, but despite everything pointing in the opposite direction, she had moments of doubt. "We can't write it off. Anything is possible."

"Okay, we'll keep it in mind." Jeff's tone sounded like it was the last thing he wanted to keep in mind.

"Let's do more than that. Let's add it to the wall." Chantal pulled another sheet of plastic from the roll and found an empty spot for it.

She took the marker from Jeff with a smile and added a title, Innocent. She looked over her shoulder at Jeff while she tapped her finger on the sheet. "If it's true, he's in serious trouble. Let's hope he's still alive."

Chantal's words sobered the atmosphere in the room.

"Don't worry. We'll remember." Jeff retrieved the marker and approached the sheet for the Mafia connection. "We still have brainstorming to do. If they're connected to the Mafia, Dion knew all along you were a cop, Chantal. They were in on the game. Why meet with us again?" His gaze moved from one cop to the other. Chantal mulled over the idea, and a chill danced along her spine.

"They wanted to control the information," Mark said.

"Yeah, and he needed to keep up appearances." As Jeff spoke, he noted his words on the wall.

Chantal placed her hands on her hips. "Did Owen orchestrate the murders? What about the attempt on our lives? It put him in danger."

"For your first question, it's possible. Or his Mafia minions took care of it. Either way, it implicated him," Jeff said. "For your second question, they could have orchestrated that too. The timing was perfect. Almost too perfect. Neither or you were hurt."

"Another thought. Why abduct me? Why did Eric rescue me? I don't understand how it fits into all of this."

Jeff's shoulders slumped. "Neither do I."

"To throw us off?" Mark said. "To make us believe it was the Mafia behind it all?"

"It seems elaborate." Chantal shook her head.

"And they killed two of their own men," Jeff said. "It makes no sense."

Mark shrugged. "I didn't say it was perfect, but it could be something. Maybe Eric went rogue."

"You're making progress, I see." They turned as Bouchard entered the room. Chantal glanced from him to the wall. The notes were impressive, but she didn't think they were any closer to Owen. It was taking longer than she would like.

Her attention turned to the captain as he cleared his throat.

"I have news for you. I just got off the phone with Lieutenant Wilson. He's Owen's supervisor in the Toronto branch of the RCMP."

Chantal wasn't sure where her boss headed with this information, but judging by his sour expression, she didn't think the rest of what he had to say would thrill her.

"He said, once again, Owen's an exemplary officer and has worked for him for ten years now. He has full trust in him."

Jeff snorted beside Chantal. She resisted the temptation to elbow him.

Her boss either didn't hear Jeff's intrusion or ignored it. "They're very concerned. A team is on its way to Quebec to join us. They'll arrive later today."

Chantal stifled a groan. What she didn't want were more RCMP officers sticking their nose in the case. Yet, she reminded herself Mark was one of them and had proven to be an asset.

"Have these people worked with Owen before? Do they have any knowledge that could help us?" Jeff asked, a hint of frustration in his tone.

"I'm sure they do. They'll fill you in when they get here."

Chantal exchanged a discouraged look with Jeff. He was no more enchanted with the news than her.

• • •

His shoulders were level with Jeff's, but that's where the resemblance ended. He wore the required dark suit, which contrasted with Jeff's uniform of jeans and a t-shirt. The man's head was a shiny, dark brown dome next to Jeff's shaggy head of hair. Chantal guessed his age to be in the mid to upper forties. A forced smile stretched his lips as he shook hands with the three police officers. There was something more genuine when his gaze fell upon Mark. Although they had never met, he knew the younger man was an RCMP officer and not from the Quebec police force. The new arrival introduced himself as Ivan Hayes.

The woman who accompanied him, Brenda Weaver, stood eye-to-eye with Chantal and was a few years older than the SQ officer. A severe bun restrained her jet-black hair. Striking green eyes seemed to pierce Chantal's soul before she shifted her attention to Jeff and Mark. Her wide smile appeared strained. Chantal knew this wasn't a pleasure trip for them. Their colleague was missing and possibly in extreme danger.

Captain Bouchard joined them for the introductions and summarized the developments so far before turning the floor over to Jeff.

The SQ officer stood by the wall and explained the theories they had put together. A noticeable chill permeated the room when he implied Owen was a possible guilty party.

Weaver strolled to the wall and peered at the notes on each sheet. She turned to face the group. Stunned disbelief covered her face. "How can you consider the possibility that Owen's involved in any way?"

Jeff, playing the diplomat, smiled. "We hope that's not the scenario, but we're considering all theories, good or bad."

The woman's gaze drifted between the Quebec officers, as if gauging who bought into the idea of her colleague's guilt. With each passing second, her disbelief morphed into concern.

"Why don't you tell us all you can about Owen?" Chantal kept her tone soft and conciliatory. "We need to eliminate theories."

Weaver and Hayes exchanged a glance, and the man took the lead.

"He's an outstanding officer. There's never been an inkling of suspicion surrounding him. Never. If anyone is straight up and honest, it's Owen."

"They chose him to take this case. Why?" Jeff said.

Hayes shrugged. "I think he asked for it when it came up."

Chantal pinned the man with a look. She felt Jeff's gaze on her and understood where his thoughts lead. "Why did he want it? It wasn't all that interesting. A lot of paper-pushing."

Hayes shrugged. "He told me he was restless, and a trip to Quebec City appealed to him."

"I realize what you're thinking," Weaver said. She set her fists on her hips, and her voice trembled with emotion. "But you're wrong. He didn't set it up."

"We're not thinking anything," Chantal said. "We just want the facts."

"It's how you interpret the facts that count."

"Agreed." Although Chantal was just as hopeful as the other woman about Owen's innocence, she worried about the RCMP officer's ability to remain objective. Was she always this emphatic toward her co-workers, or was this emotion reserved for Owen? Did she protest too much?

Chantal focused on the case. "What about the man called Eric? Any intel on him?"

"We saw the sketch you sent," Hayes said. "We have nothing. I assume you ran it through the databases."

"We did. As I mentioned before, his fingerprints showed up at two other crime scenes that Owen worked, but we don't have an identity." Jeff glanced at the notes before turning back to Hayes and Weaver. "What can you tell us about the drug bust where Owen was stabbed?"

Hayes gestured toward his partner, handing her the lead.

"I worked that one with him and Sutton. Everything went according to plan until the raid. There was a leak." Her face creased into a frown as she spoke. "Before you ask, we never found the leak. And it wasn't Owen. Someone stabbed him during that raid. He moved at the last second and avoided worse."

"And the money that disappeared?" Jeff said.

Her eyes flashed. "You're not trying to pin that on him too, are you?"

"Brenda," her partner admonished, his voice stern. The female officer glanced at him and took a deep breath.

"Two weeks later, someone noticed the initial count from the scene didn't match," she continued. "We all underwent an investigation. Nothing turned up. We still don't know what happened."

Jeff made notes on the wall. Weaver watched his moves like a cat ready to pounce on a mouse.

"Are there more questions?" Hayes said. "I think I'd like to check in and get some rest. We'll get back at it tomorrow."

"I have one last one," Jeff said. "Why were you chosen to work on this? You seem biased toward Owen's innocence."

"We're looking out for one of our own. We want him found. It's as simple as that."

CHAPTER 33

"Apart from confirming what we already knew, they don't seem to have much to contribute."

"Not yet, but they may give us more. Either way, we're stuck with them for now." Jeff's expression reflected his regret.

Chantal's shoulders slumped. They strolled side-by-side through the parking lot. She felt a pang of guilt for not escorting the two newly arrived RCMP officers to their hotel or finding them a decent place to grab a meal. Instead, she let Mark deal with them. She was too tired to make the effort, and it would strain her nerves to play nice to the newcomers.

"Eric is the key." Jeff wasn't party to Chantal's thoughts, but he hadn't jumped up to offer his role as host either. She assumed he didn't harbor any warm and fuzzy feelings for the other officers. "We need more information about him."

"Tomorrow, we'll deal with it. Between us, we'll come up with something. But it has to be soon. Too much time has gone by."

They reached Chantal's car, and Jeff waited, his hands shoved in his pockets, as she foraged in her purse for her keys.

"We have to put ourselves in their shoes," he said. "If it was one of our own missing, someone we knew and trusted, we wouldn't be receptive to conspiracy theories either."

"I get it," Chantal said. "I really do."

Jeff gave her a smile and a quick squeeze of her shoulder before he turned and headed to his pickup truck.

Within ten minutes, Chantal was at her apartment and content to be there. She kicked off her shoes, let down her hair, and made a beeline for the bathroom. All she wanted was to shower and crawl into bed. She stopped in her tracks when the buzz of her doorbell sounded behind her.

"Who could that be?"

She swung around and followed her tracks back to the security pad beside her door. Hitting a button, the screen lit up, giving her an unobstructed view of the doorstep. Her eyes widened and her heart took up a frantic beat. What was he doing here? How had he found her? She reached for her cell phone to call 9-1-1 just as his voice reverberated through the speaker.

"I know what you're thinking. We're not here to do you any harm. I just want to talk to you. And keep in mind that if I want to talk to you or if I want to hurt you, I can do it whenever and wherever I want."

Chantal froze. *Should she believe him? Was she taking a chance she'd regret? Or one she might never have the opportunity to regret?* Something told her she could trust him, at least this time, but she would be prepared. She grabbed her gun and put it in the waistband at her back before she hit the button to unlock the outside door.

Two sets of footsteps trudged up the staircase to her apartment landing. As they reached the top, Chantal opened her door to her visitors and took a step back.

Martin Dion gave her a wide grin. His bodyguard brushed past her, and without asking permission, swept through her apartment. The Mafia boss remained silent during his employee's absence, a benevolent smile on his face. A minute later, the muscular thug arrived back at Chantal's side and gave his superior a nod.

"I'm sorry for intruding so late in the evening," he said. "I'm sure you're tired after a hard day of work."

"You've been following me." Chantal strained to keep her tone level and calm. She couldn't betray her fear, nor appear relaxed.

"Of course. Did you think I wouldn't want to know this person I was to do business with? I've only taken an interest in you since our little visit the other day. You see, I've been losing people. I don't like losing people, unless it's me who decides they need to be lost. You know what I mean?"

He didn't wait for an answer.

"Now, of course, I'm aware you're a cop. And you and your friends have turned your attention to me. That doesn't make me happy, all this snooping around, trying to set me up."

He glanced around him and seemed to grasp he stood in her living room. Moving to an armchair, he bent his knees to sit before realizing she hadn't invited him to do so. He looked at Chantal with a raised eyebrow and smiled when she nodded and gestured for him to take a seat.

"Normally someone like me shouldn't associate with someone like you," he said as he crossed his legs and unbuttoned his jacket. "We're like dogs and cats, you know. But sometimes dogs and cats get along. I see these cute videos on the internet of dogs and cats being chummy. So, I said to myself, maybe I can talk to this nice lady. And we might better understand why I lost my people. I'd like to deal with the individuals responsible personally."

Chantal's mind raced. He looked at her, and she gathered it was her turn to talk. She hoped she didn't blow it. "We thought you were the one who lost your people - on purpose."

He waved his hand in a dismissive gesture. "No, not this time. Beaudet was a minor player, a speck of dust on a table, but Griggs was useful, up to a point. I suspected he had branched off and wanted to make some money on his own. I looked forward to discussing it with him but never got the chance. It irritates me when someone takes my opportunities away from me."

"What about the guys in the cabin? And the ones who took Owen? They're all dead now."

His head cocked to one side, and his eyes narrowed. "I don't know who you're talking about. You keep bringing up people I've never done business with. Who did you mention the other day?"

"Walsh and Trenton?"

"Yes. Who are they?"

Chantal knew she shouldn't believe him. It could be an act. Dion wouldn't admit to murder, not to a cop. Yet his words rang true. Chantal's gaze shifted around the room. She tried to piece together what she had learned.

"This husband of yours," he said, making quote signs in the air. "He's a cop, too. I don't go after cops. Who's the other guy? The one you talked to me about. Eric somebody."

"We don't know who he is. We're trying to find him."

"I'm good at finding people."

"I see that."

His spurt of laughter echoed through the room "I like you. You've got guts. Let's work together to find these people. If your friend is on the take, you can have him and deal with him. The other guy I could take care of for you."

Chantal returned his smile. This was, without a doubt, the most bizarre situation that had ever happened to her, she thought. "I can't do that. Cats and dogs, you know. They may get along sometimes, but they eventually draw the line. I appreciate your offer. If you ever find out who Eric is, and you'd like to share that information with me, I'd be very pleased. But we'd like to deal with him ourselves, through legal channels."

He pushed himself to his feet. "You guys and your scruples. It slows everything down. But I understand where you're coming from. Let me think on it. If I find anything, I'll decide what to do with it."

The men stepped through the doorway, but Dion faced her from the landing. "I let you keep the gun out of good faith. I trusted you. You should do the same and trust me."

CHAPTER 34

All eyes focused on Chantal when she barged into the room.

"Where were you? It's almost nine o'clock." Jeff took out and dusted off his most accusatory tone.

Chantal had paced the floor the night before until past one o'clock in the morning, itching to call him but not wanting to disturb a pregnant Tori and an exhausted friend. Yet, despite her thoughtfulness, this was the reaction she got in return.

"I've got news." Those three words wiped her morning transgressions from Jeff's thoughts and those of their guests from Toronto. "We can eliminate one of our theories." She strode to the wall and drew a large X over the notes alleging Owen's ties to the Mafia.

"What happened?" Jeff leaned forward in his chair, his palms on his knees.

She described her meeting with Dion the previous night, not leaving out any details. No one spoke as she filled them in on the visit. They stared at her with varying degrees of disbelief. When she finished, Chantal plopped into a chair, a proud smile on her face.

"You're telling me you and a Mafia boss are friends." Brenda stared at Chantal with wide eyes. She shifted her gaze to Jeff as if seeking denial or confirmation.

"Of course, we're not friends. I'm a cop." Chantal's voice held an affronted tone.

"He went to your apartment. He offered to help with the investigation." The incredulity was clear in Brenda's voice.

"I don't think you paid attention. He offered to help catch the guys. He would throw Owen to us and deal with Eric. I said no." Chantal raised her shoulders and held her arms out to her sides. "It was an innocent conversation. That's all. The point I'm trying to make is that it eliminates the theory of Owen working with the Mafia."

"Great. Yeah, that's good." Jeff forced a smile.

"What's up? I thought everybody would be happy. It's progress."

"You're right. We're happy. We can concentrate on other theories." Jeff went to the wall, standing with his arms crossed and his gaze pinned on the notes.

Chantal followed. "What's wrong?" She kept her voice low, hoping the others wouldn't hear. Something was off with Jeff, and she wanted to understand what it was.

"Nothing. I just want this damn case over with," he said between clenched teeth.

"We all do. As fast as possible. But something's bothering you. What is it?"

He turned to her, his eyes blazing. "You can't figure it out? You were alone in your apartment with two Mafia goons. Guys that think nothing of killing someone who's in their way. What the hell were you doing, letting them in?"

"I told you what he said. And he had a point. Either I talked to him there, or I talked to him in a dark alley, or they picked me off the street and shoved me into a car. I took my chances. I'm sorry if it upset you, but I had a hunch, and I followed through on it."

Jeff sighed.

Chantal laid her palm on his arm. "It worked. I got important information."

"You did, but where does it leave us?" The voice came from behind her.

Chantal spun around to face Ivan. Mark and Brenda stood on either side of him.

"We've got one less theory to run on," Ivan said. "No matter which one it is, we still don't know where to find Owen or Eric."

Chantal's spirits deflated. He was right, but that didn't make it easier to accept.

Captain Bouchard supplied another piece of the puzzle when he joined them. "We've discovered the identities of the two men who kidnapped you, Chantal."

He had seized the undivided attention of everyone in the room. This could be the next big lead.

"They were actors." The captain's lips twisted. "They told a friend about a job someone hired them to do. They said someone paid them a lot of money for it but gave no other details."

"Actors." The word came out on a breath. It clicked in Chantal's mind. "That's what bothered me about them. Their behavior was too forced, too stereotypical. They were over the top with the tough-guy attitude. And they had guns with no bullets in them. It makes sense now. They were props."

"I'm sure we'll find out someone also hired the men killed in the explosion to fill the part," Jeff said.

"Yes. They were the same. Their mannerisms, their tough talk. It was all staged." Chantal ran her hands through her hair. "And the two Mafia men we met in Montreal. There was something not right with them, too. Someone spared no expense to play games with us."

"We need to figure out Eric. That's our link. Without that, we'll get nowhere. At least not soon enough," Jeff said.

Mark shrugged. "We've searched the databases, we've circulated the police sketch, we got nothing."

"He was at three crime scenes." Chantal said. "What's the common thread?"

"Two were drug-related, one was your abduction." As Jeff said the words, Chantal detected a slight wince. It still bothered him to think of her as a captive.

"Owen," Mark said, his tone flat.

"Yes." Jeff's gaze swept across each person. "Owen was present and involved in all three cases. Those fingerprints haven't shown up at other crime scenes that we know of. There's a common thread. The first scene, a man went to prison. Someone murdered him there; it appeared unrelated. The second scene, Owen was injured and almost killed. And the third scene, he's disappeared."

"We're down to a revenge hit where Owen is the victim, or a possibility where he's working with Eric for personal gain." Chantal focused on Brenda as she spoke. A suspicion niggled at the rear of her mind, and she wanted confirmation.

"I vote for the revenge hit," the other woman said.

Chantal's lips twitched. Here was something upon which they agreed. "There's the question of the missing money. Did anyone check into Owen's finances at the time?" She directed her question to Mark.

"They checked everyone involved in the investigation. Nothing showed up."

"Eric took it?" Ivan said. "Is this guy invisible, or what?"

"If we go with the theory Eric acted out of revenge, the only person he'd seek revenge for is the guy in prison. But we couldn't find any connection." Jeff stared at the notes on the wall as if something would light up. He threw a quick glance over his shoulder at Mark.

"Did you find any pictures of his siblings?"

Mark turned to his laptop and hit a few keys. The unsmiling image of a man with a round face and thinning dark hair filled the screen. A pock-marked and dull complexion encased dark brown eyes. Another photo of an emaciated woman with dyed blond hair and the air of someone often beaten into submission followed it.

"The brother's dead, but his sister could've hired Eric to take care of Owen for her," Brenda said. Her tone was uncertain, and Chantal could understand why. The woman looked as if her own shadow frightened her. Not someone who would pay hardened criminals to carry out a hit. But Chantal also knew from experience that appearances were deceiving.

"From what I see, I don't think she has the money to pay a hitman," Mark said in answer to Weaver's comment.

"Can we track her down?" Chantal asked.

"Yep," Mark said.

"Eric might be a friend of the family," Brenda offered as an alternative.

"Something to explore." Jeff made a note on the board. "They couldn't find any friends but maybe they didn't look hard enough. Eric could be the mother's ex-boyfriend."

Chantal puckered her lips. "I think he'd be a little young, but I suppose it wouldn't be impossible."

"Mark, could you get on it? See what you can dig up?" Jeff asked.

The man nodded and turned to his beloved laptop.

"Owen and Eric would be around the same age, wouldn't they?" Ivan looked at Chantal. She was the only person who had seen Eric.

"Yes, they seem to be," Chantal said.

"Were they friends at some point? Go to school together?"

"Mark?" Jeff said.

"I'm on it."

• • •

After hours of poring over school yearbooks and college event photos, they called an end to the day. The only bright spot had been the news the RCMP in Toronto had found an address for Stone's sister. They would bring her in for questioning and let them know the results as soon as possible.

It was eight o'clock in the evening, and everyone was hungry and tired.

"I'm done. I can't look at this anymore." Ivan stood and stretched his arms over his head. He had removed his jacket and tie and tossed them over the back of an empty chair.

"I agree. How about we grab something to eat?" Jeff said. "You in, Chantal?"

"Yeah, sure." She would prefer to go home, relax in a hot bath, and crawl into bed, but she had to promote a team atmosphere, and Jeff's comment reminded her to do just that. "How about Dooly's. It shouldn't be too crowded tonight."

It didn't take any further nudging to get people to shut their laptops and arrange their papers. Brenda picked up her purse and excused herself, heading to the ladies' room. Chantal waited a few beats before moving in the same direction. She ignored Jeff's curious stare.

The door swung shut behind Chantal on well-greased hinges. She hung out around the sinks, ready to pretend an interest in her makeup. Bending down, she searched for feet in other stalls until she was certain they were alone. Chantal wanted to have this conversation before anyone disturbed them.

197

When a flush came from the direction of Brenda's stall, Chantal grabbed her purse and reapplied the lipstick she had just removed with a paper towel. In the mirror, she caught the other woman's surprised look before she replaced it with a smile. Chantal smiled back.

"So, what's your story?" She didn't have time to beat around the bush.

"My story? What are you asking?" Brenda's gaze met hers in the mirror, her eyes wide.

"Are you and Owen a couple?"

"No."

Chantal thought her answer was too fast and too emphatic. "Were you ever?"

Brenda lowered her gaze and washed her hands. "At one point, yes."

"Ah."

"What does that mean?" The woman's gaze snapped upward to meet Chantal's in the mirror.

"It means that's what I thought."

"It has nothing to do with this case."

"I didn't say it did. I just suspected you had been a couple."

"Did he talk to you about me?"

Her voice quivered and a stab of pity pierced Chantal. Perhaps she was still in love with him. It tempted Chantal to say he had spoken about her, but it was a lie. It would not only give Brenda false hope, but it could create a web in which Chantal would get caught.

Chantal also wondered why she cared. She and Owen were not a couple and never would be. He lived in Toronto. He wasn't her type. She could go on with her reasoning. But the something that niggled her mind since she met Brenda was still there, niggling away.

Chantal stuck with the truth. "No, he didn't."

"How did you know?"

"It was just a lucky guess. Anyway, it doesn't matter. Like you said, it has no bearing on the case." Chantal dropped her lipstick into her purse.

Brenda faced her, leaning a hip against the sink. "What's your gut feeling? Do you think he's dirty?"

An invisible weight bore down on Chantal's chest. "To tell you the truth, my gut and my brain aren't getting along very well right now. They can't seem to agree. We'll know when we find him."

CHAPTER 35

"We're spinning our wheels. How long can this go on?" Ivan's clenched fists sat on his hips, and his lips were tightly drawn.

"What do you suggest? A crystal ball? Maybe we could call in a psychic." Too little sleep and too much worry had Chantal on edge.

The previous evening, Chantal had done her best to be affable with the RCMP visitors. Mark had helped, telling anecdotes and encouraging Chantal to do the same. Brenda became more relaxed after a glass of wine, letting her hair down and sharing a laugh. Jeff and Ivan sat like solemn bookends at opposite sides of the table, rarely joining in the conversation. By unspoken agreement, they called it an early night, and once they settled the bills, they went their respective ways.

"You don't have to be sarcastic. Don't you realize that every minute we delay could risk Owen's life? If he's even alive at this point." The RCMP officer ran his hand over his scalp as if he wished he had hair to pull out.

"All right, let's stay calm," Jeff said. "We're all feeling the tension, but squabbling won't get us closer to finding Owen or Eric."

"I agree, but I don't think I can stare at the wall or go through photos much longer, without coming up with new ideas." Ivan looked toward Brenda, as if hoping his colleague would offer her support.

"It's frustrating, but throwing ideas around, talking about it, may bring something up. We can't declare defeat yet."

Chantal recognized Jeff's level of frustration as he tried to appease the federal officer. Better him than me, she thought.

"Great. We've got it." All eyes focused on Mark as he waved a hand at the wall. "They sent us the interview with Amelia Stone."

On the screen, a stark, sterile room appeared. A man and a woman, RCMP officers in their dark business suits, sat on one side of a gray metal table. Across from them sat a scrawny, pale woman with stringy blond hair that showed two inches of dark roots. Her eyes, filled with trepidation, looked too big for her thin face. Chantal suspected she had a history of drug abuse, which may have led to funding her habits with criminal activities. Sitting in a police station wouldn't put her at ease.

The officers introduced themselves as Dan Armstrong and Sophie Sinclair. The female cop took the lead.

"Ms. Stone, we asked you here because we have a few questions about your brother. John Wilson Stone was your brother, is that correct?"

The woman's gaze darted between the two cops. "Yeah, but I had nothing to do with him and his shit. I didn't get involved in any of that." Both legs jiggled so fast she bounced like drops of water on a hot stove.

"We aren't saying that you were. Our interest is in his murder, not his drug-dealing."

"I had nothing to do with that either. He brought that on himself."

"What do you mean by that? How did he bring it on?"

Amelia hesitated, seeming unsure. "Can I smoke in here?" She looked around as if an ashtray would appear out of nowhere.

"No, I'm sorry, you have to wait until you get outside. What did you mean when you said he brought it on himself?" Sinclair steered the woman's limited attention span back to their questions.

"I don't know. He musta made somebody mad. He was like that, always irritating people."

"Hard to get along with, was he? Did he have any friends?"

"John? No. None that were worth anything. He just cared about himself. Nobody else." Amelia Stone picked at a scab on her hand as she looked anywhere except at the cops.

"Do you have any idea who would want him dead?"

"No. How would I know that?"

"Didn't you go visit him at the prison?"

"Yeah, I guess so. A couple of times."

"Did he get along with your other brother?"

The woman's eyes took on a glazed look.

"Amelia? Did you hear me?" Sinclair persisted. "Did John and William get along?"

For a moment, Amelia focused on Sinclair before her gaze skittered to a point over the cop's shoulder. "Yeah, I guess so. But William gets along with everybody. He's so nice."

The two cops exchanged a look. Armstrong spoke for the first time. "William's been dead for about three years, hasn't he?"

The young woman's face transformed in an instant from cautious fear to shock. "William's dead?"

"You didn't know?" The man maintained a calm tone. "He died three years ago in a car accident."

"Three years?" Tears sprang to Amelia's eyes and her face crumpled. "Nobody told me. I didn't know. I thought I saw him not that long ago. I didn't know he was dead. I got nobody now." The rest of her words washed away with wails and sobs.

Chantal's gaze circled around the group at SQ headquarters when the interview wound down and the screen went blank. It was clear there was little to gain from Stone's sister except an overwhelming sense of pity, both for her grief and the circumstances that had brought her to that point.

* * * *

As Chantal's gaze moved over the words, it hung up on one line scrawled in Jeff's almost illegible script. Her thoughts swirled.

"Mark," she whispered. The voices behind her didn't cease. "Mark," she repeated, raising her volume a few notches. All conversation stopped. A hesitant 'Yes?' followed.

She swung around to face four sets of eyes fixed on her. "Eric, or whoever he's working for, seems to have a lot of information about us and our movements. We know he hacked into Mark's phone. But we haven't been using it. He must've found another way into our systems." She looked at each person before her gaze settled on Mark.

"What's that thing you do?" She snapped her fingers as if it would make the word appear in her mind. "Geo-something. What is it?"

"Geocaching."

"Yes! That's it." She looked at Jeff to see if he shared her epiphany, but all she received in return was a blank, somewhat concerned stare. She shook her head in disappointment and turned back to Mark. "You're part of a group, a membership, didn't you tell us that? It's a website. Is it possible someone got your information from there and hacked into your computer? Took it over?"

Mark's mouth dropped open. "That'd be highly unlikely."

Chantal placed her palms on the table and leaned closer to him, her voice emphatic. "But is it possible?"

The man's gaze shifted around the group. They looked at him as if he possessed all the answers.

"Anything's possible, but they're a legitimate organization. They have protections in place, firewalls…"

"And this guy hacked into company computers, took over their emails, intercepted money, and infiltrated a Mafia information system." She tapped the table and straightened, moving her gaze over the others, like a lawyer who had just finished presenting her argument to a jury.

A gleam of pride lit Jeff's face. "He could be a member. It'd make sense. He's a computer geek, into the techno stuff."

Ivan leaned forward. "We'll need a list of the members," he said to Mark, who nodded in return, his frantic gaze attached to his screen.

"They won't just hand it over," Brenda said. "We'll need a warrant."

Jeff was a step ahead of her. He picked up his phone and made a call. He spoke in rapid French and only Chantal understood he filled in their boss on their new theory and asked for help to get a warrant. Jeff's expression and the information gleaned from the one-sided conversation told her Bouchard didn't believe they would get a list from the organization in a timely manner.

She shifted her attention back to Mark. "Have you interacted with other members? Met them in person or online?"

"Well… sometimes, yeah." Mark seemed uncomfortable being the sole focus of Chantal's intensity. "But no one stands out as a murderer or a criminal mastermind."

"No one that resembled Eric?"

"No."

Chantal pulled up a chair next to Mark and leaned toward him. "It's like a game, isn't it? A challenge? A search for treasures?"

"Yes. Yes, it is. It's for fun. And to travel and connect with people."

Chantal looked up at the other law enforcement officers. "That's what this is to Eric. It's a game. He hired actors to play roles, and then he disposed of them. He played with me in that cabin, making up stories to upset me, pretending to sympathize. But it was all for fun, for his amusement."

"I have trouble believing this."

Chantal swung to face the other woman. "Why?"

"Because it's so far-fetched. How can you connect Mark's geocaching and this Eric guy?"

"Mark is part of this techy game-loving group. And Eric is some kind of techno whiz who loves to play games. The dots connect. He's accessed us through Mark and the geocaching." Chantal's gaze shifted from one to the other. As she spoke the words, part of her agreed with Brenda. It was too weird. But the guy she met in St-Raymond pushed the limits of weird. It was as if he set out to challenge them.

Ivan shrugged. "It wouldn't hurt to look into it."

"What about the treasures?" Jeff asked, turning to Mark. "Are there any hidden in Quebec City?"

"Definitely. Many."

Chantal didn't hide her surprise. "How many? Where?"

"I'll show you." As Mark returned to his laptop, the other cops gathered behind him. A website appeared, and with more clicks of the keys, a map of Quebec City filled the screen. Chantal's eyes grew at the sight of at least a dozen flashing icons.

"Those are the hiding places?" she asked.

Jeff's finger pointed at one icon. "That's somewhere on the Plains of Abraham."

"That one's in the lower-town area." Chantal pointed to another.

"Place Royale," Jeff said. "It looks like it's near Notre-Dame-des-Victoires."

Chantal stilled. Something tugged at a memory. Ivan started to ask a question, and she held up her hands to stop him. The room fell silent.

"Yes," she said in a hushed tone. "That's got to be it."

"What are you talking about?"

Chantal had piqued Brenda's curiosity and a quick glance at the others told her she had intrigued them as well.

"Eric made a strange comment when we were in the cabin. And he laughed, a weird laugh. It made little sense at the time. But maybe it does now."

"What did he say?" Mark stared at Chantal like a child sitting around a campfire listening to ghost stories.

"He said 'our lady of victories.' Then he laughed. He made it sound like he was talking about me, but he was acting crazy, and I ignored him." She lifted her gaze to Jeff's, the only person in the room who would understand the implications.

"That's it," Jeff said.

"Would someone mind filling the rest of us in? It's obvious you know something we don't," Brenda said.

Jeff did the honors. "There's a very famous, 18th century church in Place Royale, a square close to the St-Lawrence River. It's called Notre-Dame-des-Victoires, which translates into English as Our Lady of Victories. It's not much, but why would Eric mention it and find it funny? Besides, the church and all the buildings surrounding it would have lots of hiding places, secret passages, caverns. We have to look into it."

"We'll need a plan of the building, if possible." A hard expression darkened Mark's face.

Jeff grabbed his phone and called Bouchard, bringing him up to date. After he disconnected, he faced the group. "The captain agreed it's a starting point. He also knows where to get his hands on a plan. He'll contact the historical commission of Quebec City and put a fast track on it."

The tension in the room eased, replaced by anticipation. At least they had a trail to follow. Whether it would bring them anywhere was another matter.

Within an hour, the church plans arrived by email, and they printed copies.

"The underground section is what we're most interested in," Jeff said, taping the photocopied document to the wall.

Ivan peered at the detailed plan. "Is the church still used for religious services?"

"Yes, and they have guided tours of the building. If Owen and Eric are in there, it'll be in a place not visible to anyone on the tours. Or somewhere no one knows exists."

"How would Eric know?" Ivan said. He turned to Chantal. "Didn't he say he was from Toronto?"

"That's what he said, but it might not be true."

"What we know is that, when his fingerprints showed up, they were from Toronto crime scenes," Jeff said. "So that pins him, more or less, to that area."

Ivan shrugged. "Okay, so that brings me back to my question. How would he know obscure hiding places underneath an old church in Quebec City?"

"Research?" Mark offered. "Most people know old buildings often had secret passageways. People in those days needed to escape if someone attacked them."

"That's possible." Jeff turned to Brenda. "Any thoughts?"

"Thoughts? I don't understand how you can connect a few words he said in a cabin to a hiding place within a church." Her laugh was soft and strained. "I'm afraid we're wasting our time chasing our tails while Owen may already be dead."

Brenda's voice caught on the last word. She stood beside the wall and waved her arm like a game show host presenting a prize. "There's got to be something else."

Chantal felt another wave of pity for the woman. It was clear her concern for Owen had turned to desperation. Looking at it from Brenda's point of view, she realized their theory seemed to come out of nowhere, but Chantal was convinced it had merit.

Despite her own feeling of urgency and conviction, Chantal remained soothing. "We've been staring at that wall long enough. This is the best we've got."

"These plans won't help," Mark said, ignoring the exchange between the two women. "They show the areas that are accessible. We need to know what isn't."

"Maybe no one knows, except Eric," Ivan said.

"It'll take a search. We'll grab a guide and start." Chantal seized her cell phone from the table and headed for the door.

CHAPTER 36

"Are you aware of any hidden rooms or passages?" Chantal spoke to the man in English for the benefit of their Toronto visitors. They stood in the square known as Place Royale, a section of the city that had existed for over 400 years. They rebuilt the buildings making up the square in stone in the late 1600s after a fire destroyed the original wooden structures. The historic Notre-Dame-des-Victoires church, the oldest stone church in North America, stood sentinel over the square.

Captain Bouchard had arranged a private tour for the group of police detectives. Their guide, Benoit Marceau, in his early twenties, was tall and thin and dressed in the period costume of a religious man from the 18th century. The attire was unnecessary for this group, but it added to the atmosphere.

"I don't know of any, but it wouldn't surprise me. Other buildings have them, so why wouldn't a church?"

"That's what we thought." Chantal knew the authorities hadn't brought the guide up to speed on the reason for the urgent tour of the church, and she appreciated his level of calm and discretion in the company of five law enforcement officers.

"Historians and archeologists have studied this building. It's not unusual to discover something new, but unlikely." He gazed at the building with affection.

"They uncovered an underground city when they repaired the Dufferin Terrace," Jeff said.

Benoit nodded his assent. "Yes, they did, so anything is possible. Shall we proceed?" He waved them forward with a small bow, urging them across the cobblestone square toward the steps and the immense wooden doors of the church.

They told him his customary spiel was not needed, since this wasn't a conventional tour, but he couldn't resist giving the occasional comment, and he excelled at his job. It was a natural reflex for him to fall into character.

The cops had requested access to passageways and rooms at the back or underneath the building, and Benoit obliged. After covering the known areas of the church, knocking on walls and exploring crevices, the cops regarded each other with an air of despondency.

"There's nothing here," Brenda said, her shoulders slumped in disappointment. Although the Toronto cop had made it clear she wasn't keen on exploring this option, Chantal realized she had held hope.

Unwilling to give up, Chantal turned to the tour guide. "You mentioned there were other buildings nearby that had hidden chambers."

"That's right. I'm sure many of them do. The one next door does."

"Can you take us there?"

The tour guide's mouth twisted in dismay. "I'm sorry. The buildings in the square are owned and rented out by the Minister of Cultural Affairs. I'm only allowed to take people into the church."

"Does anyone rent the below-ground level of the one next door?" Chantal asked.

"There's a gourmet food store on the main floor. Maybe they use the basement."

Chantal exchanged a nod with Jeff.

As the group exited the church, Brenda spoke up. "Haven't we seen enough? Don't you think we should concentrate our energy somewhere else? We're wasting time."

Chantal, driven to the limits of her patience and worry, whirled toward the woman. "You're free to go back to headquarters if you like. Or Toronto might be a better idea."

Jeff's hand wrapped around Chantal's forearm and gave it a firm squeeze. She took a deep breath and attempted to calm her frazzled nerves.

"Brenda, I know you never agreed with this theory, but we've come this far," she said. "It won't take us long to see it through. If nothing turns up, we'll try to find something else."

The RCMP officer nodded her agreement, her lips clenched. The group followed Jeff toward the building to the right of the church.

Most of the structures in the square were attached, except those bordering a street or walkway. They were narrow and had three or four stories above ground. The top ones were apartments, and the ground floors, as the guide had said, housed boutiques and specialty stores.

The one they were interested in sold gourmet food items particular to the region. Tourists crowded the small shop, looking for that perfect *gourmandise.*

They drew curious stares from the patrons; five official-looking people standing to one side waiting to catch the attention of the owner of the store. Within a few minutes, a short, rotund man approached and enquired if he could help them. His expression concerned, he perhaps wondered if he had violated some obscure inspection regulation.

Jeff, being the person initially addressed by the man who introduced himself as Arthur Ferland, took the lead. He explained they were police officers, and they wanted to ask him questions about the below-ground section of the store. Jeff reassured him they weren't interested in his business, inventory, or the condition of the building.

The man led them to a small room that doubled as an office and storage space. It held two chairs, but everyone stood pressed together, out of necessity rather than choice.

"Monsieur Ferland, there is a basement, is there not?" Chantal asked. When the man nodded, she continued her questioning. "Do you have use of it, since you rent this portion for your business?"

"Yes, I do." His brows drew together in confusion. Chantal couldn't blame the man. It wouldn't be every day that someone took an interest in his basement.

"We heard there's a hidden room down there. Is that correct?"

"You might not call it a room. It's small. The whole area is tiny. It's only about six feet high. I use it for storage. There's a tiny passageway that leads to another, even smaller area, but I never go there."

"Why not?" Chantal asked.

The man shrugged his shoulders. "I have no need for it. It would be more of a bother. As I said, it's tiny. It's also dark. I can't imagine what they ever used it for, except perhaps as a hiding place during the wars."

"Could we see it, please?"

"What is this about?" They could only hold his curiosity at bay for so long.

"An ongoing investigation," Jeff said. "Again, there's no need to worry. You're not involved."

Doubt filled the man's expression, but he accepted he didn't have any choice in the matter.

"Before we go, I want to show you a picture." Chantal removed an envelope from her shoulder bag and withdrew the five by seven inch sketch of Eric. "Do you recognize this man?"

The shopkeeper took the paper from Chantal and studied it. He shook his head. "Many people come through here every day. I can't say I recognize him. I'm sorry."

"It's okay." Chantal realized it had been a long shot to ask.

"Shall we go?" the man said. He led the five of them through a doorway and down a steep, narrow set of stone stairs. Someone had equipped it with electricity, but since there were few bulbs, the light cast deep shadows on the steps. Chantal slid her hands along the damp wall as she descended, afraid to fall and create a domino effect upon the others in front of her.

The temperature dropped in proportion to each step taken until she shivered and rubbed her arms when they reached the bottom. Chantal noticed Brenda did the same.

Ferland didn't exaggerate when he said the space was small. The three male cops hunched their shoulders to keep from brushing the ceiling with their heads, and the six of them took up most of the floor space.

"The door to the passageway is there." Mr. Ferland pointed toward a wall that appeared constructed of solid stone. As if reading their minds, he said, "You can't see it. You'd have to know it's there. I'll move those." He pointed to a small stack of boxes piled along the wall.

"Were these always there?" Jeff kneeled beside the boxes and studied the dust that surrounded them.

"They've been there for several months. As I said, I don't use the room."

"There's no other way in or out?" Jeff stood and brushed off his pants.

"I don't think so," the man said with a shrug.

Chantal stifled a groan. Another dead end.

"We have to check it out and cross it off the list," Ivan said.

"I agree. We have to be certain." Behind her, Brenda exhaled a deep sigh, and Chantal knew the cop's exasperation level grew with each step they took.

Jeff and Ivan stepped forward to help the man move the boxes. Everyone watched in fascination when Ferland pulled a lever that was indistinguishable from the stone it imitated. A thump and a high-pitched squeak accompanied the opening of the door. Chantal took a step backward as a blast of frigid air rushed through the opening, blowing her hair behind her.

No one moved as the view of a dark, damp tunnel faced them. Chantal assumed the reason for their hesitation was the same as hers. What the hell was down there?

Mr. Ferland grabbed a flashlight from a nearby shelf and looked at them, waiting for direction. Jeff gestured for him to lead the way. Chantal fell into step behind Jeff, leaving the Toronto people to follow. There was a sense of security being close to her fellow SQ officer.

"How far is it?" Jeff enquired.

"About fifty feet." The store owner, accustomed to centuries-old buildings, continued at a brisk pace. Chantal feared he would get so far ahead of them he would leave them in the dark. She laid a hand on Jeff's back, encouraging him to move faster.

Nothing was visible in the flashlight's beam except more of the same; a dark tunnel made of stone. Until they turned a corner and an opening loomed ahead. Chantal thought the sight of a faint glimmer of light was peculiar. The shopkeeper's gasp reinforced her opinion. He hadn't expected this.

Chantal reached under her jacket and removed her weapon from its holster, knowing the four other cops did the same.

Jeff laid his hand on Mr. Ferland's shoulder, gesturing with his head that the man should fall back behind the others. The shopkeeper didn't argue.

Their footsteps slowed. Ivan instructed Ferland to extinguish the flashlight, and they used the feeble light from the room ahead of them as a guide. Ten feet from the door, Jeff raised his weapon and turned to Chantal, nodding his head toward the opening's right side. He looked at the others and gestured for them to fan out behind him. They would meet whoever was in there with brute force and hope to have the element of surprise on their side.

Jeff pinned his gaze on Chantal as they faced each other across the opening. She waited for his nod, and when it came, they swung into the stone-lined room with their guns held in front of them.

They scanned the space before them and relaxed their stances. The room measured ten by twelve feet and appeared to be empty. A table and two chairs stood against one wall. The source of light, a battery-powered lantern, rested on the table. Chantal caught sight of a pile of filthy blankets lying in a corner. She exchanged a look with Jeff before she approached the mound with care. The others shuffled into the room behind her.

Chantal stabbed at the blankets with her toe, and they emitted a faint sound, like a whoosh of breath. She glanced over her shoulder to see if everyone had heard it. Jeff sidled up beside her and held his gun on the pile as she bent over and pulled off a blanket.

She gasped at what lay underneath.

CHAPTER 37

"Where is he?"

"I don't know."

A blanket covered his shivering shoulders. With one eye swollen shut, blood crusted on his eyelids and down the side of his face. More dried blood clung to a cut on his opposite cheek that ran from his ear to the corner of his mouth. Chantal didn't think it was deep enough to require stitches, but they would need someone with more experience to examine it. Her gaze slid over him to see if there was anything else needing immediate attention.

When they had lifted Owen off the floor and onto a chair, his injured leg was stiff and almost useless, but he didn't appear to have any broken bones. Torn and filthy clothes hung from his body, and he hunched his shoulders inward.

"He didn't say anything?"

Chantal raised an annoyed gaze to Jeff. "Why don't you give him a minute? He's in pain. Can't you see that?"

Owen raised a protesting hand a few inches. "I can't help much. He said nothing significant, and I was out of it often." His voice was raspy and weak, his head bowed.

Owen lifted his one-eyed gaze to focus on Chantal until it shifted to someone over her shoulder and the eye squinted. "Brenda? What are you doing here?"

Chantal turned her head to catch the other woman's reaction to Owen's question. The look on Brenda's face intrigued her. Before she could analyze it further, Jeff spoke to Owen.

"How did he get in and out?"

"Over there." Owen nodded toward the opening through which they had come.

"How? Boxes blocked the door, and no one had moved them for months," Ivan said.

"I have no other answer for you. That's it."

"Who is he? Did he give you a name?" Chantal asked.

"He insisted I call him Eric."

"What about…?

A stifled shriek and a scuffling sound interrupted them. The cops grabbed their weapons and swiveled toward it. The man they knew as Eric appeared in the opening with the shopkeeper, his arm across the man's chest and a gun held to his head. Terror filled Ferland's eyes.

Menace dripped from the gunman's leer. "Visitors? So nice of you to drop by. You should have told me. I would have fixed up the place. But it's impolite to point guns at your host, you know. You should put them on the ground, or this poor little man might die."

Even in the dim light of the below-ground cavern, Chantal saw the blisters from his soup burns.

A tense silence stretched over the group until Jeff took the lead and laid his weapon on the floor. The four others followed suit.

"Perfect. So obedient. I like that. Now, let's keep the same level of cooperation for the next step." His gaze swung to Brenda. "You. Come here. We'll do a little trade, him for you."

The RCMP officer stood frozen to the floor. "Will… I…"

"Now! Get over here or he dies." The crazy grin disappeared, replaced by a flare of rage.

The cop took a hesitant step forward.

"Brenda, no," Ivan said.

Her gaze swung to her partner, her expression a mixture of apprehension and something else that Chantal couldn't define. "I have to."

"Stop the chatting. You have three seconds, or a bullet goes through his head."

Brenda raised her arms in the air and approached the man, her steps firm. She stopped in front of him, her gaze fixed on his. Chantal was both surprised and impressed by the woman's burst of courage.

Eric smirked at her before flinging Ferland to the side. Brenda replaced him as the madman grabbed her and pulled her against him.

Chantal's mind reeled from the speed of the exchange and marveled at Brenda's strength and determination. Chantal had been in such a position in the past, and she hadn't faced it with such fearlessness.

The echo of Mr. Ferland's running footsteps bounced along the passageway into the room. The terrified man hadn't hesitated to make his escape. In a few minutes, he'd be in his store and would call for help, she hoped.

Eric had the same realization, but if he felt concern, he masked it well. "Got to go," he said with a grin. He paced backward toward the tunnel and dragged Brenda along with him. "I don't feel up to any more visitors today. Oh and be careful about following me. I have a gun to her head. If I see or hear any of you, she'll die." They gaped at Brenda's impassive face as he tugged her into the darkness.

No one made a sound or moved a muscle as they listened to the scuffling feet of Eric and his captive. When the screech of stone rubbing on stone reached their ears, Jeff snatched his gun from the floor and moved to the opening. Chantal was behind him, taking the other side. Darkness engulfed the tunnel. Another scraping noise followed a bang. The criminal and his hostage had disappeared into a secret opening.

It was the only explanation. Eric had taken advantage of something that no one else was aware of; another way out of the passageway.

Everyone mobilized, except Owen, whose weakened state left him weaving in the chair and shivering under the blanket.

Jeff grabbed his phone off his belt and swore. "There's no signal down here. Where's the flashlight? Anyone see it?"

"Ferland had it last. It could be in the tunnel, but God knows where," Ivan said. "We'll use our cell phones. We need to find the door." A note of desperation throbbed in his voice and Chantal knew he struggled to suppress his worry for Brenda.

"Mark, stay with Owen and wait for help," Chantal instructed over her shoulder.

The rest of them fanned out through the tunnel. Chantal held the lantern, and the others used the flashlights on their cell phones to light the way.

"He didn't go far," Jeff said. "I'd say it's only twenty feet in."

Chantal ran her hands over the walls searching for a seam, a crack, any sign of a hidden doorway.

She spun to face the other end of the tunnel, her gun ready, when footsteps clattered on the stone floor to her left. The flashlight beams bobbed in time to the noise.

"Police! Stop right there!" Jeff's shout echoed off the walls, and the steps came to a halt. As hoped, the new arrivals identified themselves as two police officers. Jeff summarized the situation for them, and they joined in the quest for the doorway.

Chantal's fingertip snagged a crevice. She followed it down an inch until it turned into several inches. "I think I found it," she said, urgency in her tone.

She sensed Jeff by her side before the others followed. His hand slid down beside hers. "You're right. There's a lever here somewhere."

Seconds later, Jeff gave a victorious shout. The door creaked as it eased open a few inches and stopped. Jeff wedged his hand inside and heaved on the massive door until it revealed another dark, dank passageway. Unlike the one they were in, it rose upwards, like a ramp. It was also narrower. They would proceed single file.

Jeff took the lead, with Chantal behind him, followed by the remaining cops. They sprinted up the corridor, following its curving trajectory. The beams from the flashlights bounced off the walls and floor.

Chantal's gut clenched when the distinct sound of a gunshot echoed through the cavern. They came to an abrupt standstill, no one making a sound. The shot came from up ahead, and Chantal suspected it didn't bode well for Brenda. She threw a glance at Ivan. Horror spread over his face.

"Dear God," he said, his voice a whisper.

"She may have wrestled the gun from Eric and shot him," Chantal said. She hoped her words were more convincing than her thoughts.

With a signal from Jeff, they broke into a run, holding their guns in front of them. Rounding the corner, they came face-to-face with another stone wall.

"It's another door. Look for the lever." Jeff said.

Experience was on their side. Within seconds, they found the lever, but as Ivan was about to pull it, Chantal laid a hand on his forearm.

"We don't know what's on the other side," she said. "He might be there, waiting for us. We can't wait for backup. Every second counts, at this point."

"I'll go first," Ivan said, his mouth set in a grim line. "She was my partner."

Chantal noticed he spoke of Brenda in the past tense and understood his anger and distress. She also realized he needed to do this. She stood aside as he pressed himself against the wall and the others spread out on the opposite side, prepared to follow him with a blast of power.

Jeff turned to the city cops. "We may end up aboveground. If we can pinpoint where we are, radio for help."

The door squealed on its hinges, and Chantal cringed. It heralded their presence, and the danger increased a hundredfold. Every muscle in her body screamed with tension.

A fraction of that tension eased when the door swung open. Ivan slid through, and Chantal had a view of what they faced. Dark mahogany bookshelves lined the opposite wall from floor to ceiling, filled with books that resembled ancient tomes.

Ivan stood centered in the doorway, wheeling from side to side with his gun held in front of him. He beckoned them in with his head. He didn't relax his aggressive stance.

"Where are we?"

"I think I know," Chantal said. Jeff looked at her, his expression curious. "Somewhere inside Notre-Dame-des-Victoires."

Comprehension flooded her partner's face, and they looked around them with fresh eyes. A voice behind her called for backup and instructed someone to blockade the square and enter through the front doors.

"We didn't see this room on our tour, but it's the only explanation I have," Chantal said.

Jeff stepped forward. "There's one door out of here." He peered around the room. "That we're aware of, that is."

Ivan lowered his weapon, but tension sprang from him. "A library of some sort."

A radio squawked a message. Chantal translated for Ivan. "Backup is at the front. We can move through."

The RCMP officer took the lead. On the far side of the room was another corridor. At the end, through a glass-paned door, lay the church's inner sanctuary.

"Where did the shot come from? Not in there?" Chantal threw a worried glance at Jeff. It seemed sacrilegious to fire a weapon in a church.

"One way to find out," Jeff said.

They pushed through the door. To the right, six cops spread out at the back. Some searched the confessionals, while others peered under each pew as they advanced. Jeff and Chantal headed toward the altar.

Chantal came to an abrupt stop. "Jeff," she said.

Her partner swung around and came to stand by her side. He glanced down at the floor behind the lectern before lifting his gaze to meet that of a shocked Chantal.

CHAPTER 38

Owen struggled to hold himself upright in the chair, his eyes heavy with fatigue. They had transported him to the hospital by ambulance, and the medical staff treated his cuts and abrasions and arranged for x-rays. However, he refused to be admitted. Instead, he insisted on returning to headquarters to help with the investigation.

Chantal worried he might tumble off his chair. A half-consumed bowl of soup congealed in front of him. She had forced him to eat as much as possible, but his primary desire was for coffee. He was on his third cup.

Although concerned, she appreciated having him with them. His help could be invaluable in the search for Eric and Brenda.

"I don't understand." Exhaustion and pain slurred Owen's words. "You found a pool of blood in the church, and you assume it's Brenda's?"

"If she got the gun and shot him, she would have been there or come to find us. If he shot and injured her, he took her away."

Owen leaned his head against the back of the chair and closed his eyes. "Yeah, makes sense."

She laid her hand on his forearm. "We know she left the church alive and walking. Someone would have noticed a man carrying an unconscious, bleeding woman."

"I would hope so. But this guy is slippery. He knows things no one else does. Maybe he went through another hidden tunnel."

Owen had a good point; one they had considered. A team was in place, searching every inch of the historic church for evidence and another passageway.

"Did he say anything to give us a hint where he is?" Chantal asked Owen.

"Nothing."

"What did he want from you? Why kidnap you?" Ivan said from behind Chantal's shoulder.

"I don't know. I asked him. Many times. He raved about how he was smarter than the police, about how he escaped Chantal, how they'd never find him, or me." Owen shook his head as if trying to rid himself of the memory. "He's insane."

The police circulated Eric's likeness to the airport, train stations, bus depots, and car rental agencies. They hoped to trap him within the city.

He had brought Owen by car to the church, although the RCMP officer wasn't able to identify it; Eric had overpowered him as soon as they had set foot outside the room. He had struck him on the head with a heavy object, secured the arms of a dazed Owen, and blindfolded him.

Nevertheless, it was valuable information to know he had a car, and they set up roadblocks on all bridges and roadways leaving the area.

"Why did you leave with him?" Jeff asked. Chantal detected the undertone of accusation in his voice. "You must have recognized him from Chantal's description."

Owen lifted a bloodshot eye to peer at Jeff. "Of course, I did. The Grim Reaper could have walked in that door, and I would've followed him out. I would take my chances with anyone. I hadn't planned for him to get the upper hand."

Chantal shot a smug look at Jeff before turning back to Owen. "You're alive. That's what counts."

"What if he went back to that cabin where he held Chantal?" Ivan said.

"We thought of that." Jeff turned to the distraught RCMP officer. "We sent a team, but I think it's a long shot. He's not likely to return to a place we know of."

Ivan fought to control his frustration. His shock at seeing the blood in the church and knowing it likely belonged to Brenda hit him hard.

"Why don't I take you back to your hotel?" Chantal suggested to Owen. Not only did he need to rest, but she was desperate to leave headquarters and felt confident Jeff would call if anything arose. She half-expected Owen to refuse and insist on staying. It was a measure of how terrible he felt when he agreed.

He stifled a groan when he lowered himself into her car.

"We should have you examined. You left the hospital too fast."

"No." His tone left no room for argument.

Chantal pressed her lips together and drove to the Palace Hotel. She didn't ask if he wanted her to accompany him to his room. She parked the car and followed him inside. He must have realized there was no point bickering with her, and she didn't intend to leave him to pass out in the elevator.

Chantal leaned against the wall outside his room as he searched his pockets for his room card. He held it between his fingers and stared at it for a couple of seconds as if he wasn't sure what to do with it.

His jaw tense, he lifted his narrowed gaze to Chantal. "Did you think I was dirty?"

Chantal's heart thumped. "Why do you ask?"

He snorted a humorless laugh. "I'm a detective, remember? I'm also pretty observant, even with one eye. Jeff gave off some strong vibes. I want to know if you believed him."

Chantal cleared her throat. "I didn't want to believe him. It didn't seem possible."

"But he convinced you."

"A hundred percent convinced? No. I believed there was a strong possibility. Everything pointed in that direction." Her sentence ended with a pleading tone, and a flush rose in her cheeks. Was it shame for not trusting him or was it anger at herself for whining?

He nodded, as if he had expected her answer. No matter what, Owen remained self-contained, Chantal thought.

"Yeah, I guess the evidence was pretty damning," he said with a shrug.

"We have to put it behind us and move forward. We can't let anger keep us from catching this guy."

"Don't worry. Nothing will keep me from that. It's my number one goal."

•　•　•

By noon the next day, the team struck pay dirt.

The membership list of the geocaching website came through. The bonus was that each member had a photo uploaded into their profile. Some people used avatars, but many, like Mark, used their own photo.

221

A half hour into the perusal of the list, Chantal picked out the photo of Eric, with his trademark grin, reddish blond hair, and charming blue eyes. She knew how deceiving those good looks could be. They masked an insane and devious mind.

The name that accompanied the photo was Bill Shelton. The profile only supplied an email address, but it sent the tech teams into a frenzy of research.

Of particular interest and significance was the fact he had become a member of the group a few days earlier, after Mark's incident at the bar and the temporary loss of his phone.

Chantal paced to the window. "It seems too easy. His photo, his email. He's too smart to put that information out there."

"He may never have expected us to track him this far." Jeff's voice was the epitome of reason. "He could've joined the group to gain access to Mark."

"At least we may have a legitimate name to work with," Ivan said.

When Jeff turned toward him, Mark held up a hand, palm facing forward. "I'm on it," he said, not bothering to look up from his laptop.

"There has to be more," Chantal said. "He's connected to Quebec City. He knows too much."

"That's one thing," Ivan interjected. "There's also his connection to the other crime scenes to find."

Mark glanced up, his eyes bright. "We're getting some info. He's a computer geek, works in software development. And we have an address."

Chantal took up a position behind Mark's right shoulder, while Jeff planted his palms on the front of the table and leaned forward. Owen didn't move from his chair. Chantal didn't know if he still hurt from his beating or if he wanted as little to do with them as possible. It was hard to tell with Owen, but she got a strong vibe of animosity from him.

"They're looking into his family and friends now," Mark said. "He took three weeks' leave from work. Something about a death in the family, and he needed to leave town."

"There was a death involved. That part was true." A grimace formed on Jeff's lips. "Anything else?"

"It's coming in. No criminal record, but we already knew that."

"Can you speed it up?"

Mark exchanged a glance with Jeff, who rolled his eyes at Chantal.

He circled around the table and put an arm across his partner's shoulders. "Why don't you take a walk? Give the man room to work and breathe."

"All right. I get it. I'll calm down."

"It's going to happen, but you can't expect it to be instantaneous."

"I know. I got it." She sat at another table, grabbed her phone, and scrolled through it with no real purpose other than to take her mind off the waiting game.

"Hmm."

Chantal was on her feet and by Mark's side in a flash. "What do you mean, 'hmm'?"

"This is interesting."

Chantal wanted to shake him. Her hands lifted from her side to do it as Jeff spoke. "Mark, if you value your life and your body parts, I suggest you be more forthcoming."

The RCMP officer cast a nervous glance over his shoulder. "Bill Shelton is untraceable until three years ago."

Chantal's eyes widened. "The same time William Stone died."

"The master hacker," Jeff said. "He fabricated his own death and switched identities."

"You think his death and the photo are fake?" As Chantal spoke the words, she knew what Jeff's answer was. He didn't disappoint her.

"This guy is capable of anything. How hard would it be for him to hack his way into a system, record a death, and switch out a picture? And remember his sister's reaction? She thought she had seen him recently. Because she's a drug addict, we didn't believe her."

"But why would he put a legit picture on that site if he's trying to hide his identity?" It didn't add up for Chantal.

"Maybe he didn't think we'd find him there," Mark said.

"Either that, or it's just another part of the game for him. He's teasing us."

Chantal nodded her head. Jeff's theory made the most sense to her.

"Photos," she said. "We need photos of William Stone."

Mark shot her a look. "I know. I'm working on it."

Chantal swung toward Jeff. "He must be John Stone's brother. It could have been a revenge hit. The attacks on Owen and this entire case could be an elaborate set-up."

Jeff considered her statement. "It looks that way."

They turned their attention to the man slouched in the chair at the other table, a coffee cup held in his hand. His complete stillness concerned Chantal.

"What do you think?" she asked Owen.

He lifted himself from his chair with obvious effort, leaning on the table to keep from tumbling over. Once he had straightened, he limped over to the other cops.

"What do I think? I think it's a shame you wasted time and resources investigating me when they'd have been better spent doing what you're doing now."

The bitterness in his tone sent Chantal's spirits into a downward spiral.

"You're right, of course," Jeff said. "But you know like I do, we needed to explore everything, whether or not we're happy with it. I'm sorry if it hurt your feelings. I'd feel the same way, but we'll kiss and make up later. We have an officer that's missing, probably injured, possibly dead. That's what we deal with."

The two men exchanged a hard stare for several long seconds until Owen nodded. "Fair enough, although I'll forego the kiss, if you don't mind."

An invisible weight lifted from Chantal's shoulders.

"Is he familiar to you?" She pointed to the photo from the geocaching profile. "Do you remember him from either of the drug busts?"

Owen shook his head. "No, even when we had the police sketch, he didn't ring any bells. At the time, there was too much action. People got away. Besides, just because they found his fingerprints, doesn't mean he was present. It means he'd been in the building at one point. If you want my opinion, I think he's close by. He wasn't always in the cave." Owen looked at the map spread out on the table. "He wouldn't have commuted for more than a ten or fifteen-minute drive."

Chantal breathed an inward sigh of relief. There was a time she wasn't so eager to hear his voice, but now she welcomed it.

"You're right." Jeff paced with his fists in his pockets, his head lowered. "But that covers a lot of area, a lot of apartments, hotels, and condos."

"Mark, did you check his credit card transactions?" Chantal asked.

"Nothing. He hasn't used his card for over a month. No airfare, car rentals, nothing."

"Did you check under Eric Sutton?"

Chantal snapped her fingers and pointed at Owen. "You're right. He could have taken over Eric's identity. Passport, credit cards, everything."

"He planned this for a while. How did he set up everything in Quebec City? How did he know of the secret passageways?" Jeff asked.

Owen shoved his hands in his pants pockets. "If he was after me, how could he be sure I'd get this assignment?"

"Could he have a mole in the department? I mean, he's a hacker, but a computer didn't assign you to the case."

Chantal conceded Jeff had a good point. She turned to Owen. "Didn't you request it?"

"I did, but there was never a guarantee I'd get it."

Chantal went to the wall and grabbed the pen. Another mystery to solve, she thought.

Chapter 39

Two hours later, Mark had what they wanted. As Owen had suggested, Shelton had created a new identity under the name of Eric Sutton, including passport and credit cards. The charges on the card led them to a payment for a vacation rental, which led them to an address on St-Joseph Street in the lower-town area, a short drive from Place Royale.

St-Joseph Street was in the St-Roch district of the city, an area that had been known as the rough section of town. But recent efforts by the city had turned it into a trendy area filled with popular restaurants, bars, and shopping, not to mention upscale condos and vacation rentals.

They pulled a SWAT team together and erected barricades at each end of the street. Chantal and Jeff donned vests and helmets. Owen wanted to join them, but Bouchard was emphatic. The RCMP officer wasn't strong enough to take part in the infiltration and might hamper the effort. Owen didn't argue, but his scowl left no doubt of his displeasure.

The authorities evacuated the surrounding buildings, cops slipping people out of the premises without fanfare. They didn't know if Shelton was there or how much firepower he had, but they couldn't take chances.

The goal was to immobilize him and take him alive if they could. They needed to find out if he worked alone. They also had to discover Brenda's whereabouts.

The owner gave the layout of the rental to the police. It was a three-room apartment on the second floor with a view to the back alleyway. The team could enter from the front without being seen.

Four SWAT team officers, in full gear, led the way up the stairs. Jeff and Chantal followed behind. Once they immobilized Shelton, they would interrogate him; with any luck, before he insisted on the help of a lawyer.

The four men positioned themselves on the landing, two on either side of the door. At a signal from the team leader, a heavy booted foot knocked the door open against its hinges. The team barged in, yelled at the occupant to get on the floor and put his hands behind his head.

Chantal's heart throbbed against her chest. Shelton was in the room. They had him. She moved to step forward, but Jeff's hand reached out and clamped on her shoulder.

"Something's wrong," he said.

Chantal's body stiffened, and her ears strained. There was no sound, no yelling, no scuffling of booted feet, and no struggling suspect. She tightened her hold on her weapon.

A voice, Eric's voice, said, "All it takes is for me to press this button. I'm not afraid to do it." An eerie chuckle followed. "Where's my friend? Chantal? Are you there? I give you ten seconds to get in here or many people will die."

Her gaze met Jeff's. It held fear, but it also held determination. Her intentions were obvious. His nod told her he would be right behind her.

Her spine stiff, her expression grim, Chantal stepped into the room. Jeff's footsteps trailed close behind her.

The space was small and basic. The door opened into a kitchen furnished with white laminate cupboards and aging appliances. Chantal's memory of the floor plan told her the living area was on her right, with a bedroom to the side of that.

A small rectangular kitchen table stood six feet away, in front of them, surrounded by four wooden chairs. A bright floral tablecloth, draped over the table, hid everything underneath it. On the other side, facing the door, sat Eric, now known as Bill Shelton. With disheveled hair and a torn t-shirt, he didn't seem the worse for wear, apart from the blisters and a fine sheen of sweat.

"Ah, there she is. The lovely Chantal." His maniacal grin was familiar—too familiar.

The SWAT men stood to each side; their guns aimed at the suspect. Eric didn't seem to notice or care. Instead, he looked as if he wanted to welcome them in for drinks. "I thought you'd never get here. And you brought your sidekick with you. How nice."

Chantal's gaze went to his right hand, which he kept raised by his side as his elbow rested on the table. He held a dark object. She wasn't an expert, but she recognized the detonator. Without turning her head, her gaze shifted around the room.

"It isn't here. That would be silly, wouldn't it? I don't intend to die today. I plan to live a long and healthy life, somewhere sunny and warm. Or perhaps it will be in a historic European city. After spending quality time in Quebec, it's given me a taste for the European flavor."

"Where is it?" she asked.

"The bomb? I can't tell you that. I will say, if you let me go, I won't set it off. If you don't, hundreds, if not thousands, of people will perish. It would be a terrible tragedy."

"What's your game, Bill?"

"You discovered my name. Very good detective work. I'm impressed. Was it the geocaching website?" he asked with a wide, excited smile. "That was special, wasn't it? I took a big risk, but what fun is a game if there are no challenges, right?" He didn't wait for an answer. "Just to let you know, I prefer you call me William."

"We also know you're John Stone's brother, and you tried to kill Owen six months ago to avenge your brother's death." Chantal threw the theory at him. She needed to see how he would react. She also wanted to keep him talking as long as possible. They needed to discover where he had planted the bomb.

"Brilliant," he said. "I promised my mother to look out for the others. She felt I was the responsible one, though I was younger. Are you surprised?" He paused, as if expecting an answer. "I take my promises seriously. I didn't appreciate our friend's work on that case. By the way, how is Owen? I hope he's not too tuckered out after our time together. It was nice to get to know him. I think he has a thing for you. It upset him when I suggested torturing you."

"You set up the fraud and made certain they assigned him to the operation. Who did you have on the inside to help you?" Chantal tossed the pieces of the puzzle at him, hoping they would tumble into the proper place. All she understood at this point was Shelton played an intricate game to seek revenge against an imagined enemy.

He held up the index finger on his left hand. "A slight correction there. I didn't set up the fraud. That was all Griggs and the Mafia, but I reaped the benefits, in more ways than one. People don't realize how easy it is to do these things." A smug smile lit his face. "As for having inside help, some things I'm not able to share with you. I make it my business to learn the weaknesses of many people, including those in law enforcement. I like to have fun with other people's failings. You learned that first-hand, didn't you?"

His smile, once charming, sickened her.

"Where's Brenda?" Chantal sensed Jeff's presence beside her, encouraging her to take the reins and deal with the monster. Her confidence increased.

"Do you care? I didn't think the two of you would get along. Did she tell you she had a little fling with Owen? That girl got around." His leer was chilling.

Shelton's expression took a serious turn. "I know everything about all of you. That shouldn't surprise you. Knowledge is power."

Chantal ignored his comments and forced a firm, calm tone. "Where did you leave her? Is she alive?"

"I think I'll keep that information in my back pocket, just in case I need it at some point. I'm not having fond memories of her right now."

"Even if you get away, we'll find you. You know that, don't you? Make it easier on yourself, before you harm too many people. Give yourself up."

A harsh laugh burst from his throat. "You're good, Chantal. Very delightful, but I think I'll take my chances with my own plans instead of yours. Thank you for the generous offer."

"What about your goal?"

"What goal would that be?"

"Getting back at Owen," Chantal said. "You still think you should punish him, don't you?"

"Don't worry. I have a contingency plan for him."

"What can I offer you that'll convince you to give up the detonator?"

"Freedom. Money. I'm not asking for much."

"How much money?" His demands didn't surprise Chantal.

"Let's see. I'm a reasonable man. A million dollars is not much to ask. In cash, of course. I prefer small bills."

"It'll take a while to get that much cash. In the meantime, your hand could get cramped, holding onto that detonator. Why don't you give it to us, we'll get you the money, and you can be on your way?"

"You're so funny." William turned his attention to Jeff. "You must get such a kick out of working with this girl. She's a laugh a minute." His gaze hardened and shifted back to Chantal. "No, you'll arrange for the money, it'll arrive, and I'll walk out of here a free man. Trust me when I say I won't blow up a good portion of Quebec City. Besides, I know you can work miracles." He exposed his teeth in a malevolent grin.

"You haven't proved trustworthy."

"I'll be good this time, I promise. Why don't you take care of your end of the bargain, instead of wasting time? The bomb squad won't be able to do anything to help you. Your babysitters can wait here while you're taking care of business."

Chapter 40

"We have to find out where he planted the bomb." Chantal ran both hands through her hair. "Even if we give him the money, there's no guarantee he doesn't have another detonator hidden somewhere and will set it off anyway."

"What would be the point?" Jeff asked.

"He doesn't need a point," Owen said. "He's crazy."

They had regrouped at headquarters, leaving Shelton in the company of the SWAT team.

Their expressions grim, they had made their way to the car, pushing through the crowds of curious bystanders and reporters without saying a word.

"It would mean combing all the buildings in the city. It's almost impossible," Bouchard said.

"Security cameras?" Jeff asked.

"We're on it. So far, we've found nothing," Mark said. He left his computer to stand beside Bouchard.

"We also have to find Brenda," Ivan said.

"Don't worry. We haven't forgotten about Brenda. So far, he doesn't want to tell us anything. She may be in the apartment, for all we know." Jeff's voice was harsh.

Owen slumped in a chair. The tightness around his eyes showed the pain he still suffered. Chantal had tried to convince him to rest at the hotel, but he wanted nothing to do with the idea.

"Can you think of anything he said, Owen?" Chantal had asked him this question before, but she couldn't restrain herself.

"He was careful. We're lucky he slipped up in the cabin and hinted at the name of the church. He has a thing about religion. I guess that's why he hid me underneath one of the most famous churches in Quebec."

"What do you mean, he has a thing about it?"

"He knew all the history of French-Canadian culture and religion. The guy said so many towns in Quebec are named St-something or other, and how it used to be so religious, run by the Catholic Church. He was full of anecdotes about Notre-Dame-des-Victoires. You'd swear he was a tour guide."

"Maybe that's it," Jeff said. "He could have worked here as a tour guide." He turned toward Mark, but the captain forestalled him.

"That's something I can deal with. I'll call my contact in the historical commission," Bouchard said, pulling his phone from his pocket.

Chantal sat opposite Owen and leaned forward in her chair. "This is excellent information. What about his attitude? Did he seem to respect and admire the church? Or was he resentful?"

Owen lifted his battered face to meet her gaze. The swelling around his left eye had diminished somewhat; enough to see how bloodshot it was.

"I see where you're going with this." His expression turned pensive. "He vacillated between the two, admiration and resentment. He seemed intrigued by the history and power the church used to have. But then he'd veer off about how immorality within the ranks poisoned the church."

Chantal turned to Bouchard. "Did we send a bomb squad to Notre-Dame-des-Victoires?"

"It's the first place we looked. Nothing."

"Anything else?" Chantal swung back to Owen.

"It always ran along the same lines. How Quebecers had been firm believers in miracles, but miracles didn't exist and never would. He said you needed to create your own happiness and not depend on someone else to hand you a miracle."

The Quebec natives exchanged wide-eyed looks for a space of two heartbeats. Bouchard grabbed his phone and shouted orders into it in rapid-fire French.

Jeff and Chantal strode to the door.

"Hold up. You're not leaving without me." Owen hobbled after them.

• • •

They raced for the patrol car in the parking lot.

"We have to evacuate the area."

"Jeff, wait." Chantal grabbed his forearm. "It's a long drive. We have units to do that. The squad is already on its way."

"What are you saying?" He swung around to face her.

"We have to talk to William, distract him, and keep him talking and thinking about other stuff, while our teams do their thing. We'd only be able to stand around and watch." As Chantal finished her plea, Owen caught up to them.

Jeff hesitated a second before running his hands through his hair. "You're right. It makes sense. Let's go."

Chantal swung around to face Owen. His face was flushed and his breathing raspy. "You should stay here."

"No, I'm coming with you. You can explain on the way."

Chantal didn't have time to argue with him. As the car sped toward St-Joseph Street with Jeff at the wheel, she filled Owen in on their theory.

"It was what he said about miracles that tipped us off." She pointed over her shoulder. "About twenty-five minutes east of here, there's a town called Ste-Anne-de-Beaupré. It's not a big place, but it has a famous Catholic Basilica. People from everywhere go there to pray for miracles; they make pilgrimages. Just inside the front doors, people have left behind their canes and crutches because they're able to walk on their own after visiting. Around here, when someone mentions miracles, it's what we think of."

"That could be it." His tone was uncertain.

"It's the most we have at this point. During the tourist season, if he wanted to hurt or kill a lot of people, it's a good choice," Jeff said, as he maneuvered through the late afternoon traffic.

"He may also have left Brenda there," Chantal added.

"Why is Brenda in Quebec?"

Chantal twisted in her seat to Owen. "They sent her and Ivan to help us search for you. Either they chose her to come, or she volunteered. I didn't ask."

Owen's face wore a puzzled frown.

By the time the group arrived at the vacation rental, they were composed and prepared to face the mad man. The same four men were on duty. They straightened as the detectives entered the room.

Shelton sat in the same spot, the detonator still in his right hand, resting on the table. Chantal noticed his complexion had paled since an hour earlier, yet when he spoke, his voice held vibrancy.

"You're back. And you brought Owen with you. How nice. Are you feeling better?"

Chantal glanced at Owen and caught his grim expression. He remained silent, refusing to respond to the malevolent prodding.

"Did you bring my money? I don't see you carrying bags of cash."

"We don't have it yet, but it shouldn't be long," Chantal said. "Someone will text us when it's ready."

"So, you decided to pay me a little visit. How sweet of you."

"We have questions."

William waved his left hand in the air. "Go ahead. But there are no guarantees I'll answer them."

"Tell us where Brenda is." Chantal said.

"I already told you. Forget about that. I'll tell you if I want to."

Chantal glanced at Jeff, hoping her frustration wasn't obvious. If the female RCMP officer was alive, they needed to find her and get medical help fast.

But Chantal also needed to keep him talking long enough for the bomb squad to work their magic.

"How do you know so much about Quebec? How did you learn about the underground chamber in Place Royale?"

"Ah, yes, I figured you'd be curious about that. I outsmarted you there, didn't I?"

Chantal didn't correct him. He may have delayed them, but they discovered where he was. She would allow the narcissist his moment to gloat. If it helped them achieve their goal, it would be worth it.

"My uncle lived here," he said. "You didn't know that, did you? Your little computer gurus didn't get the connection. I know they didn't. I spent several summers here as a teenager. My mother couldn't wait to get me out of the house, and honestly, I couldn't wait to leave. Uncle Frank was the curator at Notre-Dame-des-Victoires. He introduced me to all the little nooks and crannies in and around the church; places people weren't aware existed. It was very educational."

Chantal fought to keep her expression neutral during his revelation. She watched, fascinated, as his face flushed with a red tinge.

"Good old Uncle Frank came to a terrible end. Life is full of irony, isn't it?"

Here was another thread to follow as they unraveled William Stone's past, she thought.

"I suppose that was his cabin you took me to," she said.

William smiled and winked at Chantal. "You catch on fast, my dear. I was familiar with that area too. Everything worked out perfectly."

Again, Chantal decided not to remind him of his slip-up in the cabin that had helped her latch onto the fact he was an imposter. But she wanted to keep him on point.

"Why did you take me? Were you going to kill me?"

Shelton chuckled. "You don't know how much fun that was, setting it all up. Those two imbeciles thought they would make an easy buck. All I asked them to do was capture and harass a woman for a couple of days. Then I would come in and be a hero." His chuckle morphed into a loud guffaw. "They never saw it coming, and neither did you. At first." He focused a serious look on Chantal. "I'd kill you and the police would blame the Mafia. Meanwhile, the bigwigs in the Mafia would get a tip that Lockwood killed you and pointed the finger at them. They wouldn't appreciate that. What a delightful mess I had planned."

Shelton gave an elaborate shrug before continuing. "But you figured it out, so I went to Plan B."

Chantal felt the tension radiating from Owen behind her. She was certain he wanted to jump across the table and strangle the man with his bare hands. But she wanted more information.

"Which was?" she asked.

"To make him look like my accomplice, my buddy, my lifelong friend. I had a few loose ends to tie up before I exposed his vicious plot. Killing him would have been too kind. I wanted him to go to prison, like my brother." The killer's gaze shifted and drilled into that of the man behind her. "But, of course, that backfired too. So here I have Plan C." He waved the hand that held the detonator.

Chantal tried to absorb all that she heard. The shock of seeing inside the mind of a madman rolled over her.

Yet she felt they might gain the upper hand. He seemed to tire. His blinks lengthened, and his eyes glazed over until he shook himself to alertness.

"You're wasting my time with this," Shelton said. "I'm tired of answering questions. Where's my money?"

"I told you. We're waiting for a text to tell us the money is ready," Chantal said. "Someone's going to deliver it to the door. But I want your assurance that you're going to give us the detonator. We don't want anyone to get hurt."

"Aren't you curious about where the bomb is?"

"Yes. We already asked you. You said you wouldn't tell us."

"And you leave it at that?" His gaze moved from Chantal to the other cops. "You know, don't you? You've figured it out." An angry red flush climbed up his neck and into his face.

"How would we know? There are thousands of places you could put it. We assume it's somewhere between here and Place Royale, but that only narrows it down slightly. Of course, we're searching. You must've expected that."

"I did. But I'm thinking you're smarter than I thought." Shelton pushed his chair back several inches but stayed seated, once again holding the device in the air, his thumb poised over the button. He swayed a few inches.

Chantal held out her hands. "William, don't get upset. Your money is on its way." She pulled her phone from her pocket. "I'll text my boss to find out where it is."

"Give me your phone." Shelton held out his left hand.

"I can't do that."

"Give it to me! Or I swear to God, I'll push this button."

"Okay, calm down. I'll give it to you. I'll enter my password first."

Chantal punched in four numbers to unlock her screen as the device vibrated and the text from Bouchard appeared. It was the all-clear signal. She hid her sense of relief and her innate curiosity. She would get the details later. For now, Chantal needed to deal with a lunatic.

"There. I told you he'd text me." Chantal took a step forward, intending to hand the phone to Shelton. The message was ambiguous enough for him to interpret it as a sign the funds were ready.

"Set it on the table and step back."

Chantal did as he said, shoving the phone in his direction before taking two steps back. She poised herself to leap across the table at him if the opportunity presented itself.

William grabbed the phone and stared at the screen. "What does…"

A heavy weight catapulted into Chantal's side, accompanied by a loud grunt of pain in her right ear. She landed on the floor with the weight on top of her. The sharp bark of a gunshot echoed through the room, followed by a split second of stunned silence.

Owen rolled off Chantal and onto his back beside her, drawing his gun as he did so. Chantal sprang to her feet and grabbed her weapon from her shoulder holster. Instinct led her to train her sights on William, considered the most threatening person in the room. He slumped forward on the table, a pool of blood forming under his head. His arms hung by his sides, the detonator on the floor by his right hand.

Chantal swung to her right, her weapon poised, and faced the source of the bullet.

Brenda.

The RCMP officer stood like a statue, her gun held in both hands in front of her, aimed at the dead man.

Chantal witnessed the disturbing gleam in the woman's eyes. As Brenda swiveled her body to the left, her arms still extended, Chantal dived toward her.

Her shoulder connected with Brenda's stomach, taking her down. A second gunshot rang out as both women landed on the floor. A grunt came from Chantal's right. She wrapped her hands around the woman's wrists and pinned her arms above her head as she straddled her.

"What are you doing?" Chantal demanded. Her heart raced with adrenaline. In her peripheral vision, she made out masculine feet surrounding them and knew they trained weapons on the women beneath her. Frantic shouts for medical assistance echoed throughout the room.

Chantal registered the message that an officer was down. Confused, she swung her head and saw Owen, Ivan, and Jeff, all safe. Who was it? Was there a mistake?

Brenda bucked underneath her, drawing Chantal's focus. The woman's eyes were wide and wild. A madness reminiscent of that of the dead William lurked in her gaze.

"Why did you shoot him?" Fury filled Chantal's voice, shaking the woman by the wrists.

"I had to." Brenda focused on Chantal. A spark of hysteria shone in the other woman's eyes. "He was dangerous. He was going to kill people."

The RCMP officer prepared her defense. Chantal leaned forward until her face hovered a couple of inches from Brenda's. "Who were you going to shoot next? Me or Owen?"

"Neither. I was looking for another threat."

"You already removed the threat," Chantal said through gritted teeth.

An officer spoke from behind her. The words baffled Chantal. Looking up at Jeff, his confused expression reflected her own feelings.

"Somebody already shot him?" Chantal asked. She waited in frustration while her partner moved across the room to investigate the body of William Shelton/Stone. Owen remained by her side, his gaze fixed on the woman who struggled to get out from underneath Chantal.

Shuffling and mutterings came from behind her until Chantal couldn't stand it any longer. "Jeff, what is it?"

"He already had a gunshot wound in his side."

Chantal's gaze reconnected with Brenda's. "It was his blood in the church. You shot him and took off. Did you think he was dead?"

The other woman's lips tightened. "I'm a cop."

"Where have you been? We were looking for you."

Brenda's face was red from either anger or exertion, but she refused to meet Chantal's stormy gaze. "I've been searching for him."

The woman's words made little sense to Chantal. She was with him. Had he escaped her, even with an injury? Why didn't she report back to headquarters and join the team?

"He told us about blackmailing you into helping him." Chantal tossed another puzzle piece into the air to see if it fell into place.

"No, of course not. It's not true. You can't believe anything he said. You know that. How many times did he lie to you?"

The answer was 'many', but Chantal's trust had evaporated, and Brenda's tone rang with desperation. The film in her mind of Brenda turning to the left, perhaps to shoot Owen, was vivid and impossible to erase. Many things were wrong with this picture.

"What did Owen do to you? Why were you going to shoot him?"

"You can't talk to me like this."

Chantal wanted to argue, but the voice of her boss stopped her. Bouchard had arrived on the scene.

"We'll confiscate her weapon, and she'll have a lot of questions to answer. You can let her up now."

Several seconds passed while the two female cops exchanged venomous stares.

Chantal stood and grew aware of the pandemonium happening in the hallway. Two booted feet were visible as paramedics and SWAT team officers blocked her view of the victim.

She grabbed the elbow of the closest officer and asked who had been shot. The man's answer floored her.

Paul Morrisette.

CHAPTER 41

The pouncing and crashing had resulted in multiple bruises on Chantal's frame, but a glance in Owen's direction convinced her his pain exceeded hers.

His jaw tense, Owen met her stare. Chantal didn't know if it conveyed regret, anger, or solidarity. She sensed it was a mix of the three.

They had reconvened at headquarters.

Chantal's hunch about the bomb's location had been on point. After evacuating the site, the bomb squad and search dogs located the explosive in the altar of the historic church in Ste-Anne-de-Beaupré. The team defused it before the detonator slipped out of the dying man's hand and hit the floor.

The CSI team examined and photographed William Shelton's body before they transported it to the morgue. Brenda Weaver waited in an interrogation room. A representative from the RCMP office in Toronto was on his way, along with an internal investigation expert.

And Paul Morrisette was in a hospital. He suffered a bullet wound to his upper arm. It wasn't critical but he would be off-duty for a while. He had stepped forward to intervene as Chantal had dived toward Brenda. He had taken the wild shot from Brenda's gun.

Chantal tore her thoughts away from the look they had shared as they placed him on the stretcher. With difficulty, she focused on the activity in the conference room.

The group of detectives would sift through what they knew to piece together a case that had started with bank fraud and ended in death, with several bodies in between.

The earlier burst of adrenaline developed into an exhausted slump among the group. Mark was the only person hyped and full of questions; he had stayed behind during the intervention on St-Joseph Street.

"Why did she shoot him in the church and disappear? It makes no sense."

"That's what I thought," Chantal answered. "And then she shot the suspect a second time and killed him. He was the only person who could tell us who his partner was, if he had one."

"Owen, what are you thinking?" Bouchard asked.

All eyes turned toward him. Tension hardened his face. He focused on Chantal as he spoke. "I don't know what to think. All I know was it surprised me that Brenda showed up in Quebec. I assumed she asked to come because of our past association, but somehow it didn't ring true for me."

Despite how hard he attempted to hide it, the pain and betrayal vibrated in his words.

"We're all tired," Bouchard said. "There's nothing more for us to do. They'll be questioning Brenda for hours. I suggest we get some sleep, and we can start again tomorrow."

No one argued, although the likelihood of falling asleep was low, as far as Chantal was concerned. Her mind would race long into the night.

"I'll give you a lift to the hotel," she said to Owen.

"No, thanks. It's too far out of your way. I'll take a taxi."

"I don't mind," Chantal said.

"No thanks. I'll see you in the morning."

She watched him leave the room, his limp conspicuous and his shoulders slumped. Her heart wrenched.

"He'll be okay. He has to deal with it in his own way."

Chantal looked at Mark. "I know. I just wish I could help, that's all."

She slung her purse over her shoulder and headed home.

• • •

The late-night air cooled her skin. It was a stark contrast from the humidity of the day, and she welcomed it. Too much had happened;

too much had gone wrong on this horrible day that seemed to never end. Escaping the tension indoors helped to lift a weight off her shoulders. Tomorrow would be another round of questions, arguments, and finger-pointing.

From the sidewalk, she watched the cars race by. Everyone seemed to have somewhere to go, even at this late hour.

A sleek black car pulled up to the curb. She squinted to see inside, but the tinted windows prevented it. Instinct made her take two steps back. She wasn't fast enough. The doors swung open, and two men jumped out. Powerful hands wrapped around her wrists. She struck out with a foot, but it missed its mark as they twisted her right arm behind her.

Her forehead banged against the doorframe as they shoved her in the backseat. She landed in the lap of another man. A sinister laugh accompanied his leer as he thrust her upright.

Her mind raced with outcomes, none of them optimistic. The group of four did not hide their faces. That was never a good sign.

She didn't ask questions. She knew who was behind this.

Her eyes shifted around the car for a means of escape. Four men surrounded her, three of them muscular and burly, all of them probably armed. There was no way of escaping, not at this point.

The car sped along the highway to an unknown destination. Twenty minutes later, it bumped along a narrow path, rocks bouncing off the underside of the vehicle. The only light came from the headlights. They remained lit when the car came to a standstill, and a propelling current of water glinted under their glare.

She drew a deep breath, knowing this was the moment where she would escape or die.

CHAPTER 42

Chantal arrived first at headquarters. She shuffled through papers on her desk, not making headway. When the sound of footsteps reached her ears, she dropped all pretense of work and went to meet the arrival.

Chantal attempted to keep her expression neutral but realized she failed when Jeff said, "You're disappointed to see me? Who were you expecting?"

His grin irritated her, but a calm expression stayed on her face.

"I thought it might be the captain. Maybe he has news about Brenda."

"Uh-huh," Jeff said with a wink. "He should be here soon."

Chantal wasn't sure which 'he' Jeff referred to, and she didn't waste her time asking. She knew from experience his teasing could be relentless.

Both heads turned toward the door when another set of footsteps approached. Chantal realized she should have known Jeff was not Owen. The uneven gait announced the man's arrival.

The RCMP agent's appearance spoke of a night with little sleep. Which type of pain he suffered, either emotional or physical, only he knew.

Mark completed the foursome, his mood upbeat compared to the others, but everyone was on edge, wanting to learn what Brenda's interview had revealed. When Bouchard entered the room, the mundane surface conversation came to an abrupt halt.

Chantal knew her boss, and though he could be tough and sometimes severe, he now carried a disheartened air she had rarely seen before. She took a step toward him. "What's wrong?"

"Brenda has disappeared."

Of all she expected, that was the most shocking. Her gaze swung to Owen. The man who had impassivity down to an art form appeared stunned.

Chantal spoke first. "I don't understand. How could she disappear? She ran away?"

"No, we have camera footage. It happened right outside this building, shortly after one in the morning. She called an Uber to take her to the hotel, but when she set foot on the sidewalk, a car drove up, two men threw her in the backseat, and drove away."

Another long, stunned silence followed his words until Owen spoke in a low voice. "Plates?"

"They obscured the license plate, of course," Bouchard said.

"Why would someone take her? What's the purpose? Who could it be?" Chantal looked at each person, hoping someone had an answer, no matter how unlikely.

Jeff looked at his boss. "What came out of the interview?"

"Nothing new. Brenda stood by her story of eliminating a threat and wouldn't say anything more without representation. She was to report this morning for more questioning."

"Eliminating a threat?" Jeff said, his tone both incredulous and furious. "The man held a detonator. It could have gone off and killed hundreds of people."

Chantal couldn't absorb the fact that the woman had disappeared. There had been friction between them, but she would never wish something like this upon her. She looked at Ivan, who had arrived seconds after Bouchard. He had yet to speak, but the news shook him.

Chantal faced Owen. "Had she ever acted like that before? Was she known to make risky, last-minute decisions?"

"No, of course not." Owen shook his head without turning around. "They would have suspended her or relegated her to a desk job."

"Maybe she was involved in Shelton's game." Jeff voiced Chantal's chief concern.

"The investigation will continue. We may turn up something." Bouchard's tone held conviction, but it seemed forced.

Owen limped to the window. He stared outside, his hands on his hips.

Chantal's mind raced over everything she could remember about Brenda Weaver since the moment they had met. She snagged on one memory.

"Owen and Ivan, I have a question for you both. You're the only two who ever worked with Brenda."

Owen turned, and Ivan straightened from his slouch.

"What do you think she meant?" Chantal sensed everyone in the room focused their attention on her. "When Shelton said he wanted to trade her for Mr. Ferland, she said 'Will I'. Will I be hurt? Will I be freed? Was she trying to give us a message?"

Ivan shrugged. "I don't know. I didn't think about it." His gaze moved to Owen, as if he could solve the puzzle.

"She said, 'Will I'?" Owen said. "That's it? I don't remember."

"Could she have been calling him Will?" Chantal asked. "If so, it would prove she knew him." Her head pivoted back to the man beside her. "Ivan, could that be?"

"I have no idea. I haven't worked with her that long, only six months."

"Owen, what's your take on it?" Chantal asked. "You knew her well."

"Apparently, not well enough. I have no way of knowing if she ever met this guy. But it would solve a few mysteries."

"Yeah, like his contact on the inside to assign you to the case," Chantal said as she paced to the wall of notes and stared at them without seeing them.

Jeff came up beside her. "It looks more and more like Shelton and Brenda worked together."

Chantal ran her fingers through her hair. "What is it you say? *Le renard avec les poules?*"

"The fox in the henhouse," Jeff said. As he spoke, the anger in his tone intensified.

Chantal snuck a glance at Ivan, who looked like someone had hit him with a shovel.

"But that doesn't explain why someone took her. Shelton is dead. If she worked with him, he was the only one to want her to keep quiet."

"It's obvious he's not the only one," Owen said from behind her. "Shelton may have seemed like a loose cannon, working on his own, but someone else had to be behind it. Someone that needed to eliminate Brenda."

"Or someone with a personal grudge against her." Chantal's gaze met Jeff's, and she realized he read her thoughts.

"Mafia," he said.

"It could be. Dion said he didn't like interference in his business, making him look responsible for something he had nothing to do with." Chantal chewed her lip. "I'll go see him."

"I'll go with you," Owen said.

"You don't need to."

"There's no way you're going alone. Either Owen goes or I do." Jeff's tone left no room for negotiations.

Everyone looked toward Bouchard. His expression held concern, and Chantal worried he would refuse her proposal. When he spoke, Chantal repressed a sigh of relief.

"Okay," he said. "Dion knows you're cops. There's no reason for a cover story anymore. Keep in mind what you want to find out."

CHAPTER 43

They went through the usual channels to meet Dion, even though their facade was no longer necessary. It was the only known way for them to reach him.

There was also no need to dress as a wealthy couple and drive a high-scale car. Chantal wore jeans and a light sweater, and she and Owen arrived at the meeting driving her five-year-old Honda Civic.

As luck would have it, Dion was in Quebec City, eliminating the drive to Montreal and a wasted five hours on the road.

"Lovely to see you again, Mademoiselle Pouliot." Dion gave her his most charming smile.

Chantal didn't grasp the reason behind his unusual good humor. She hoped it was clear by the time they left.

"Please, sit." Dion waved his hand toward two chairs.

They were in a private room at a steakhouse. It was mid-afternoon, and the place was almost empty, but Chantal appreciated the solitude for their discussion with the Mafia boss.

"To what do I owe the pleasure?" Dion's gaze included both cops, but it came to rest on Chantal. Since they had expected he would show deference to her, they agreed beforehand she would take the lead in the conversation.

"I wanted to bring you up to date. As you can see, we found Owen."

"Yes, the husband that ran away with all your money." Dion laughed out loud, and the sycophant bodyguards standing on each side of him joined in the laughter. Owen and Chantal allowed themselves a slight smile.

"Well, we were fortunate to find him alive and my money intact," Chantal said with a chuckle. "We also found the man named Eric. We believe he was behind the deaths of Griggs and Beaudet."

"Ah. And what was his excuse for eliminating them?"

"I don't think he needed an excuse to kill people. He seemed to do it for fun."

"Past tense?"

"Yes, he's dead. Killed by an RCMP officer."

Dion frowned, appearing disappointed to hear this news, but Chantal didn't think his sorrow was for the loss of a man's life. His next words spelled out his true feelings.

"That's too bad. I know people who'd take pleasure in the task."

The two goons beside him exchanged a grin.

"Strangely though, another problem developed." Chantal studied the man's face. His reaction seemed genuine; a curious lifting of a brow, perhaps a spark of interest at the prospect of another chance to engage his hitmen.

"Someone abducted the officer, Brenda Weaver, who shot and killed him during the night," she said.

"Why?" Dion's brows changed direction and formed a perplexed frown.

Chantal hesitated before taking the calculated chance of angering the mob boss. "We wondered if you knew anything about it."

The frown remained for several seconds before it disappeared, and he threw his head back in laughter. "You think I had something to do with it? Now you're pulling my leg, aren't you?"

"We're not accusing you of anything," Chantal hastened to add. "We thought, with your extensive connections, you may have heard something."

Dion chuckled again, before lifting his glass of wine and taking a sip.

"I'm afraid not. I had a minor interest in this Eric person because of what he did to my people. But, if someone killed him, it wouldn't upset me. Not enough to threaten a police officer. You can remove me from your list of suspects."

The trace of a smile rested on his lips, but it no longer reached his eyes. They hardened and sent a powerful message to the two cops.

• • •

"You're sure they're not involved?" Jeff asked.

"No, I'm not one hundred percent sure. But I feel it's not a Mafia job. That's the best I can do."

Jeff turned his gaze from Chantal to Owen. "Do you have the same feeling?"

"Yeah, I do. Unless we find a link between Brenda and the mob, there's no reason for them to go after her."

"What we have to find is a stronger link between Brenda and Will Shelton. All we have is suspicion." Chantal paced the room, wishing something would materialize soon.

As if reading her thoughts, Mark came through the doorway. "I've got it."

All eyes swung toward the cop, but Chantal was the first to surge forward. "What is it?"

"We didn't find a direct connection to Shelton but get this. Someone hacked her emails six months ago."

"William's specialty," Jeff interjected.

"Exactly," Mark said. "And, from what I discovered, she had an affair with a married man, a bigwig in the RCMP, although we don't know his identity. But the hacker blackmailed her."

Chantal clenched her fists. "That's it. That's how Shelton made sure they assigned Owen to the case. He used Brenda. Just as we suspected." She turned to look at Owen. He fixed his stare on the floor, but she realized the wheels turned at warp speed in his mind.

"She whispered in someone's ear, and I landed the operation," he said. "And that's why she came to Quebec. It wasn't to find me. It was to find Shelton and eliminate him before he revealed her secret."

"And Shelton's purpose was to get revenge and to make a little money on the side," Chantal said.

"And games," Mark added. "He was into games."

Jeff's brows furrowed. "It was for fun?"

Mark lifted his shoulders. "It's a guess. We might discover he was into a lot of games, either high-tech or not."

"Mark's right," Owen said. "I have the same sense. He was an egomaniac who loved to play with people's minds."

"Okay. Let's say that's it." Chantal strode to the wall. "Who took Brenda, and why? How are we going to find her?"

Bouchard listened to the exchange between the cops but moved to the corner of the office to find privacy when his phone rang. He ended the call, slid the device into his pocket, and turned back to the group. "I think we've found her."

All conversation stopped, and Bouchard became the center of attention. His slumped shoulders foreshadowed his next words.

"They've pulled a body matching her description out of the St-Charles River."

A whoosh of air left Chantal's lungs as she sank onto a chair. The worst had happened. Although Brenda seemed likely to be a dirty cop, it was still a blow to hear of her death. The death of any law enforcement officer was difficult for a cop to accept.

"It sounds like a Mafia hit," Owen said. "Dion already told us being implicated in Shelton's game annoyed him. Maybe he sent a message."

"Or silenced a witness," Jeff added.

Owen nodded his acknowledgment of Jeff's statement. "Yeah. Both William and Brenda are dead. We don't have any other witnesses to point the finger at Dion."

"I don't agree," Chantal said. "He may have been involved at the beginning. He admitted he worked with Griggs and Beaudet. But that's where I think Dion's involvement ended."

"You believe William inserted himself into the Mafia's business and redirected it to himself? That takes guts," Jeff said.

"Guts or insanity. I vote for insanity." Owen's cuts and bruises helped him reach that decision, Chantal suspected. But he had a valid point.

"At least we know where Brenda came into it. She eliminated a witness to save her career," Ivan said.

"She wasn't a bad cop. But she let herself get into a dangerous situation, and she realized it. Shelton would never have let her go. He would have continued to blackmail her for his own ends for the rest of her days." The sorrow was clear in Owen's voice.

"She could have called his bluff," Chantal said.

"Her career still would have been over. I think I know who she had the affair with, and believe me, he would destroy every ounce of reputation she had. Being an RCMP officer was everything to her. She wouldn't have taken the chance."

"If you could figure it out so easily, that may be the reason she wanted to kill you. Tying up another loose end," Chantal said.

"You could be right," Owen's lips turned down. "I don't condone what she did. She came to Quebec intending to put an end to Will

Shelton, or Stone or whatever you want to call him. It was wrong in every sense of the word, but I know why she did it."

Put like that, Chantal understood and felt a smidgeon of sympathy for Brenda. It was another reason to avoid relationships within the police force, she thought.

• • •

All eyes turned toward Mark as he joined them.

"I've got something. Whether it's good or bad, I'll let you judge for yourselves."

"It must be about Stone's uncle. That's who you looked into, wasn't it?" Jeff said.

"It is, and it was. Frank Holmes, William's maternal uncle, was the curator at the church from 1992 to 2002. They considered him deeply religious. He was an esteemed historian until they discovered he had a penchant for pedophilia." Mark paused as his fellow police officers groaned in unison. "His first victim was his own sister. She was six years his junior."

Chantal closed her eyes in disgust and horror. She hated hearing this. She forced herself to concentrate on Mark when he spoke again.

"Several years ago, Uncle Frank met with an unfortunate hunting accident close to his cabin, the one where William led Chantal. It was even more unfortunate since he wasn't a hunter, and it was his first time trying the sport."

No one spoke a word for several long seconds until Owen's deep voice broke the spell. "I take it young William found his uncle's body."

"Correct," Mark said. "There was an investigation, but since Frank was inexperienced with a firearm, they ruled it an accident."

Chantal attempted to absorb all the information, as terrible as it was. William Stone grew up in a severely dysfunctional household, where they sowed the roots of his mental illness a generation earlier. He had been an intelligent, functioning member of society, but he used his intelligence to hide a personality disorder and a sense of vengeance that was his downfall.

"I wasn't expecting that," Jeff said. "It came straight out of left field."

"It's tragic. Everything about it is tragic," Bouchard said. "Of course, there'll be an investigation into Brenda's murder. The RCMP will handle it in their organized crime division. As for the email fraud, the banking experts and insurance companies will track the funds. The culprit is no longer among the living."

Chantal nodded. For her, the case was over. Her superiors would judge her performance and decide if she was ready to carry on in the homicide division. No matter what their decision was, she knew she had done her best. She had her moments of fear and doubts, but she had overcome them. In her opinion, those moments hadn't compromised the operation, and that's what mattered to her.

Chantal also knew it was time to part ways with the RCMP contingent, bringing a new set of emotions to the stage.

EPILOGUE

"Chantal, my relationship with Brenda was a while back and short-lived. I considered her a friend and a colleague, and that's why her death hits me hard. That, and a betrayal of her badge and her friendship."

Owen's gaze held Chantal's as they stood outside Quebec airport's security gate. Mark had said his goodbyes and left the two of them alone.

"I understand," she replied.

"Do you?"

"Yes, of course." And she did. Chantal didn't see any signs of heartbreak in Owen's behavior, but the sadness at her death and the sense of hurt stemming from her disloyalty was a common factor among the officers involved in the case.

Owen's gaze shifted to the line of people getting their passports checked before proceeding to the scanners.

"We'll be in touch," he said as he looked into her eyes, a question lurking in them. "Toronto's not that far."

Chantal forced herself to smile. In her mind, it was at the far side of the earth. She knew their memories, good or bad, would fade with time, and the effort it took to keep a long-distance relationship alive would be its death toll.

When Owen lowered his head and kissed her, she understood it would likely be the only kiss they would share.

He strode to the security queue with a last glance over his shoulder before he disappeared from Chantal's sight.

As she walked toward her car in the underground parking lot, she pulled her car keys from her purse and let her mind linger on the kiss. Her smile disappeared when she spotted the man standing beside her car, two burly men at attention on each side of him.

Chantal took a step back and thought of her weapon in her bag. There would be no point in trying to retrieve it. These were armed men, and they wouldn't hesitate to protect their boss and themselves. Although she and Dion had parted on good terms the last time they met, she kept in mind who he was and who he would always be. Cats and dogs.

"I'm sorry to intrude on your thoughts. It must have been difficult to say goodbye to your friend," Dion said.

Chantal shrugged in response. She wasn't comfortable with him knowing her every move.

"I just wanted to keep in touch with you. I like you. I like your spunk. And you seem like an honest and trustworthy person. I appreciate that. There are many untrustworthy people in the world."

Chantal wondered if he referred to Brenda, but she didn't ask.

"There's been a lot of action in Quebec City the past few days. Very unusual. I hope it's going to calm down and go back to its quiet, pleasant ways. And I hope people don't think I'm involved in all the action. I like to have quiet time, away from suspicion."

Chantal's mind raced for an appropriate answer. She was eager to learn more about the mob's involvement or non-involvement, but she didn't want to instigate any further tension with the organized crime boss, not while she was alone with him in an almost deserted parking lot.

The man raised his hand. "No need for an answer." Dion read her mind. "I just wanted you to understand we don't feel the need to involve ourselves in everything."

The man turned and walked away, his minions following him.

Chantal squeezed the keys in her hand as she tried to parse Dion's enigmatic words. The authorities had uncovered most of the answers in the Shelton case. They would hypothesize the few that remained and relegate them to another category.

The assignment had been momentous for Chantal. Not only had it freed her from the clutches of a boring desk job, but it had helped to release her from her fears and lack of confidence.

It was impossible to say all is well that ends well, given the number of deaths involved, but she had reaped benefits from it.

Chantal settled into the driver's seat and started the ignition. Her phone beeped.

She rummaged in her purse for the device and stared at the lit screen. A frisson ran up her spine.

The text message read: Can you handle another one without choking?

THE END

About the Author

A.J. McCarthy grew up with books by Agatha Christie, Sidney Sheldon, and many other masters of mystery and suspense. She's an award-winning author with five published suspense mysteries to her credit and plans to have many more to come. She's a member of International Thriller Writers, Sisters in Crime, and Crime Writers of Canada. For more information about A.J. and her work, please go to www.ajackmccarthy.com.

Note from the Author

I wrote the largest part of this novel during 2020. At the beginning of the year, I naively believed that, by the time I submitted my final manuscript to Black Rose Writing on the first day of 2021, the global pandemic would be a thing of the past. Since it would be released in June 2021, I originally set the novel in the summer of that year.

As time wore on and the date for my final submission approached, the pandemic still ran rampant, and I became less optimistic for my setting of July 2021. I rewrote a few sections to move it forward into the following year.

I wanted my characters to live and work without masks or social distancing.

If this is not the case in 2022, I apologize for not having the foresight to move it farther ahead. I also will be deeply saddened by the fact such a terrible global event still holds us in its clutches.

Word-of-mouth is crucial for any author to succeed. If you enjoyed *Faux Friends*, please leave a review online—anywhere you are able. Even if it's just a sentence or two. It would make all the difference and would be very much appreciated.

Thanks!
A. J. McCarthy

Thank you so much for reading one of **A.J. McCarthy's** novels.
If you enjoyed the experience, please check out our recommended
title for your next great read!

Sins of the Fathers by A.J. McCarthy

"McCarthy perfectly weaves together suspense, dangers, and
an intriguing storyline that will compel readers from start to
finish...an enthralling and energetic writing style that is sure
to enrapture any reader."

–The Red-headed Book Lover

View other Black Rose Writing titles at
www.blackrosewriting.com/books and use promo code
PRINT to receive a **20% discount** when purchasing.